form, and succeeding volumes will bring the story down to 1960. Each volume is a self-contained unit tracing a specific phase of the complete story. This second volume covers the period from January, 1948, through December, 1950, turbulent years that imbued Toda and Soka Gakkai with a renewed sense of mission.

Toda's unshakeable faith and crusading zeal stand out in sharp relief against the dramatic background of the Tokyo War Crimes Tribunal, the privations under the economic policies of the occupation government, the failure of two more of Toda's business ventures, and the outbreak of the Korean War. The deepening bond between Toda and Shin'ichi Yamamoto (Mr. Ikeda) is revealed warmly; and vignettes telling of the sorrows and joys of Soka Gakkai members clearly show Toda's strong character, the caliber of his leadership, and the depth of his faith. While an inspiring story of the power of faith, the book at the same time does much to explain what Toynbee has called the astonishing postwar resurrection of Soka Gakkai.

THE HUMAN REVOLUTION

DAISAKU IKEDA

The HUMAN REVOLUTION

VOLUME TWO

with a foreword by Arnold J. Toynbee

and illustrations by Teikichi Miyoshi

New York • WEATHERHILL • *Tokyo*

This book contains a condensed English translation of Volume 3 and Volume 4 of the original Japanese version of *Ningen Kakumei* (Human Revolution) as first published serially in the daily newspaper *Seikyo Shimbun,* Tokyo, during the periods of October, 1966, to January, 1967, and January, 1968, to May, 1968, and then published in book form by Seikyo Press, Tokyo, in March, 1967, and July, 1968. An earlier English translation was published by the Seikyo Press in March, 1967, and July, 1968.

First edition, 1974
Second printing, 1977
(with corrections)

Published by John Weatherhill, Inc., of New York and Tokyo, with editorial offices at 7-6-13-Roppongi, Minato-ku, Tokyo 106, Japan. Copyright © 1967, 1968, 1974, by Daisaku Ikeda; all rights reserved. Printed in Japan.

LCC Card No. 72-79121   *ISBN 0-8348-0087-x*

CONTENTS

FOREWORD

IN THE present volume of *The Human Revolution,* Mr. Ikeda continues his narrative of the postwar history of Soka Gakkai, the lay organization for the propagation of Nichiren Shoshu. This is Buddhism as presented by the Japanese "prophet" Nichiren, who lived in the thirteenth century of the Christian Era but still lives on in the church that he founded. I use the Jewish and Muslim term "prophet" and the Christian term "church" because Nichiren and his followers look to a Westerner as if they were more closely akin, in spirit, to Jews, Christians, and Muslims than to non-Nichirenist Buddhists. Adherents of Nichiren Shoshu call their faith "Buddhism" without any distinguishing epithet, because they hold that this is the sole true and right form of Buddhism and, indeed, of religion. This uncompromising confidence strikes a Westerner as being Judaic. At any rate, it is something with which he is familiar in his native tradition. At the same time, Nichiren Shoshu is manifestly Buddhist in its tenets and its aims. One of its fundamental tenets is the Indian belief in karma: an ever-open spiritual profit-and-loss account. The account is not closed by death, for another tenet of Nichiren Shoshu is a belief that a deceased holder of a karma account is eventually reincarnated after an interval of dormancy and that the account runs on from one life in this world to another in a series of lives that may be endless.

In the course of any one of these lives, the holder of the account has it in his power to change the balance, either for better or for worse. This belief is a spur to strenuous spiritual endeavor, and it has an important social corollary. Social improvement on any plane—political or economic—can come only through the spiritual action of individual members of society. An individual's improvement of his own karma by his own efforts is the key to the spiritual advance of mankind as a whole. For adherents of Nichiren Shoshu, this means that the spiritual conduct of every "church member" is supremely important, and so is the winning of each single convert to what the adherents of Nichiren Shoshu believe to be the only true and efficacious faith.

The first volume of this book started with the release of Josei Toda from prison just before Japan's capitulation at the end of the Second World War. Soka Gakkai had resolutely opposed Japan's participation in this war, and its leaders had been imprisoned by the wartime Japanese government. Josei Toda's teacher, Tsunesaburo Makiguchi, the first president of Soka Gakkai, had died in prison. Josei Toda had come out alive, and the responsibility had devolved on him for taking the initiative in reestablishing Soka Gakkai.

In the present volume, Josei Toda is the protagonist. Mr. Ikeda records Toda's spiritual and intellectual struggle to grasp the meaning of Nichirenism; Toda's attainment of a new vision of the meaning of it; his "evangelizing" work (another appropriate Western term); the failure of two of his business enterprises; and his consequent resignation from his postwar post of director general of Soka Gakkai.

This stage of Toda's career is placed in its setting of both private and public life. There are numerous accounts of the lives of individuals and of families—always apropos their relations to Soka Gakkai and to Toda. This selectivity is required by the subject of the book. The cases here described may not be average samples of contemporary Japanese life; yet they are interesting for students of both the phenomenon of religious conversion in general and Japanese postwar social history in particular. The contemporary background of public affairs is monetary inflation, a disappointing start in parliamentary government, the outbreak of the Korean War, and the United States' consequent pressure on the Japanese government to whittle away Article 9 of Japan's postwar constitution, in which Japan has renounced not only war but armaments. Soka Gakkai has consistently stood out against war, armaments, and political corruption.

In the first phase of the postwar period, the Japanese people had to restart life from the beginning, both individually and collectively. They had been defeated militarily and had been ruined economically. This tribulation evoked in Japan a number of new religions and of new versions of old religions. Soka Gakkai was attractive because its faith inspired confidence. This is an uncontroversial statement of an evident fact. The adherents of Soka Gakkai would add that the reason Nichiren Shoshu is inspiring is because this is the true and right religion. They have set out to convert not only the rest of the Japanese people but the whole of mankind.

Arnold Toynbee

PREFACE TO THE
ENGLISH EDITION

NO OTHER human being has influenced my life as much as Josei Toda. Because he was the teacher who helped me find the path I was destined to follow, I am naturally eager to share with the rest of the world the triumphs and trials of his life. With this goal in mind, I have tried to tell Josei Toda's story and the history of Soka Gakkai, to which he devoted his entire being. For ten years I have been laboring on *The Human Revolution*, and the eighth volume of the Japanese-language version has recently been published. Looking back on the book, I can see that although it contains a great deal of information somehow, in spite of its bulk, it says too little. The life force that was Josei Toda is an immense entity, one that is difficult, if not impossible, to describe in toto. But I cannot be content to give a mere factual account of the life of this great man. Instead, I hope to explain to people everywhere the full extent of his activities and the vital importance of what he stood for.

To all of us who are members of Soka Gakkai and believers in Nichiren Shoshu, the Buddhism to which Toda devoted his life is destined to change the fate of mankind. Though some people may regard this statement as boastful, I know it is not. I am certain of our role in history, and in many parts of the world today I see clear evidence that our efforts are having results.

Inspired by our progress, I have resolved to do the best I can to complete this biography of the man without whose courage and determination our task would be infinitely more difficult. I realize that my efforts may not have produced entirely satisfactory results, but I am determined to see this task through to conclusion because of its importance to me, Soka Gakkai, and the whole world.

As with the first volume of this English-language edition, some condensation was necessary but the story does not suffer for it. And here, again, the vocabulary of Buddhist terminology has been simplified so that people with no knowledge of Buddhism can easily understand the value of Toda's counsel, as well as the import of Nichiren Daishonin's teaching. A comprehensive glossary is included as a further aid to readers who may be unfamiliar with some of the Buddhist personages and terminology in this book. And of course, I must offer my thanks to a group of people whose endeavors helped make this second volume of *The Human Revolution* possible. I express my gratitude to Richard L. Gage and the international group of translators who prepared the English manuscript and to Rebecca Davis of John Weatherhill, Inc. for her patient editing. In addition, I extend my appreciation to Meredith Weatherby, Takeshi Yamazaki, and the editorial and production staffs of Weatherhill.

BOOK THREE

1. FRESH STARTS

EARLY on the bright morning of New Year's Day, 1948, Josei Toda and several of his followers joined in morning Gongyo services before the Gohonzon in the unheated second-floor room of his publishing company, Nihon Shogakkan, in the Kanda district of Tokyo. As Toda listened to the rhythmic unity of the voices, he said to himself: "This is as it should be; we are all in harmony with each other." His thoughts passed beyond the shabby walls of the building and traveled into the limitless universe. The earth is only a small planet in the solar system, itself merely a speck in comparison with the vast, constantly moving galaxies rolling in unspeakable grandeur through the unknowable spaces of the universe. Through the ages, mankind has amassed an astounding amount of knowledge about his planet and about other bodies in the solar system. He knows how far it is to the most distant of observed planets. He knows that the frigid cold of Pluto and the blazing heat of Mercury forbid the existence of life as we understand it. He possesses many concrete data on distances, speeds, sizes, and orbits in the solar system. But in spite of his amazing knowledge, man has never been able to free himself of misery and unhappiness.

"Here I sit," thought Toda, "in a small room on an island country in the Pacific Ocean, only one of billions of human beings. By comparison with the overwhelming vastness of the universe, I am tiny and puny. But I have a task to accomplish, and I vow to see it through. I am on this earth to do battle with the forces of evil and to help mankind find salvation through Nichiren Daishonin's teachings, which are as boundless as the whole universe itself."

Just as his thoughts reached this point, the chanting of the Daimoku came to an end. Everyone exchanged congratulations on the new year and asked that Toda lead them in the future just as in the past so that they could continue to do good work. This gave Toda an opportunity to interject a few words of caution as a spur to more energetic activity in the coming year.

"Do you really want to carry on with the same old kind of good work you did last year?" Toda asked. "I certainly don't want anything of the sort. If you do the same kind of work, do you know what we'll have? Yoshizo Mishima will continue grumbling, Takeo Konishi will sulk, and Hisao Seki will never get that pale, worried look off his face. No more of that, if you please!" Toda laughed and everyone joined him.

Becoming serious, he went on: "We are now entering the third year of the reconstruction of Soka Gakkai. I am deeply moved by the misery of the people in this country and even more deeply impressed with the immensity of our duty in alleviating that misery. As I have told you in the past, nothing in life can remain the same. Either you go forward or you regress. And we can't afford to go back by so much as a single step.

"You may think you did pretty well last year. Perhaps in some respects you did, but there is one thing I want to warn you about. I have often worried because you show signs of true eagerness only when I am around. Simply following my lead is a far cry from practicing your faith in an active way.

"Our organization is fairly well set up now; and that's very good. But sometimes when a group achieves stability, inertia sets in. People in leadership positions act under nothing but force of habit. This is not the way to send our faith to peoples everywhere. Each of you must act on his own initiative. And to do that, you need to have a broad picture of all life force and of your own part in that life force.

"Consider the nature of the universe. It is in a continuous state of flux. Nothing in it remains the same. From the immense rolling and swirling of countless galaxies to our own small solar system, an immutable universal law governs everything. From the blazing sun and Mercury, where intense heat makes life impossible, to the frigid, distant Pluto, gripped in unimaginable cold, everything fits a pattern. Here we sit in a shabby little room, in Kanda, on an island that is a tiny part of a smallish planet. But we too, as insignificant as we may seem, are part of something infinite. That something is life force, which Nichiren Daishonin distilled into the fundamental universal law of Nam-myoho-renge-kyo and then gave physical embodiment in the Dai-Gohonzon. This marvelous life force operates throughout the entire universe, in the most distant stars and in the life of each individual being. This is the basic truth on which everything rests. Without knowledge of this truth, faith is impossible. But with faith arising from the knowledge of the nature of all life, we have the power to work changes in karma, the law of cause and effect that governs the actions of everything in the universe.

"But to change karma requires deliberate action on our part. And this in turn demands unwavering faith in true Buddhism. A person enjoying a happy life might be deluded into thinking that his good fortune will continue always. However, unless he has faith, his lot will change for the worse, because, as I said, it is the nature of all things to alter. But by like token, sound faith put to practical use can convert a life apparently destined to unmitigated misery into one of happiness.

"If it is possible to revolutionize an individual life—from misery to joy—by applying faith to action on a wide plane, the same kind of revolution can be carried out even more broadly in the life of an entire nation. At present, conditions in Japan are so bad that some people despair of recovery. But I do not despair. In light of the great truth of Buddhism, the current situation cannot last. Now that we of Nichiren Shoshu and Soka Gakkai have taken the first steps toward the universal propagation of our faith, a change for the better in the karma of Japan is bound to take place.

"In the history of the world, no religion, philosophy, or ideology, no matter how great, has ever completely saved even one man from unhappiness. Psychological comfort is the best that past philosophies have been able to offer the individual. It is scarcely surprising, then, that no philosophy has ever saved a whole nation from predestined downfall. But Nichiren Daishonin has promised that we will succeed where others have failed. To the best of my knowledge, the words of Nichiren Daishonin have never been proved wrong: they embody every universally valid truth.

"The task before us is immense and difficult. Our inevitable success will not result from our own powers—we must never be so conceited as to think that we can do it alone. We will accomplish our mission because, and only because, the true Buddhism as taught by Nichiren Daishonin has given us the power.

"But to return to my original thought, with such a vast job ahead, none of us can afford to work by mere force of habit. And this is why, when I began talking—some time ago, come to think of it—I insisted that simply doing as well as you did last year will not be good enough this year. I seem to have talked a long time about doing things the way you did them before, but don't think that I am merely splitting hairs. Even the slightest things you say reveal your true state of mind to me with almost too much clarity. Faith enables me to see into the heart of things. Life force is intangible and has no form or color, but it makes itself known subtly in its true state, which is the law of life force. I want you to understand the importance of our work and the heavy responsibility resting on the shoulders of each of us. The time has come to put you through a strenuous training course. You must not complain about it, because in all fields of endeavor—art, technology, business, politics—no one has achieved greatness without training. The revolution that we are going to bring about obviously demands the most intense training of all of us because it is unparalleled in the history of man.

"But for now, let's relax. I've got some very good sakè here, and we can toast the new year."

Toda brought out cups, handed them around, and filled each with the fragrant spiced sakè called *otoso,* the traditional drink on New Year's Day. Exchanging holiday greetings, everyone drained his cup. The sakè was delicious, but its flavor was greatly enhanced by the atmosphere of teacher-disciple, father-child warmth that Toda always generated when he was with fellow believers. He was their teacher, but more important, he was almost a parent to them. He understood their problems. He knew their strengths and weaknesses, and he always knew just how to bring out the best in each of them.

After the toast, the perpetually amiable Miss Katsu Kiyohara said: "New Year is such a warm, happy time. But I sometimes wonder how Nichiren Daishonin felt about the holiday."

"There is a very interesting passage in the *Gosho* dealing with New Year," said Toda. "A certain Lady Omosu, the wife of Ishikawa Shimbei Sanetada, Lord of Omosu, sent a box of delicacies and cakes called *mushimochi* all the way to Minobu, where Nichiren Daishonin was living. To thank her, Nichiren Daishonin wrote a famous letter that, because of the cakes, is called the 'Mushimochi Gosho.' Seki, you'll find it in your copy of the *Gosho*. Please read it for us."

Thumbing through his worn and well-read copy of the book, Hisao Seki found the letter, toward the end of the *Gosho,* and began to read:

"I have received a hundred *mushimochi* cakes and a box of delicacies. The morning of the first of January is the beginning of a day and the beginning of a month, as well as the beginning of spring and the year. Those who celebrate it will increase their virtue and be loved by others, just as the sun becomes brighter as it travels from east to west and the new moon waxes as it moves from west to east.

"Your sincerity in offering contributions to the Lotus Sutra at the beginning of the new year is as admirable and beautiful as the blossoming forth of flowers from trees, the budding of the lotus from a pond, the fragrance of the sandalwood tree, and the rising of the new moon. Today Japan has made herself an adversary of the Lotus Sutra and thus has invited calamities and disasters from three thousand miles beyond her shores. Judging from this, those who believe in the Lotus Sutra will invite good fortune from thirty thousand miles away.

"The shadow comes from the substance. A nation of people who disrespect the Lotus Sutra will be visited by calamities, just as the shadow follows the body; whereas the adherents of the Lotus Sutra are like the august sandalwood tree, yet more fragrant. I shall write to you again."

"Yes," said Toda. "Now I think I should give you a clear explanation of this letter. Nichiren Daishonin, touched by the considerate gift of Lady Omosu, wrote to her to explain in a symbolic way some very important doctrines. He says that the first day of January is a beginning. Since the sun and moon mentioned in this passage symbolize the universe, he is referring to the beginning of everything. The sun, the moon, and the mood of spring represent universal movement, which is an expression of the Buddha's compassion, which in its turn is the Myoho. New Year's Day is a time to remind people of the eternal movement that is the law and pulse of the universe. The New Year festival, then, is a time for man to remind himself of this all-pervasive universal motion, which he always tends to forget.

"When he overlooks the great universal law, man and his actions are doomed. Often humanity runs counter to the law, and it is this violation of universal principles that breeds misfortune and unhappiness. Fortunately, however, the true Buddhism taught by Nichiren Daishonin clearly explains the universal law. If an individual grasps the fundamental truth of universal movement and understands his place in it, he becomes a small universe in himself. Learned people have sometimes described man as a microcosm within the macrocosm.

"As I said, however, since man tends to forget this principle, New Year is an important time for making fresh starts and resolutions for the future. It recalls to man the nature of his relationship with the universe, more so since it is the day on which the earth begins a new revolution around the sun. People feel that it is a good idea to make resolutions to alter their ways of living on this day of beginnings. But no resolution can have effect unless the person who makes it is in touch with the universal rhythm through faith in the Gohonzon. Even in small matters like making New Year's resolutions there is a vast difference between those who believe in Nichiren Shoshu and those who do not. Our faith gives us the power to abide by whatever resolutions we make.

"Nichiren Daishonin told Lady Omosu that she would increase her virtue and would be loved by others. This seems to indicate that she had made a resolution for that particular new year and that Nichiren Daishonin was gratified by her earnestness and sincerity in doing so. He goes on to prophesy happiness for her and to contrast the fates of believers with the calamities invited by other people who are adversaries of the Lotus Sutra —in this case Japan herself.

"The passage about inviting calamities by refusing to believe in the Gohonzon and about enjoying good fortune as the result of unwavering faith offers great insight into the law of cause and effect. When Nichiren Daishonin said that Japan would bring calamity upon herself by remaining an adversary of the Gohonzon, he had in mind more than the Mongol invasions, which did in fact afflict Japan seven hundred years ago. He was thinking of the defeat of Japan at the hands of the Allied Powers in the twentieth century, as well.

"The ideas expressed in the 'Mushimochi Gosho' are stern but inspiring. They teach us that the law of cause and effect, karma in other words, is irrevocable and that unless we do something to change the karma of this nation, the Japanese will find no relief from their present suffering. Desperate and miserable in defeat, the Japanese are in a grave situation. Who can save them? General MacArthur? The Japanese government? Of course not. The only people equal to this task are those who hold high a great philosophy and who devote themselves mind and body to putting that philosophy into practical action. That is what Kosen-rufu, or the universal propagation of our faith, means; and we are the only ones who can bring it about."

The passage from the *Gosho* was familiar, but Toda seemed to have given it new meaning for all the people present that morning. Because his throat was a little parched after his long talk, he drained what was left in his sakè cup and reached to refill it, but the bottle was empty.

"Pretty good at drinking while you listen, aren't you?" he said with a chuckle. "Well, then, let's start our New Year's pilgrimage to the head temple. It's a long ride from here to Mount Fuji, and I'm willing to bet the trains are packed. But remember, there is no good fortune as great as a New Year's trip to Taiseki-ji."

As they left the office and started toward Kanda Station, Toda noticed that there were no signs of holiday decoration in the neighborhood. The occupation forces had forbidden the display of the Japanese flag, a traditional way of celebrating special occasions. All in all, this cold, windy first of January was bleak for most of the citizens of Tokyo; but Toda's group was warmed and gladdened by a sense of comradeship and unity in dedication to a mission.

Leaving at eight thirty, the train from Tokyo took about three hours to reach Fuji, a station near Taiseki-ji. The windows of the coaches were boarded up. It was pitch black and extremely stuffy inside, where as many people as could possibly sit, stand, or lean were crushed together. Worn, shabby, tired, and disgruntled, many of the passengers were so-called evacuation widowers, men whose families had remained in the rural areas to which they had evacuated during the war. The men themselves came to Tokyo to find work but could not bring their families with them because of the acute housing shortage. Occasional holidays provided them with their only opportunities to be with their loved ones. Naturally they did not want to miss these chances, and they boarded all available conveyances in huge numbers. So crowded was the train Toda and his group were riding that when it finally chugged wearily into Fuji Station they were forced to climb off through the windows: a solid mass of people blocked all doorways.

Out of the train at last, they enjoyed intense relief. On the low hills near Mount Fuji the air was exhilarating. The sacred mountain itself glittered white in the sun, as though it too had taken on fresh beauty for the new year.

A battered old bus was the only transportation to the temple, and it was none too reliable. About halfway up the steep road it stopped and would budge no farther. Jumping from the bus, Toda and his group urged everyone to help push. Finally, the bus started moving again with barely enough energy to transport the passengers to the gate of Taiseki-ji just after dusk. Exhausted, the small group went directly to the lodging building called the Rikyo-bo, where sixty other members of Soka

Gakkai were already waiting. This was twice as many as had made the New Year's pilgrimage the previous year and ten times the number two years before.

After a hearty supper of rice cakes and boiled vegetables, the refreshed pilgrims began animated informal discussions of a number of important issues. When the discussions were finished, a young man stood up and started singing. At first Toda listened in silence; but then, moved by the music and the lyrics, he joined in and finally led the chorus himself. The singing continued late into the night until at last Toda brought the evening to a close with a stanza from one of his own poems:

> "All I have is my single life,
> And that I give without regret.
> Now I call the young, the banner bearers.
> Where are you? Appear!
> Can you not see the pure and
> Lofty peak of Fuji?"

On the following day as the sun glinted on the white splendor of Fuji, Toda and his party first worshiped the Dai-Gohonzon at the Treasure Temple. Toda made his New Year's pledge at that time; and later he had an audience with High Priest Nissho Mizutani, who was eager to discuss plans for the reconstruction of two important buildings, the Kyakuden and the Mutsubo, both of which were still in ruins after a fire that occurred in 1945. Other Nichiren Shoshu temples throughout the country were already being rebuilt, and plans called for work on a new functionally organized Kyakuden and Mutsubo to begin in the autumn of 1948. Trees in the Taiseki-ji grounds were to be felled to provide lumber for the project. The high priest admitted that the difficulty of the times and the sad state of temple finances would make it extremely hard to raise the vast sum needed for construction, but he was determined to set up a special committee to canvass funds. Touched by the high priest's devotion to the rehabilitation of the head temple, Toda made a contribution pledge at once.

As an extra inspiration for increased activity, before they departed Toda guided his small group to the charred remains of the old Kyakuden. There he disclosed the high priest's reconstruction plans and declared that Soka Gakkai would make

the greatest efforts to see that the dream was realized. Toda said, and everyone agreed, that the rebuilding of these two important structures would usher in a new age for Taiseki-ji and become a milestone in the march toward the universal propagation of the faith.

Pilgrims to Taiseki-ji usually experience a sharp sense of contrast between the purity and serenity of the mountain temple, devoted to the betterment of mankind and to eternal peace, and the vicious, sullied life of the city. After the New Year trip in 1948, Toda found Tokyo more than usually depressing. Because of a paper shortage, newspapers in those days consisted of only two pages; but this limited space was filled with distressing information. For instance, in late January of 1948, for several days the leading story in all the major newspapers concerned a shocking mass murder. A middle-aged man who identified himself as an employee of the Tokyo Metropolitan Sanitation Bureau walked into a bank in the Shiinamachi district of the city and convinced a number of people to drink a white liquid that he claimed was a precautionary dose against the possible spread of the dysentery that had recently stricken several people in the neighborhood. The unsuspecting people in the bank drank the potion, and eleven of them died of poisoning.

Still another saddening group of news items was related to the international military tribunal for the Far East. The trials of alleged Japanese war criminals were entering the final stage, as prosecutor Joseph B. Keenan interrogated General Hideki Tojo, the man held primarily responsible for the Pacific War. Verdicts were to be handed down later in the spring. The entire issue of the trials aroused profound doubts about their justness and validity.

In the midst of the turmoil symbolized by the senseless mass murder and the doubts surrounding the war-crimes trials, the government found itself in a most ticklish position. After less than six months in power, the Socialist cabinet headed by Prime Minister Tetsu Katayama began to show signs of collapse because of internal strife. By February 10, the squabbles for power that split the party into left and right factions forced the Katayama cabinet to resign in a body. A month later, Hitoshi Ashida of the Democratic party formed a cabinet, but because of a general mood of political corruption and degeneration, it did not seem likely to last long.

From Josei Toda's standpoint, the most heartbreaking reflection of the public moral slump was to be found in the economic and financial sectors. Because of the overwhelming power of the black market, inflation grew steadily worse, while the people remained very poor. The greedy rich, many politicians, and leaders in financial circles cruelly victimized the masses. The wretched living and business conditions stirred up deadly competition, and any means was considered satisfactory if it achieved its aims. People turned on each other in ugly, cut-throat struggles to survive. Toda viewed such battling as virtual war between brother and brother.

Seeing this grievous fate that had befallen the Japanese people, Toda felt more convinced than ever that the time was ripe for the universal spreading of true Buddhism. Reflecting on the situation, he thought: "Let the authorities do as they wish, they are certain to wind up in a dead-end alley. We who believe in the teachings of Nichiren Daishonin are the only people who can bring salvation to this age. We are going to be very busy in the years to come, because we must devote ourselves to the study of all aspects of philosophy and to the practical activities of our society."

Toda worked indefatigably. With equal kindness and sincerity, he taught, advised, and guided all who came to the discussion meetings. Even people attending the gatherings for the first time were treated by Toda as if they were old acquaintances. Personal problems and dilemmas presented to him were numerous and varied. To each he gave his undivided attention and as much time as it took to work out a solution. This amount of time was great, since each individual's distinctive karma presented extremely complex problems.

No matter how constantly poised and assured he appeared to others, even Toda had moments of weakness. This is not surprising: the task of guiding even one person out of misfortune and into happiness is formidable, but Toda was faced with many such tasks. Whenever his immense burden of work seemed too heavy to bear, however, he knew exactly how to regain his composure: he invariably turned to the Gohonzon and the Myoho for help. Through his faith, Toda had gained complete self-mastery. In his heart he could always say: "This is the way. The important thing is to believe in the Gohonzon with unwavering faith. Then all problems—personal, family, or social—will be solved." This conviction gave him the strength to bring courage and self-confidence to his followers when they were troubled. From time to time, the problems were of a very delicate personal nature. But even in the face of such issues, Toda knew what kind of guidance to offer because he considered it both his mission and his responsibility to prove the Buddhist law in terms of the lives of individual human beings.

On January 31, 1948, a discussion meeting was held in the roomy house of Tetsuyuki Matsumura, an active member of the Youth Division who lived near Koiwa Station. Present that evening were Mr. and Mrs. Hiroshi Izumida, also active in membership campaigns and other Soka Gakkai activities in the Koiwa district. On that particular night, Toda was in a very relaxed mood. After the meeting started, he said that he thought it would be a good idea to forgo the usual formalities and simply enjoy a few friendly hours together discussing things in general. "If you have anything on your minds, speak up. Let's just chat for a while."

The more than a dozen people seated around Toda included familiar faces and new people, some of whom had not yet accepted the faith of Nichiren Shoshu. Toda's geniality conveyed itself to everyone present with such intensity that no one seemed to have any problems to discuss. After a few minutes of aimless talk, however, Toda glanced at Mrs. Kinu Sasai, who, sitting silent in a corner, had a worried look on her face. Turning to her, Toda said gently: "Well, Mrs. Sasai, you seem glum tonight. What's troubling you?"

Toda knew precisely what was worrying Mrs. Sasai, because he was aware of her background and the discord in her home. The small factory owned by Mr. Sasai was on the point of bankruptcy. Her husband was sick, and to make matters worse, he had a tyrannical disposition. They had several children, and it was all Mrs. Sasai could do to provide for them, take care of the home, and nurse her ailing, cross-tempered husband. Not long before, she had joined Nichiren Shoshu in the hope of alleviating conditions that had become almost too harsh to cope with.

For a while, her new faith gave her confidence in the future, but her husband soon began to find fault with her religious activities. At first he only grumbled and pressed her to renounce her faith. Later, however, he became violent and even resorted to brutality. The psychological burden imposed by her husband's attitude, added to everything else she had to suffer, caused Mrs. Sasai to waver for a while. She wondered if she had been mistaken to join Nichiren Shoshu. But on further reflection, she could find nothing wrong with the religion itself. She therefore concluded that her husband's fierce opposition might be a sign, not that she should abandon her faith, but that she should leave him. With her children to shelter and feed and without a husband to provide for them, she knew that her life would be hard. Still, it could not be any worse than it already was. Feeling she must take some steps to put an end to her almost unbearable sufferings, she had come to the meeting in Koiwa to ask Toda's advice.

As Toda looked at her intently, Mrs. Sasai, with head lowered, said in a strained voice: "I've made up my mind to leave my husband." For a few minutes no one in the room made a sound. Many of the people present knew Mrs. Sasai well. Though they understood the trying conditions of her life, they were startled that she had decided to take so drastic a step. Toda gazed at the obviously troubled and nearly exhausted woman for a few minutes, before saying in a calm, even voice: "I understand how upset you are, but I am afraid that I cannot interfere in your marriage problems. Still, there is one thing that I want to tell you. You are bound to your husband by karma. Unless you change that karma, if you remarry, you'll probably get the same kind of man. You've put up with this one for a number of years now, and you have several children. Why not stick with him. Who knows, he may be as good a husband as any other you could have."

Toda's mild humor brought chuckles from some people and a wan smile even to the face of Mrs. Sasai. But realizing that the woman's problems were no laughing matter, he continued in a steady, measured voice: "I have said that you must change your karma and I have said that your husband might be as good as you can get. I am perfectly serious in both instances. Let me explain. As a member of Nichiren Shoshu, you know that it is possible to change karma by means of steady, constant faith, because—as I often say to you—everything in the universe is a changing phenomenon. If you remain true to your faith and in that way alter your karma, your husband too will change for the better. If he does not improve, I am certain that he will leave you of his own accord.

"If you insist on divorcing him, I cannot try to dissuade you. I do, however, suggest that you continue to be diligent in your religious faith and try to make things work at home for at least six months or a year longer. If you do that, I am confident that you will bring about a kind of revolution in your own house, change your karma, and turn misery into happiness for your whole family."

The look on Mrs. Sasai's face revealed her disappointment. What Toda had said did not seem to satisfy. There ought to be an easier way out of her predicament. But reluctant to seem forward by pursuing the matter further, she lowered her head in silence. Toda immediately sensed what was on her mind.

"Perhaps you don't understand the true meaning of what I'm telling you," he said. "I suspect that right now in your heart you are saying: 'But what about my troubles? How can I get out of the mess I'm in right now? That's what I want to know.' "

Mrs. Sasai nodded with a bashful smile.

Toda went on: "You're looking for a kind of spiritual panacea that will heal the suffering of your marriage. There isn't one.

You can take medicines for headaches and colds, but there is no medicine to patch up a family.

"I've asked you to be patient and to remain true to your faith for six months or a year. I suppose that seems like a long time to you. But when you think of all life and its endless three existences, surely you can see that a year is less than a passing moment. The law of karma extends through all three existences, and it is this law that has produced the situation you find yourself in. It's no accident that your husband became violently opposed to your religion immediately after you joined Nichiren Shoshu. He wouldn't have cared if you'd become a member of some inferior, misguided sect. The very violence of his opposition shows that ours is a powerful, living faith. Bear in mind another important thing. The more intense your husband's objections, the sooner you will be able to purge your life of the evil consequences of your karma.

"But to turn to a very basic point, I suspect that you have already asked yourself why you should have been afflicted with grave difficulties as soon as you accepted true Buddhism. Believe me, it is not because you have an impure heart or bad intentions. Nor is it because your husband is a bad man. It is because the law of karma binds us all, whether we are aware of it or not. This is the fundamental truth, the basic teaching of the Buddha. And I imagine you understand this to an extent.

"But knowledge of the law of karma alone will not solve your problem. There is a way to do that, however, a way that Nichiren Daishonin has prepared for us all. He left us the Gohonzon and the Daimoku as a way of worshiping the Gohonzon. If you faithfully chant the Daimoku and remain true to the teachings of Nichiren Daishonin, you can change your karma and solve your difficulties because you will work a kind of revolution in your life. This will take time, of course, because just as a sapling doesn't become a full-grown tree in a day, a change in karma cannot be accomplished overnight.

"It's up to you to decide whether you will face your karma and alter it by means of faith. But I can offer you these words of comfort from the Lotus Sutra: 'All sins are as frost, for the merciful sun shall dispel them.' I can promise you that the mercy of our religion will banish all your troubles if you are steadfast and faithful."

As Toda finished, Mrs. Sasai wiped tears of gratitude from her eyes. No one, not even her closest friends and relatives, had understood her problems as deeply or shown such compassionate concern as immediately as this tall man with thick glasses. Somehow she knew that she could rely on him for the spiritual guidance she needed. Her voice quavered slightly with emotion as she thanked him and apologized for taking up so much time.

"Don't apologize," said Toda. "I only want to show you that you must face your hardships with patience, courage, and above all, firm faith. You'll be all right, I'm sure." He was convinced that Mrs. Sasai was ready to face whatever lay ahead because, from the look on her face, he could already sense the increasing faith and courage.

When Toda had finished talking to Mrs. Sasai, Mrs. Tamè Izumida asked if she might introduce Mr. and Mrs. Yoshito Yamakawa, a couple she had met when they moved into her neighborhood recently. Mr. Yamakawa was in his forties; and his frail, tubercular wife was in her middle thirties. In presenting them to Toda, Mrs. Izumida said: "Mr. and Mrs. Yamakawa would like to join us. Mr. Yamakawa is out of work right now, and Mrs. Yamakawa has been suffering from tuberculosis for some time. They have six children, and their family suffered a great deal during the war."

"Well," said Toda, "look at this, Mrs. Sasai, we have another quarreling couple on our hands."

"How did you know they quarreled?" asked the surprised Mrs. Izumida.

"When a husband is out of work in a family with six children and a tubercular wife, there are bound to be quarrels." Then Toda asked the Yamakawas to tell him about themselves.

During the war, Yamakawa had made a small fortune as the owner of a munitions plant. In the last years of the conflict, when American air raids became intense, he was compelled to evacuate his plant to a rural area. Preparations were made, and all his machinery and tools were packed in crates and hauled to the railway yard to await transportation. Suddenly, in two air raids, he lost his house and factory and all the equipment that had been standing in the freight yard. Still, he had been wise enough to put away a large amount of cash in a safe place. This remained, and he estimated that he and his family would be able to live on it for almost ten years. They were by no means wealthy, but they managed to rent a small house on the banks of the Edogawa river in Tokyo.

But Yamakawa's calculations of the degree of security his cash would provide turned out to be faulty. At the end of the war, prices soared and money depreciated to the extent that what he had thought would last for ten years was almost all spent in three. His ill wife stubbornly refused to interpret their financial difficulties as anything but the result of his mismanagement. There was never enough food, and the children constantly complained of hunger. Just as Toda had surmised, quarrels occurred frequently. Yamakawa's only solace was to walk along the banks of the river in order to escape the cramped, unhappy surroundings of his home.

One day, by accident, Mrs. Izumida happened to meet Mrs. Yamakawa. Sensing at once that the frail woman was spiritually as well as physically unwell, the good-hearted Mrs. Izumida struck up a conversation in the hope of leading the now poverty-stricken family to a better life through religious faith. On several subsequent occasions she had discussed Nichiren Shoshu and Soka Gakkai with Mr. and Mrs. Yamakawa, who showed interest and finally asked to be introduced to Josei Toda.

Removing his glasses and rubbing his eyes for a moment when Yamakawa had finished his story, Toda said heavily: "I'm afraid that something—my intuition perhaps—tells me that you are in for darker days yet. If you hope to win good fortune, you will have to use your religious faith as a weapon in a long battle to change your karma. And in your case, I suspect that it will be a difficult fight. Do you think you are up to it?"

"We're used to poverty," said Mrs. Yamakawa as her husband sighed and lowered his head.

"I don't want to cause you anxiety, but I have a suspicion that things will get worse than they have been. Remember, you have the Gohonzon and the Daimoku. Don't let your faith weaken for a moment, and I can promise that you can look forward to brighter times when your long battle is over." Turning to Mrs. Izumida, Toda added: "If they have difficulties, you and your family must give them all the advice and help they need."

Though the Yamakawas' story was not one of unmixed happiness, it did not end in tragedy. As Toda had foreseen, still more severe poverty struck the family not long after the discussion meeting; but warned by Toda, they employed their great faith to overcome their troubles. Even during their financially darkest times, Mrs. Yamakawa was granted a divine reward for her steadfast faith. She had long suffered fits of coughing up blood. At one stage, her doctor had given her up as incurable; but shortly after her conversion to Nichiren Shoshu, she miraculously recovered from tuberculosis and from the neuralgia and bladder inflammation with which she had been afflicted. Finally, after a long struggle, the Yamakawa family regained financial security and in time reached a considerable level of prosperity.

2. THREE TRIPS
TO SHIMODA

IN SPITE of the turbulent conditions in Japan immediately after World War II, Josei Toda had managed to revitalize Nihon Shogakkan, the publishing firm he had established in prewar days. He and his staff worked very hard; but inflation, shortages of materials, and government controls continually threatened small- and medium-size businesses with disaster. Toda was forced to act always with the greatest caution, since a moment's carelessness could undo all that he and his fellow workers had managed to achieve.

Constantly aware of the needs and possibilities of the contemporary publishing world, Toda frequently shifted the emphasis of his publishing projects in keeping with changes in the market and general prevailing conditions. When he reopened his company, he had concentrated on correspondence courses in mathematics, science, English, and other subjects because, due to the long closing of schools during the war, young people were hungry for knowledge. The national education system had not yet been put into satisfactory working order, and response to the courses exceeded all expectations. Enrollments poured into Toda's office in a virtually unending stream. Still, as time passed, rising costs of paper and printing forced Toda to abandon the correspondence courses.

At that time, fortunately, the production of books was less affected by inflation. Furthermore, in their state of spiritual emptiness, the people of Japan were starved for serious reading material. For example, when a publishing firm announced a reprinting of a famous book called *A Study of Goodness*, written by the most influential Japanese philosopher of that time, Kitaro Nishida, prospective buyers gathering in the predawn hours in front of bookstores formed queues stretching for as much as half a mile. Realizing that the time had come to place greater stress on book publication, Toda launched several serious projects.

For a while, this policy worked well; but later it became apparent that in spite of good sales book production too faced a grave difficulty: procurement of paper. Because of extreme shortages, a government agency controlled all paper supplies. Publishing firms were obliged to submit publication plans to the official Japan Publishing Association, which decided whether a book was desirable on the basis of the amount of paper it required, as well as on the merit of its contents. Similar controls had been applied during the war, when such measures were unavoidable; but it was a sad sign of the times that they continued in effect for three years after the cessation of hostilities.

Nevertheless, paper was not impossible to obtain. It was generally available on the black market—like many other commodities. And from time to time, new printing paper appeared on the open market. When this happened, publishing firms rushed to purchase as much as possible, even at exorbitant prices. The paper shortage, no matter how dire, had not curtailed the mushrooming of small publishers. Ironically, in their frenzy to remain active and solvent, these companies readily paid whatever was demanded for materials and in this way only contributed to the inflation that was the primary obstacle crippling their endeavors. But this was not the only unfortunate effect of the paper shortage. Because paper was absolutely essential to their business, publishers resorted to all kinds of trickery and unethical practices to obtain necessary supplies.

Toda's company too was hampered by these difficulties. Though he worked hard to obtain paper and printing services and though his multivolume *Courses on Democracy in Japan* and several of the popular novels he issued were successful, he soon saw that book publishing had temporarily reached an impasse. Publishing firms rely on reprints of their titles for profit, but as production costs mounted, it became commercially unsound to try to sell second editions at the prices at which first editions of the same works had been issued. The situation seemed impossible.

Soon, however, Toda's judgment and business acumen suggested a way out of the difficulty. At this time, because of the paper shortage, none of the major prewar magazines had yet been revived. The only things sold in this line were skimpy, low-quality magazines, none of which catered to women or young boys. After considering all the factors involved in publishing magazines and after finding that such a project would be feasible, Toda set to work expanding his editorial staff, acquiring materials, and hiring writers and illustrators. Soon he was able to launch a youth magazine called *Boys' Adventures* and later a women's journal named *Ruby*.

Magazine work is busy to the point of frenzy. These two new projects injected tremendous vitality into the offices and staff of Nihon Shogakkan. People were constantly rushing to and fro picking up and delivering manuscripts, procuring printing supplies, negotiating with printing plants, and promoting sales. Toda directed and supervised all these activities with his usual attention to the minutest of details. Thanks to everyone's efforts, *Boys' Adventures* was soon selling more than a hundred

thousand copies monthly, and *Ruby* was selling tens of thousands. The company was making money again, in spite of the
numerous copies of the magazines that were returned unsold
each month.

All in all, the firm made considerable profit, but its financial
condition remained unsatisfactory for a very important reason:
Toda insisted on repaying all the debts he had incurred as a
result of his tremendous wartime losses. In those days, business-
men commonly either temporarily shelved or completely renounced debts of this kind; but Toda argued that he could not
adopt such an attitude because he considered it a point of
honor to acquit himself of his financial burden. It did not matter to him that the amount he owed was a staggering sum of
more than two and a half million yen or that the debts had
been incurred because of his unjust imprisonment at the hands
of the militarist regime.

Not all of the employees of Nihon Shogakkan saw eye to eye
with Toda on this matter. In fact, some of them, shocked that
he should try to repay his debts, went so far as to call him
honest to the point of foolishness. Even the gentle, amiable
Okumura, Toda's office accountant, could not restrain a critical remark.

"You are too good-hearted," he said, expressing his aver-
sion to devoting hard-won postwar profits to wartime debts.
"But the creditors have some nerve even coming here to ask
for the money. They know perfectly well that you are not really
bound by the IOUs they have against you."

"Well, I'd rather be called good-hearted than bad-hearted,"
Toda replied with a smile.

"Maybe, but still there's a limit," said Okumura, by no
means convinced.

"Think a minute," said Toda. "We must repay the debts
because we can afford to. Remember, these men were once
well-to-do, but they are now in financial trouble. They lent me
the money while I was still in prison. And that money kept

many of my employees from starving. I'm grateful to them, and you ought to be. After all, you benefited from those loans too. We should repay as much as we can without running the risk of putting ourselves in the red again."

Okumura saw that Toda was right and willingly did as he was told, though the repayments meant that he and everyone else, including Toda of course, had to work harder.

Nor was Toda's workload confined to the business of the daily running of the office. At night his time was taken up with the activities of Soka Gakkai. Three nights a week he lectured on the Lotus Sutra and the *Gosho,* and on three other nights he participated in discussion meetings where he gave guidance and counsel to both old members and the increasing number of new converts. Everyone around him marveled at his boundless energy, the source of which was his faith in Nichiren Shoshu. Six nights a week he was busy with meetings, and on weekends he often left Tokyo to go on membership campaigns in rural areas.

One of these trips had special nostalgic associations for Toda. Early in the spring of 1948, he traveled to Shimoda, at the southern tip of the Izu Peninsula, a place of great significance because it was there that Tsunesaburo Makiguchi, Toda's master and the first president of Soka Kyoiku Gakkai, had been arrested on false charges by the police of the militarist government.

In July, 1943, when he was seventy-two years old, Makiguchi traveled to Rendaiji village, located near Shimoda, to hold a discussion meeting with a small group of local believers in Nichiren Shoshu. In taking this step, Makiguchi ran a serious risk because only a few days earlier several leading members of Soka Kyoiku Gakkai had been arrested on trumped-up charges of so-called subversive activities. It was generally thought that Makiguchi's arrest too was imminent. Still, Makiguchi did not try to hide but went ahead with his plans for the meeting and membership campaign because he believed that to cancel the trip would be admitting defeat for both his faith and the lay society that represented it.

In fact, the trip to Shimoda was doubly important to Makiguchi, since it symbolized his relentless determination to protect his own faith and that of the many followers of Nichiren Shoshu, which had been a frequent target of attack from the government over the previous several months. In January, 1943, the authorities began a campaign of persecution of Soka Kyoiku Gakkai. In response to accusations of subversion, Makiguchi resolved to issue a remonstrance against the government. In doing this he was following the example of Nichiren Daishonin, who, seven hundred years earlier, bravely withstood savage persecution by the Kamakura shogunate, then ruling the nation.

Nichiren Daishonin openly denounced the government at a time when Japan faced a grave crisis that was to culminate in the Mongol invasions of 1274 and 1281. In his own day, when Japan was again confronted with a critical situation, Makiguchi treasured in his heart the passage from Nichiren Daishonin's *Kaimoku Sho* that says:

"Though the heavens forsake me, though all persecutions assail me, unless my belief is refuted by a wiser man, I will not give up my faith, for I have consecrated my life."

These words of Nichiren Daishonin inspired Makiguchi to criticize the government and to try to enlighten it on the gravity of its errors, especially in its disregard for the truth of Nichiren Shoshu. The government, however, saw fit to reject Makiguchi's ideas and went ahead with its persecutions. At first it had attempted to force Taiseki-ji, the head temple of Nichiren Shoshu, to acquiesce in a merger with the misguided Minobu Nichiren Shu. When the head temple persisted in resisting this merger, the government directed its attention to Soka Kyoiku Gakkai with renewed vehemence. Though he was alone in his resistance, Makiguchi refused to recant and intensified his efforts to strengthen and build the society. The trip to Shimoda was an important part of his plans.

On July third, after a discussion meeting at Rendaiji, Makiguchi and a few companions continued their trip to Shimoda, where they were to hold a similar gathering. In the evening, he went to the house of Miss Kishiko Hayashi, a believer in Nichiren Shoshu who had asked Makiguchi to speak with her father about the possibility of conversion to the faith. The Hayashi home was located in Suzaki at the tip of a headland jutting into the sea immediately southeast of Shimoda at a point where Sagami Bay joins the Pacific. Makiguchi was very fond of this place and of the magnificent view it commands.

Following a long discussion with Miss Hayashi's father, Makiguchi accepted an invitation to spend the night. The next morning, just as they were finishing breakfast, two detectives from the Shimoda police station arrived looking for Makiguchi. Miss Hayashi turned pale as she asked: "What do you want with him? Why have you come here? This is Shimoda, not Tokyo. What do you want to see him about?"

This brief exchange took place on the porch of the house, but Makiguchi heard it inside. Coming to the door, he asked: "What can I do for you?" He was dignified and unperturbed, but his sharp eyes examined the detectives closely.

"You'll find out what we want when you get to the police station. You're wanted there," said one of the detectives.

"Now?" asked Makiguchi, continuing to scrutinize the men.

"Yes, now."

"Very well, I'll get ready. Please wait a few minutes."

Makiguchi returned to his room, where Miss Hayashi helped him dress. Her hands were trembling.

"Don't be nervous; it's nothing to worry about. I've enjoyed my stay with you." Makiguchi tried to set her mind at rest.

After bidding the Hayashi family goodbye, Makiguchi went to the porch, where he apologized to the detectives for keeping them waiting. Then, just as they were about to leave, one of the detectives turned to Miss Hayashi and said: "You come with us too."

"Me?" she asked, startled. "Why?"

But then reflecting for an instant, she made up her mind immediately to do as she was told. First, she thought she might be able to be of some assistance to Makiguchi. Second, she was very much afraid that her father had informed the police of Makiguchi's visit to their home.

"Father—" She started to say something but could not go on. Confused and uncertain, she was unable to find words; but her look told her father that it was more than just the sudden appearance of the detectives that was upsetting her greatly. Completely unaware of her suspicions, Mr. Hayashi could only stare at his daughter helplessly. Saying no more than goodbye, she left, walking beside Makiguchi, who was using his umbrella as a cane. Her father's reticence convinced her of his guilt. She felt sure that his antagonism toward Nichiren Shoshu had led him to betray Makiguchi to the authorities.

"I'm very sorry," she said to Makiguchi.

"But why should you be sorry, Kishiko?" Makiguchi asked. "You have nothing to do with this. It's only that the time has come at last."

Miss Hayashi did not understand Makiguchi's meaning because she did not realize that for months he had known he would be arrested soon. He was mentally prepared to face whatever fate held in store. Throughout the three-mile walk to the Shimoda police station, Makiguchi was silent. As he walked proud and erect, his face showed no sign of fear or anxiety. His greatest concern seemed to be to enjoy the glittering blue expanse of the sea stretched out below the cliffside path along which they walked.

Apparently absorbed in the beauty of the scene, Makiguchi strode on with the dignity of a sage; but he was in fact deeply troubled about the safety of the many members of the society and especially of the leaders, including Director General Toda.

If the authorities were now pressing their campaign against Soka Kyoiku Gakkai to the extent that they would track down Makiguchi in this remote area, in all likelihood they were preparing to move against other members, as well. In his mind, he could see Toda's face; and he silently prayed for Toda's safety and that of all other members in this time of crisis. But he found strength in the words of the *Gosho:* "The disciples of Nichiren must never be cowardly." Repeating this sentence silently several times, he resolved that even at the risk of loss of life he would not be defeated.

For a moment, as Makiguchi chanted the Daimoku to himself, he became aware of the brilliance of the world around him, of the deep greens of the pines and cedars, and of the sweet singing of the birds. But then another cloud darkened his spirit. His family, his granddaughter, what would become of them? Once again a passage from the writings of Nichiren Daishonin gave him strength. In one of the eleven letters in which Nichiren Daishonin predicted both the Mongol invasions of Japan and the intensified persecution of his followers he wrote: "Each of you must be prepared. Never give thought to your wives, children, or relatives. Never be afraid of power or of the authorities."

As Makiguchi reflected on these words, once again the darkness vanished; and he saw the splendor of nature, the purple shadows of the Izu Islands in the distance, and the mighty breakers crashing on the beach below.

The walk to the police station had given Makiguchi an opportunity to analyze and understand the crisis confronting him. Instead of filling him with dread of what lay in the coming days, it strengthened his resolve.

"From now on, it will seem to the outside world that the authorities are putting me on trial, but I know that it is they who are to be judged," he thought. "I shall condemn the state for its sinful persecution of true Buddhism and its mistaken allegiance to Shinto. The days to come will give me my chance to attack the powers in authority and to prove my philosophy of value and the essence of Nichiren Shoshu."

As an outward sign of the vitality this thought inspired, Makiguchi raised his umbrella and struck a stone at the roadside. The detectives were puzzled by his action.

Makiguchi arrived at the police station with pride: he was no sheep being led to the slaughter, but a lion about to face a formidable enemy. After one night's detention, Miss Hayashi was released, much relieved to learn that her father was in no way implicated in the betrayal of Makiguchi. In fact, shortly after Makiguchi's arrest, Mr. Hayashi was converted to Nichiren Shoshu. Makiguchi himself, however, was never again to be a free man. After two nights in Shimoda, he was transferred under detective guard to the Tokyo Metropolitan Police Department.

During the trials that dragged on for eighteen months after his arrest, Makiguchi fought valiantly for his release. He confronted the authorities with the unjustness of their persecution of true Buddhism and used his time on the witness stand to lecture his judges on the significance of the philosophy of value. But his efforts brought no improvement in his chances for liberation. He was subsequently sent to Sugamo Prison, where he remained until his death in 1944.

With memories of all these moving events in his heart, Josei Toda was naturally excited when he arrived in Shimoda in 1948. A discussion and membership campaign conducted in the Shimoda district in 1947 had already produced impressive results. Instead of the mere handful of believers that Toda found there on his earlier trip, this year the town had a Soka Gakkai chapter of eighty households.

Among the many enthusiastic people welcoming Toda when he got off the bus at Shimoda station was buxom, gray-haired Mrs. Tomi Honda, whom Toda did not recognize at first. Nor was it surprising that he did not, because when he had seen

her only a year earlier she had been a defeated, haggard creature in such desperate spiritual condition that she frequently
contemplated suicide.

Before World War II, the very religious family of Mrs. Tomi
Honda lived in Tokyo and were members of a Nichiren sect

called Nakayama. Its head temple was Hokekyo-ji, in a place
called Nakayama, in Chiba Prefecture. The guardian deity of
the sect was Hariti, whom Mrs. Honda and all her family
worshiped faithfully and often. Mrs. Honda was so interested
in religion and especially in the Lotus Sutra that she made it
a rule to attend all kinds of religious meetings, even those
outside the immediate sphere of the sect she followed.

One July night in 1941, she was present at a discussion meeting sponsored by Soka Kyoiku Gakkai. But what she heard at
that meeting did not please her. During the course of the evening, in her eagerness to defend the viewpoint of her own religion, she got into a heated argument with Miss Katsu Kiyohara,

representing Nichiren Shoshu and Soka Kyoiku Gakkai. Miss Kiyohara carefully pointed out to Mrs. Honda documentary, theoretical, and actual proof of the Nakayama sect's mistakes and demonstrated that Nichiren Shoshu is the only true Buddhism.

Mrs. Honda disagreed. Growing more and more irritated at what she considered the obstinance of Miss Kiyohara, Mrs. Honda tried to counter her arguments by claiming that, since the members of the Nakayama sect chant the Daimoku and worship the Lotus Sutra, their faith was in every respect as true and orthodox as that of any other Nichiren sect, including Nichiren Shoshu.

The equally ardent Miss Kiyohara insisted that though the Daimoku chanted by all Nichiren groups is the same, the only true object of veneration is the Dai-Gohonzon. Consequently, no matter how assiduously people repeat the chant itself, if they direct it to the wrong object of worship, they cannot expect to be on the right path. But more serious than this was the danger of punishment believers in the Nakayama sect were courting by misdirecting their worship. All who neglect the worship of the Dai-Gohonzon inevitably suffer. When she heard this, Mrs. Honda could restrain herself no longer and angrily stalked out of the room. Intending to warn of harm that might soon befall her, Miss Kiyohara called out to the departing Mrs. Honda: "Be careful on your way home!" Mrs. Honda said nothing but she thought: "What nerve!"

Still, apprehension clouded her mind as she walked to the streetcar stop. She waited for a while and then, oddly frightened by Miss Kiyohara's warning, decided to walk home. But by the time she arrived safely, she felt foolish for having given in to doubt. To make up for what she considered religious negligence, she went immediately to the family altar, where she offered fervent prayers to Hariti for continued protection.

For a while, the sense of foreboding aroused by her discussion with Miss Kiyohara preyed on Mrs. Honda's mind, but as weeks and months passed without mishap, she completely forgot the unpleasant meeting and worshiped her deity with renewed devotion. Indeed, her faith seemed to be a source of blessing for her and her family. The clothing business that she and her husband had started from virtually nothing thrived. She employed five seamstresses to fill the orders that came to her in large numbers, and she and her family soon became so prosperous that they were the envy of their neighborhood. When the war situation grew worse, she entrusted her business to her daughter and moved for safety to the city of Numazu, where she and her husband settled down comfortably.

But the comfort and calm of her life were soon to be destroyed. One day as he was carrying a wardrobe to the second floor of their house, Mr. Honda tripped and fell down the flight of stairs. As he lay stunned on the floor, the wardrobe teetered and came crashing down, striking him on the head and killing him instantly. After this tragedy, Mrs. Honda's happiness vanished; but she was not to be spared further loss and misery. Soon she and her eleven-year-old grandson moved to a village on the outskirts of Shimoda, where Mrs. Honda's parents had once lived. The war had already driven thousands of people from the large metropolitan centers. Evacuees flooded small villages like the one where Mrs. Honda lived and created an acute housing shortage. She and her grandson were forced to lead a miserable life in the loft of a barn without electricity or any of the conveniences to which they had been accustomed.

On March 10, 1945, a massive air raid on Tokyo destroyed her house and business there. Her daughter and son-in-law, who had been taking care of the family's interests, were killed in the ensuing fire. Heaped atop all the other suffering, this calamity reduced Mrs. Honda to a state of complete mental and physical lethargy. For months on end, she locked herself in her loft, refusing to do more than eat what scraps of food she was able to acquire and seeing no one but her grandson.

When the war ended she was destitute. Without money enough to buy even the meager food on which she and her grandson had subsisted, she found herself compelled to venture into the world again to try to make a living. She began peddling clothes from village to village. The arduous work meant carrying heavy bundles on her back and walking many miles. Though it brought in some money, Mrs. Honda had no interest in the task, which seemed as futile as everything else. She could force herself to work for no more than about ten days a month. The remainder of her time was spent locked in the barn, where she worshiped Hariti, whom she considered her sole support. But her guardian deity inspired her with so little hope that she often thought of killing herself to end her misery. On her long treks from one village to another, she would stop under a tree and think how easy it would be to hang herself from one of the boughs. Or while walking along a seaside cliff she would be tempted to hurl herself into blessed oblivion in the waves below. Only her beloved grandson, who would be left unprotected if she died, prevented her from committing suicide.

As bad as they were, matters were to grow still worse. Toward the end of 1945, her grandson caught influenza and developed a high fever. While nursing him, Mrs. Honda too fell ill with the disease. Now forsaken, sick, and wretched, she began to wonder whether the deity in whom she had placed complete trust had abandoned her. She recalled the words spoken by Miss Kiyohara in the Soka Kyoiku Gakkai meeting years ago and for a moment entertained the fear that she was suffering the punishment prophesied for mistaken religious faith. But no; that could not be. After all, the Daimoku that she chanted daily was the same one chanted by the followers of Nichiren Shoshu. There must be some other reason. If only someone would help her understand why things had gone wrong and show her how to extricate herself and her grandson from the wretchedness of their life.

Then, one day in January, 1947, Mrs. Matsu Oya, a Nichiren Shoshu believer, called on Mrs. Honda in her barn loft to invite her to attend a meeting to be conducted by an important leader in their religious movement. Though she was not fully recovered from her illness, Mrs. Honda decided to go. She would try anything that offered some hope of improving her circumstances.

There were about ten people in the dimly lighted room in the Oya home when Mrs. Honda arrived. Among them she recognized the same Miss Kiyohara who had attempted to convince her of the truth of Nichiren Shoshu six years earlier. Mrs. Honda avoided the younger woman's gaze. Soon she was introduced to a tall, distinguished-looking man named Josei Toda, who greeted her warmly and asked her to tell him about her life and her religion. In a sudden outburst she related everything that had happened to her, insisting always that she could not understand why she had been so rigorously punished when she had been unflaggingly devoted in chanting the Daimoku and in praying to Hariti. When she finished her story, everyone in the room was grieved at her suffering and profoundly moved by the relentless law of karma as manifested in her miserable life. After a few minutes of silence, Toda said gently: "You have worked hard and have been faithful to your religion in the hope of becoming happy, but instead of happiness you have found only sorrow. Do you know where you went wrong?"

"No," she said, "I wish I did."

"Your earnest devotion to your faith is a fine thing, and you are a fine person. But I can tell you why, in spite of your goodness, you are suffering such great misfortune: you have put your faith in the wrong thing. Nichiren Daishonin taught that the object of worship determines whether we are happy or unhappy. It is your object of worship, not you yourself, that is to blame for your tragedy."

Quoting from the Lotus Sutra, Toda explained to Mrs. Honda that Hariti is an evil goddess who, though promising to protect the faithful of the Gohonzon, must not be regarded as an object of worship.

Still unconvinced, Mrs. Honda repeated the question she had asked herself and others on many occasions.

"Aren't people who chant the Daimoku protected?"

"Yes," was Toda's reply.

"I chanted it constantly for many years. Why wasn't I protected?"

"From your point of view," said Toda, "you have done everything you could. But I must repeat that you chose the wrong object of worship. As Nichiren Daishonin carefully warned, in the Latter Day of the Law the Gohonzon is the only source of faith."

"But I don't understand," said Mrs. Honda. The combination of the misery of her life and the clear, uncompromising instruction of Nichiren Daishonin to select the one and only object of veneration had weakened her assurance and had made her question the religion to which she had been unquestioningly faithful for many years. Within her heart, a struggle was taking place: "Is what he tells me true or false? Even if it's false, it seems true; on the other hand, it is too simple to be true."

Moved by the woman's suffering and stricken with shame that she had not been more persistent in her attempts to convert her in the past, Miss Kiyohara tried to come to her aid: "As much as it grieves me to say this, Mrs. Honda, I'm afraid that you have wasted six precious years. And I cannot tell you how sorry I am that I did not visit you after that discussion meeting long ago. If I had helped you then, you might have had a happy life. But it is still not too late. You can start all over again now."

Mrs. Honda asked herself if taking the young woman's warning to heart six years earlier would have made so great a difference. Of one thing she was certain, however: the religion she had followed had brought her more grief than joy. Turning again to Toda she asked softly: "Is this Gohonzon you worship really as great as you say?"

"It is the only true object of worship in this world. And you will discover this for yourself if you will accept and practice our faith, even for only a year."

"Time is very valuable. I am old now," Mrs. Honda said. "I haven't much longer to live. But I worry about my grandson. I could not die in peace without knowing that he is provided for."

With a smile of understanding, Toda said: "I tell you what, Mrs. Honda, if you accept and practice the faith of Nichiren Shoshu for a year and do not find it rewarding, I will assume responsibility for your grandson and his education. I will see that he is brought up to be a fine man."

"Do you really mean that?" asked the surprised old woman.

"I am always true to my word," replied Toda.

Still harboring doubt, Mrs. Honda persisted: "But you live in Tokyo. That's far away. And suppose, when the year has passed, I need to find you? I don't even know where you live."

Toda gave her his card and his word. Thanking him and tucking the card carefully into her kimono sash, Mrs. Honda said: "I promise to abide by my part of the bargain. From this day on, the Gohonzon will become the center of all my religious worship."

The troubled and haggard Mrs. Honda who had made that promise in 1947 was a very different person from the smiling, healthy Mrs. Honda who greeted Toda at the bus in Shimoda in 1948. As they walked together to the Oya home for the discussion meeting, Mrs. Honda thanked Toda for opening her eyes to the great goodness of the Gohonzon. She had kept her promise to Toda, and as a result she had not only regained her health and mental stability, but also made considerable strides forward in business and was thinking of building a new home soon.

Later Toda had to admit that the great success of the discussion meeting that evening was due to Mrs. Honda and her vivid tale of the blessings she had received as a consequence of faith in the Gohonzon. Though the room in which the gathering was held was unheated, all hearts were warmed by Mrs. Honda's testimonial and by that of a young man whose faith had cured him of a bone infection so serious that his doctors had given him up as hopeless. Late into the night the older members and several newcomers talked about many important aspects of human life and sought Toda's guidance on various issues.

On the following day, Toda and his party broke up in order to visit isolated areas where Mrs. Oya had talked with a number of prospective new members. Several important contacts and conversions resulted from this trip. Each person won over to true Buddhism in this and other membership campaigns soon became a small vortex generating waves of reaction that spread over a constantly widening field. As always, one of the major driving forces behind the success of undertakings of this kind was personal contact. And here Toda's charm, kindliness, and perception played a leading role. Successful personal relations are vital to the fundamental goal of Nichiren Shoshu and Soka Gakkai, because the human revolution that is the first step in the worldwide propagation of the true faith is an intensely personal matter. The great torrent of religious revival that was later to sweep throughout Japan began with individual human beings. And no one knew better how to reach individuals than Josei Toda.

3. PORTRAITS

THE PERSONALITY of Josei Toda is difficult to analyze in terms of conventional thought. He was, like all human beings, a creature of complicated, multifaceted elements. He knew when to remain outside of strictly personal matters while suggesting a broad philosophical basis for specific action. He could be compassionate and generous, as he was with Mrs. Honda and her grandson. He could be extremely charming on a personal level, as he generally was with new members and people seeking help. Perhaps the one trait that characterized him most vividly, however, was his uncompromising truthfulness and his abhorrence of hypocrisy. When he encountered insincerity and falsehood in others, he often flew into rages of scorching intensity. People who did not know him well found this anger incomprehensible in one generally so calm and considerate. But on closer acquaintance, they learned that his wrath was always detonated by and directed against such traits as hypocrisy, vanity, and bigotry, but not against the individual human beings displaying the characteristics.

Though he never attempted to manipulate people, he knew how to inspire his followers to exert their best efforts. Sometimes, kindness and encouragement were required to help a despondent man find himself, reinforce his faith, and thus contribute to the cause of Nichiren Shoshu. At other times, rigor had to be applied to shock a person out of lethargy or self-pity and show him his responsibilities. Like a father who knows when to praise and when to chastise, Toda dealt with each case according to its circumstances and needs. He was able to judge these needs accurately because his faith made of him a mirror, reflecting with undistorted clarity the inner worlds and feelings of the people with whom he came into contact. So accurate were his estimations of the conditions of his followers that he was usually able with a few apt words to set to rights situations that seemed headed for disaster. Toda's genius for guiding human relations bore rich fruit for Soka Gakkai.

Of course, by the late 1940s several of the society's leading members no longer required direct guidance from Toda to inspire them to work hard. For instance, the so-called Trio from Kamata—Koichi Harayama, Takeo Konishi, and Hisao Seki—devoted much of their time to membership campaigns and discussion meetings with immense success. Though they were fortunate to have at their disposal two houses, both located in Tokyo in places very convenient for discussion meetings and other gatherings, the work of these three men covered the whole metropolitan area and extended to Yokohama, to Urayasu in Chiba Prefecture, and to other regions. Thanks to the efforts of the trio, Kamata produced a large number of vigorous, hard-working young men who eventually became the nucleus of the Youth Division. Among them were Chuhei Yamadaira, Juichi Iwata, and Giichi Sakata, who had been disciples of Makiguchi; the college instructor Hiroshi Yamagiwa; and Miss Hideko Mikawa.

This group's favorite way of winning new converts was to attend meetings of misguided or deliberately misleading religious sects, where they employed irrefutable logic and brilliant debate tactics to prove the fallacies of the religious doctrines propounded by the erroneous groups. Consequently, the leaders of these sects came to dread the appearance of Soka Gakkai members in their midst because the inevitable outcome of encounters was a decline in their own membership and further new converts for Nichiren Shoshu.

In other parts of Japan, as well, devoted followers busily spread the news of true Buddhism. Perhaps most notable among these workers were the Morikawa family in Tsurumi, Kanagawa Prefecture; the nineteen-year-old fisherman Akio Nakamichi in Chiba Prefecture; and young Kunio Shiroya in northeastern Honshu. Largely because of the energetic efforts of these and other faithful members, by the spring of 1948, membership of the society had grown to five hundred households, or approximately thirteen hundred individuals. But things did not always run smoothly for all Soka Gakkai members. Some suffered much hardship before and during World War II and needed great help to put themselves on a path of development in postwar Japan.

Hiroshi Izumida was such a person. He was born in the remote mountains of the Izu Peninsula in 1910. When he was only three years old his mother died and his father ran away, abandoning him to the care of his grandparents, who belonged to a Zen temple in their village. They raised young Hiroshi to the best of their ability and tried to instill in him the reverence they felt for the teaching of Zen Buddhism. But he was more interested in outdoor activities and sports than in religion. Consequently, though he neglected his spiritual life, he developed a powerful physique. When Hiroshi was twenty-one, both of his grandparents died, bequeathing him a small property and a mass of debts. Paying off the financial obligations of the family left him penniless. He decided to leave Izu and become a professional soldier, in which occupation his strong body would be a considerable asset. His reasons for joining the military had more to do with a desire for security than with any sense of devotion to the nation or the emperor, toward whom Izumida was relatively indifferent.

Once in the army, he found that he did not like military life at all. He especially disliked drill and the rigid discipline, but he persevered and in time became a warrant officer. This rank carried certain privileges, among them the right to request transfer from the regular army to other branches of the military. Izumida promptly availed himself of this right and joined the military police. The cruelty for which prewar Japanese military police were notorious was repugnant to him, however; and Izumida immediately began seeking a way to remove himself from the direct stream of police activity. Before long, he had a chance to work as a paymaster. This job was to stand him in good stead later in life, but for the time being it kept him away from the unsavory side of military duty and provided him with enough security to be able to save money each month.

Japan was not at war at the time, and general conditions permitted Izumida to lead, if not a happy life, at least one of modest contentment. He was still young and wanted to marry and have children. After some time passed, he met a girl named Tamè, whom he courted and soon married. A son born to them in due time died only four days after birth. This blow dashed Izumida from the joys of fatherhood to the gloom of mourning. But worse was in store for him: only months after the death of her infant son, Izumida's wife became gravely ill. Protracted hospitalization and medical care quickly consumed all the money Izumida had been able to set aside. Still, youth is resilient, and these young people were able to survive their trials and even to hope for a new start with another child. Tamè Izumida recovered her health and after a while became pregnant again. Once more, the thrill of parenthood filled the hearts of husband and wife, until they learned with grief that their newborn daughter was a victim of congenital cerebral palsy. She would never cry, smile, or even grow normally.

So much effort, so much suffering; and what had it done

for Izumida and his wife? What had they known of married life together but sorrow and suffering? What gods or Buddhas could be cruel enough to give human beings life and then to make it a burden almost too heavy to bear? Izumida cursed his fate, reviled all religion as empty and meaningless, and fell into a dark despair where there was no glimmer of hope.

One day, quite by accident, he happened to meet Tsunesaburo Makiguchi at the home of a friend. Izumida's unfortunate experiences were briefly discussed. As he heard the story, Makiguchi realized immediately that Izumida urgently required something reliable in which to put his faith and trust. But perceiving Izumida's precarious mental condition, Makiguchi knew that rational discussions of religion would be out of place. He contented himself with saying that he knew of one thing, and only one, in this world that could give strength to the stricken and assist them in finding a way out of misery and defeat. That one source of strength is the Gohonzon. Izumida was fascinated by what Makiguchi had to say.

Izumida was then thirty. Though healthy and still powerfully built, he had gone bald. He felt time slipping through his fingers, and he shuddered at the mere contemplation of his past sufferings and of the meaninglessness of the future of his paralyzed infant daughter. At the time, he had no interest in religious orthodoxy. When he became a member of Nichiren Shoshu, it was solely out of a desperate hope of helping his child. It seemed a last resort.

As a conscientious man, after he became a member of Nichiren Shoshu, he recited the daily Gongyo prayers and chanted the Daimoku often. He requested guidance from Makiguchi, whom he first came to respect as a person and then to love as a substitute for the father that he had never had. Though his daughter's condition remained unchanged, Izumida gradually grew in faith and in knowledge of the meaning of the teachings of Nichiren Daishonin. So important did his religion become to him that two years after his conversion he vowed never to abandon his faith, even if no improvement should take place in his daughter's health.

On a late summer day in 1942, the child died. Freed at last from the agonies of disease, she lay still, an oddly peaceful shadow of a smile on her small serene face. Sitting beside his daughter, Izumida chanted the Daimoku silently and then fell into profound meditation. Two tremendous questions occupied his mind. Could it be that this poor child came into the world and suffered intense pain from birth for the sake of opening the eyes of her stupid father to the greatness of the Gohonzon? If this was true, in what way could he thank her now that life had fled her body. The second question for which he could find no answer involved the very nature of life. Only a few moments earlier his child had been alive. Now she was dead. But where did her life go? Where does life come from, and what becomes of it at death?

He sobbed for a loss that he could not understand. Suddenly he realized that something greater lay at the heart of his quandary. Somehow, he felt he must try to grasp the meaning of the mystery of living. The only thing he had encountered that held out hope of explaining this universal question was Nichiren Daishonin's Buddhism and his philosophy of life force.

A few days later, as he offered incense in his daughter's memory, Izumida realized the chain of misfortunes that had made up his existence from childhood and that had culminated in his crippled child's death had been part of a purposeful development. It had all happened to bring him to recognize the vital importance of Nichiren Shoshu. In the quiet cemetery, before the memorial to his daughter, he vowed that he would intensify both his study of Nichiren Daishonin's teachings and his practice of the faith until he found answers to the supreme questions of human life. He discussed the matter with his wife, who joined him in pledging to devote more energy and more time to their faith. The wounds of their suffering were not completely healed, but grief had abated. They now had hope and something to live for. But in the coming years, their pledge was to be sorely tested.

When Izumida's daughter died, Japan was in the heat of World War II. Thousands of Japanese soldiers were being shipped to remote corners of Asia to fight under conditions of extreme hardship. At the end of 1942, the battalion to which Izumida belonged was ordered to New Guinea, at that time the bloodiest front of the fighting.

For a time following Pearl Harbor, the Japanese won victory after victory; but the battle of Midway was a turning point after which they were on the defensive throughout much of the Pacific zone. Counteroffensives launched by the Americans at Guadalcanal in August necessitated dispatching large fleets of Japanese troop transports to the South Pacific. Many of these ships were destroyed by the United States naval forces. Though official Japanese news releases to the public minimized the losses in order to improve morale at home, word about the fates of individuals and miraculous stories of soldiers who drifted to uninhabited islands after their ships were sunk leaked into the home islands and naturally caused great concern.

Izumida too heard these rumors and was most skeptical about his chances of returning alive from New Guinea. The very human fear he felt in the face of orders that seemed tantamount to a death sentence shook his religious faith for a brief while. He had been faithful to the Gohonzon for over two years. During that time his daughter died. Now he was being sent to almost certain death. But in the midst of his doubts, he recalled something he had read in the writings of Nichiren Daishonin: "Realize, therefore, that it is pure wonder to be content and happy and a matter of course to be in difficulty." Perhaps these words did not comfort him, but they did dispel his doubt, give him courage to face the inevitable, and inspire him to make a pilgrimage to Taiseki-ji.

On January 2, 1943, he was granted an audience with the Dai-Gohonzon at the head temple. Reverently bowing his head, he asked forgiveness for his lapse of faith. He begged for protection during the frightening experiences that lay ahead and for a safe return to his homeland when the war ended. The solace he found in his trip to the temple enabled him to embark on January 28 with courage and hope.

Because the entire South Pacific was dominated by enemy submarines, after setting sail from the port of Ujima, near Hiroshima, Izumida's ship was forced to take a long, circuitous route first to Taiwan, then to Singapore, and then from island to island until it at last landed, in February, at Surabaja, in Java. Throughout the entire arduous journey, Izumida observed morning and evening Gongyo services without fail and chanted the Daimoku regularly, in spite of jeers from some of the other soldiers. Gradually, his religious fervor came to be recognized as sincere and meaningful, and those who had formerly teased him learned to respect his faith.

After remaining on standby status in Surabaja for a short while, Izumida's ship set sail again, this time to Ceram, a West Irian island, and then to Amboina, where his outfit was forced to wait for several months. Japanese troops had already begun to retreat from Guadalcanal. Though this was the first time the government publicly admitted a retreat, even in this case the move was euphemistically described as a transfer. Nonetheless, during the move, the Japanese suffered heavy casualties and narrowly missed being totally annihilated at the hands of superior enemy forces.

In fact, the American navy had gained such complete control of the seas around New Guinea that Izumida's battalion was stranded on Amboina. The outlook was grim, for food continued to diminish and there was no chance for additional supplies to reach them. In deprivation and isolation, they waited until, after some months, they seized an opportunity to sail for Sorong, their ultimate destination. It had taken them ten months to reach this island; and through good fortune, for a while they suffered no serious attacks. Matters elsewhere, however, were going badly for the Japanese. In April, Admiral Isoroku Yamamoto, commander in chief of the Imperial Navy, was killed in action. Later the same year, garrison forces first on Attu in the Aleutian Islands and then on Tarawa and Makin in the South Pacific were completely crushed. On Sorong, Izumida's group could do nothing but wait in fear of an enemy offensive as they tried to stretch their diminishing food supplies. They were almost completely unaware of the battles raging on New Guinea and in other parts of the Pacific. In the strangely isolated calm of Sorong, Izumida remained faithful to his religion, often climbing a hill to look homeward and envisage the head temple in its grove of green cedars.

In October, 1944, something extremely mysterious occurred. Izumida alone was ordered to leave Sorong and return to Amboina. He felt certain that this sealed his fate. Even should he manage to reach the island through waters infested with enemy submarines, death would await him on its shores. On a tiny island like Amboina there was no way to escape enemy bombardment. This new, and apparently final, crisis once again awakened doubt in his mind. Why had he been singled out for a mission as dangerous as this when he had been faithful under the most trying and perilous circumstances? But, as on other occasions, the answer came to him clearly and suddenly, revealing to him the futility of doubt. Faith, continuous and strong, would see him through somehow, though admittedly, at that moment, hope seemed futile.

One dark night, Izumida set out alone in a small boat. The tropical sea glittered eerily with noctiluca. Ordinarily, he would have been fascinated by the loveliness of the sight, but now terror obliterated everything but the single desire to navigate safely through waters made treacherous by the constant threat of enemy attack. He was forced to travel warily by night and to hide his boat among the many small islands in the vicinity by day. At all times, he kept a watchful eye on the horizon for signs of enemy ships. Finally, after a full month of fear-fraught navigation, he arrived at Amboina, where he soon settled down to work with his new organization. Life on the island was peaceful. Izumida thanked his Gohonzon for this and for having brought him thus far in safety.

Gradually the war situation grew worse. Like other Japanese soldiers of the time, Izumida was torn between a desire to end the struggle by surrendering to the Americans and a sense of duty to fight to the very last. But before long the Americans captured his outfit and thus did away with the need to debate the issue. In their numerous and lengthy discussions of capture and surrender, the Japanese soldiers had convinced themselves that life in an American prisoner-of-war camp would be harsh. To his surprise, however, Izumida found that he alone was both treated well and given a private room. In July, 1946, he was repatriated and demobilized at Tanabe, in Wakayama Prefecture.

Before beginning his return trip home, Izumida spent a few days at an inn in the port town. While there, he met a thin, sunburned young soldier who recognized him, though Izumida could not recall the man at first. It turned out that the young man, named Yamagiwa, had been in the organization with Izumida on Sorong. As always happens with military men who have shared experiences and then parted for a while, the two immediately struck up a conversation about what had happened since their last meeting. During the talk, Izumida learned something that threw his whole war experience into proper perspective.

The news received from his old friend amazed and inspired Izumida. He could not share it with anyone until he had had a chance to talk to Josei Toda, but he knew that the first step he must take was to go immediately to Taiseki-ji to give thanks to the Dai-Gohonzon. Though his funds were meager, he scraped together enough money for the trip. When he arrived at the beautiful main gate of the temple and saw at last the towering cedars he had so often envisaged during his travels throughout the Pacific, he knew that he was home.

The next important thing for him to do was to locate his wife and start a new life. Both tasks seemed impossible. After a long absence with no news from home he had no idea what might have happened to his wife. And conditions in war-torn Japan were so bad that making a living of any kind presented immense difficulties. Once again, however, faith showed the way. By chance, he happened to be examining the temple pilgrim register when he found his wife's calling card in the book. He immediately cabled her to come to Taiseki-ji, and while waiting the week that the trip took in those days, he helped the priests harvest the winter wheat. After a joyous reunion, the Izumidas returned to the small apartment in Koiwa, Tokyo, where Mrs. Izumida had lived while working at a city council office during the war.

The day after his return to the city, Izumida hastened to

visit Toda, who was the only man likely to understand the importance of the news passed on by his war companion. Izumida also believed that if anyone could help him get a fresh start in life, it was Toda. Toda was overjoyed to see Izumida and congratulated him on returning safe from his harrowing experiences. Unable to contain the truly miraculous nature of his escape any longer, Izumida told Toda what he had learned.

The day after Izumida had set sail alone in his small boat for Amboina, a United States transport plane had made a forced landing on Sorong. Twelve survivors from the plane were taken prisoner. A request for instructions about handling the captives was sent to battalion headquarters, but the small outfit that had taken the prisoners was remote and isolated. For one reason or another, no instructions were received before the war ended and the Americans landed to take over the island. The Japanese, about to become captives themselves, felt compelled to do something with the American prisoners to prevent them from complaining to their compatriots about the maltreatment they had received at the hands of their captors.

The solution they elected was simple: they spirited the prisoners away to a small island and shot them. Before long, however, the United States forces on the island got wind of the execution, rounded up the responsible Japanese, and shipped them to Australia, where they were to await military trial and, most probably, execution.

These men had been Izumida's subordinates on Sorong. Had he not been mysteriously ordered to Amboina, he would certainly have been held responsible for the fates of the twelve Americans. Clearly the power of the Dai-Gohonzon had miraculously brought about his transfer at just the right moment to remove him from danger. Even as he thought of his salvation in retrospect, Izumida felt a chill run down his spine. The workings of fate are amazing: only one day and two or three sentences in a set of military orders had saved him from disgrace and death. Throughout the long misery of the war he had been faithful. And the Gohonzon had rewarded him not only by protecting him in perilous conditions, but also by extricating him from a set of circumstances that would have inevitably spelled his execution even after the conclusion of the war.

Toda listened silently and attentively to everything Izumida told him. Then with a smile of happiness he confirmed what Izumida already knew in his heart.

"The Gohonzon has saved you," said Toda. "You are still healthy and, I trust, still devoted to your faith. I think you should see how important it is to preserve that faith no matter what happens."

Izumida agreed, but he could not help asking for aid in building a new life for himself and his wife. He was by no means saddened at the loss of his military job. But where was he to find another? Work was scarce. To make matters worse, professional soldiers were included under a purge directive forbidding any kind of work except that provided by the occupation forces general headquarters or by the repatriation relief bureau. Most of these positions were already filled. Izumida had some savings in the bank; but deposits were frozen, and he was able to draw only a small amount monthly. In any case, the money he had could not last more than about six months. Still Toda did not seem discouraged, even in the face of apparently insurmountable obstacles.

"After everything you have already come through safely, minor matters like this shouldn't trouble you too much. Be patient for a week. Something will turn up."

Believing firmly that everything would somehow be all right, Izumida left to make another important call that same day. While at Taiseki-ji, he had been grieved to learn of the death of Tsunesaburo Makiguchi. It was to the Makiguchi house that he went next, to offer his condolences. The loss of the man who had been a father to him was so great that even the tears streaming down Izumida's face as he prayed before the Makiguchi family altar failed to be an adequate expression of his sorrow.

After about a week or so, the something that Toda promised would turn up did materialize. Thanks to a few words of recommendation from Toda, a small newspaper office hired Izumida as an accountant, a job for which his paymaster work in the military had trained him. Now the days of poverty were over. With them went the petty disagreements that had sometimes arisen between Izumida and his wife when they were uncertain of how to make ends meet. Convinced that their faith was so firm that they had nothing to fear, both of them set out to convert other people to the saving teachings of Nichiren Daishonin. Being only human, they still argued from time to time, but the sources of disagreement were now only religious matters that two people of strong faith could easily reconcile. As time passed, Izumida and his wife converted several people in their apartment building and then others throughout their neighborhood until, before long, they had brought many people in the Koiwa district to an understanding of the effects of the power of the Gohonzon and the strength the individual human being can derive from unwavering faith.

Sometimes Toda's counseling consisted of no more than words of encouragement and gentle coaxing, as in Izumida's case. Other people required sterner treatment. Miss Katsu Kiyohara, a person who played an active part in the postwar reconstruction of the society, was an intelligent organizer and a serious student of the Lotus Sutra. Her personal life, however, was not untroubled.

She had suffered from tuberculosis when she was younger, and her domestic life was frequently marred with discord. Her family was of the upper middle class and comfortably situated. But Katsu did not get along well with her younger sister, whom she considered temperamental. After her two older brothers graduated from college, Katsu thought of getting married, but her plans were always thwarted at the last minute. As time passed, she came to pity herself. Fits of despondency would last for days, sometimes weeks. Attributing all her misfortune to the evil influences of her karma, she brooded and, in an attempt to find consolation, often confided her woes to others. For instance, once in a discussion with Toda she suddenly said: "It's been seven years since I joined Nichiren Shoshu; and you know, I'm a far cry from happiness. In fact, I think I must be one of the unhappiest women alive." When he heard this, Toda's face assumed an unusually severe expression.

"Stop complaining," he said. "What do you think religion is? A ticket to comfort and happiness? You are really on the wrong track if you are practicing the faith of Nichiren Shoshu for that reason. You know as well as I do that enlightenment and knowledge about the ultimate meaning of life and eternity are what we're striving for. Your basic trouble is that you have set your aims too low. Your complaining spirit is stifling all you have to offer. Stop grumbling. Become one of the finest women in Japan. Go ahead; give it a try."

Oddly enough, no one had ever spoken to her in so sharp a manner before. But instead of taking offense, she knew instinctively that what Toda said was true. She recognized where she had been weak and where she had set up obstacles in her own path to fulfillment. Like the intelligent woman that she was, she saw that keeping a firm grip on herself to avoid falling into self-pity was her only hope of happiness.

In the next few weeks, her life seemed to have started afresh. She worried much less about herself and more about those around her. This concern for others led her to try to convince as many people as she could that Nichiren Shoshu offers saving power to the individual. It was to her fellow faculty members at the primary school where she taught that she turned, in the hope of bringing new converts to the true faith. Hideko Oshima and Chisako Irie, two other women teachers at the school, were the first to agree to accompany Miss Kiyohara to a discussion meeting at which Toda was to preside.

At the meeting, Toda's words on the Lotus Sutra, the philosophy of value, and the meaning of life were so moving that Miss Irie joined Nichiren Shoshu that very night, much to Katsu Kiyohara's great joy. Miss Oshima, who was by nature timid and retiring, was unconvinced. Still, the three teachers soon became good friends and traveled together frequently.

Teachers in Japan in those days were underpaid. In order to improve their lot and increase their earnings, they frequently staged demonstrations to protest the prevailing system. One afternoon, the three friends left school early to participate in a demonstration organized by the teachers' union and scheduled to take place in front of the Imperial Palace. For some weeks, Miss Oshima had been noticing, with a certain wistful envy, that her two friends were always laughing and enjoying themselves; whereas she herself could not shake off a gloom that plagued her because of discontent with her life at home.

On the day of the demonstration, her friends seemed more alive and full of energy than ever. Miss Oshima asked herself if perhaps the faith of Nichiren Shoshu were the source of this happiness. And if this were true, maybe she had been wrong to reject it on first encounter. During a break in the demonstration activities, she timidly asked Katsu Kiyohara and Chisako Irie to tell her about their faith. Nothing could have delighted the other two more, and they immediately launched into explanations of how much more fulfilled a life it was possible to lead with the support of a sound religion. This time Miss Oshima seemed more interested than she had been before. When asked if she would like to attend another discussion meeting, she was delighted.

It seemed odd to Miss Oshima that, at the small gathering about a week later, other women as unhappy as she openly shared their troubles. Each of them explained her situation and received words of support and guidance from Toda and from the other members of the group. At first, when she realized that people were going to expose their personal miseries openly, Miss Oshima had resolved that she would never do a thing like that. She could not submit herself to the ridicule of strangers. Gradually, however, she saw that congeniality and sympathy characterized the attitudes of everyone present. They

all seemed to be saying: "If there is a way to solve your difficulty, we want to help you find it." Encouraged and heartened by what she heard, Miss Oshima asked if she might join Nichiren Shoshu. Of course the answer was a warm yes and a friendly welcome.

Four days after Miss Oshima's conversion to Nichiren Shoshu, her younger sister attempted suicide. She had become unable to tolerate conditions at home any longer. Miserably upset and alone, Miss Oshima called on Katsu Kiyohara, the only person on whom she felt she could rely. Miss Kiyohara, however, realized at once that matters were grave enough to require greater assistance than she could give. Though it was rather late at night, she took Miss Oshima immediately to Toda's offices, where she knew a meeting was in progress. There had been a power failure in the neighborhood earlier in the evening, and Toda was conducting an informal gathering by candlelight when the two women arrived. In the flickering light, Miss Oshima quietly explained the situation to Toda.

Hideko Oshima's mother died when she was very young. Later, hoping to find someone to help him care for Hideko and her sister and two brothers, Mr. Oshima remarried. A son was born of his second marriage. Hideko's father died, leaving his children in the care of their stepmother for the past ten years. The second Mrs. Oshima was a mean-tempered woman. When no longer under the control of her husband, she quickly made it clear that she considered her own son the true heir of the house. At first she treated her stepchildren with mere neglect, but gradually she became severe to the point of cruelty. Because she had managed all family matters, her stepchildren were completely dependent on her.

When they were younger, the children sometimes became so irritated by their stepmother's behavior that they flared up in resistance. Whenever this happened, Hideko, the eldest, tried to shield them. But there was little any of them could do to better their circumstances. Gradually, as time passed, the stepmother succeeded in reducing the younger three to a state something like the passivity of trained animals. Hideko finished school and immediately found a teaching position, which made her at least financially independent.

When the war ended, the family had no money and very little to eat. This did nothing to sweeten the stepmother's disposition. The tension at home was often so unbearable that Hideko hated to return after work. But it was not only on Hideko that the strain showed. Her younger sister, like her brothers superficially passive to their stepmother's tyranny, finally became so hopelessly desperate that she tried to kill herself. She did not succeed, but her attempt brought matters to a head. Separation from the stepmother and her son seemed to be the only solution now. But how was Hideko to manage on no more than her meager teacher's pay?

At this point in her story, Hideko broke down and cried softly. Toda, attempting to calm her, said: "Perhaps the solution to your problem is easier than you think. I'm not in a position to know who is wrong and who is right in this case, but I can assure you of one thing: you have the Gohonzon on your side. And that means that you have strength. So why do you sit and weep to yourself?

"When Nichiren Daishonin was about to be beheaded or when he was sent in exile to the island of Sado, did he cry? Of course not. He vowed to fight for true Buddhism and to become a pillar of strength for the whole nation. You are a child of Nichiren Daishonin. You can become the pillar of your whole family. But you've got to act. What good will you be to yourself or to your family if you sit timidly crying in a corner?"

No longer sobbing, Hideko looked at him for a moment and said: "We must leave that house."

"Then leave it. Rely on the Gohonzon. You'll be protected. But you must act too. Remember, be calm but firm. Your faith, if it is strong, can be a source of happiness for your whole family."

After consulting Toda, Hideko found that the strength of her faith in the Gohonzon gradually transformed what he had criticized as timidity into a quiet dignity supported by deep spiritual assurance. She was to need these sound traits in the near future, for the situation with her stepmother was now approaching a climax.

One evening, on returning from work, Hideko found her stepmother talking with the manager of the store where she worked. Having already filled the man's head with her own biased version of the family's unhappy life together, she now asked that he convince Hideko that she and the other stepchildren should find another place to live and give to her and her son the house and whatever other property remained. This was not a new demand; the stepmother had made it on several previous occasions. But this time she was determined to see that she got her way.

After greeting Hideko very formally, the store manager reprimanded her for what he, in his ignorance of the truth, took to be her unnatural behavior.

"You know," he said, "stepparents are often fonder of their foster children than real parents. After all she's done to keep you and your brothers and sister in food and clothes, do you really think you are right to be so selfish and willful? You say that you think you ought to separate. And from what your stepmother tells me about the way you act, I think you should too. But since the move is your idea, you must leave and let your stepmother and her boy have this house."

Seeing this as a good opportunity to strengthen her own position, the stepmother began trying to make Hideko see things her way. But with dignity and calm the girl explained that it would be folly to put four people out of a house for the sake of two and that finding a small place for the stepmother and her son would present comparatively little difficulty. This infuriated the short-tempered woman. She began to abuse the girl and heaped allegations of all kinds on her head. Even in the face of this tirade, Hideko remained unperturbed. Thanks to the grace of the Gohonzon, she was in command of herself and therefore in command of a trying situation. Turning to the store manager, she coolly outlined the outrageous behavior of her stepmother over the past few years.

The woman had subjected her stepchildren to all manner of perverse inconveniences and humiliations in order to drive them from their own home. She had sometimes nailed shut the doors connecting her stepchildren's rooms to prevent them from indulging in what she called plots against her. Once she had forced Hideko's younger sister to work as a live-in maid but had refused to tell Hideko the address of the girl's place of employment.

As the strange story of the stepmother's cruel practices unfolded, the store manager gradually realized that he had heard only a distorted half of the argument. Scandalized at the deceit of the stepmother he suddenly confronted her.

"You deliberately lied to me," he said.

The stepmother lost control of her mounting wrath. In an outburst of rage, she picked up a teacup, hurled it against the wall, and shouted wildly: "Who the hell'd want to live in this dump! I'll get out. Right now!"

The store manager now understood why the younger sister had tried to kill herself. He saw that for the sake of the welfare of the family and for the preservation of the stepmother's sanity something had to be done at once. Fortunately, as store manager, he was able to dispose of some housing that his store owned. After calming the older woman, he offered her a house at a modest rent that she could afford. Then turning to the still composed Hideko he said: "This is one way out of this mess. You four live here together. I'll see that your stepmother gets along all right. And you'll all be much better off if you go your separate ways."

They did go their separate ways and in peace. Hideko Oshima saw clearly that the quiet strength that had enabled her to endure her stepmother's abuse had been stimulated by her faith in the Gohonzon. From that time onward, she cherished faith as the most important thing in her life. It was to stand both her and her two good friends Katsu Kiyohara and Chisako Irie in good stead in another serious battle that was about to begin.

These three young ladies went everywhere together. They attended the same discussion meetings and lectures and they went together when calls were made on prospective Nichiren

Shoshu members. Ultimately their inseparability gained them the affectionate nickname of the Trio from Suginami, since they all lived in Suginami Ward, in Tokyo.

As members of the teachers' union, the trio attended meetings and participated in frequent demonstrations throughout the city, but the socialist aims of the union were much less meaningful to them than their religious beliefs. Consequently, they spent more time trying to help dejected people find the the right path to salvation and happiness than they did in the organizational affairs of the union. The union's leaders considered the religious activities of the young ladies irregular and at a periodical teachers' conference publicly reprimanded them. The union chairman, a middle-aged man with communist leanings who took pride in the fact that his beard and bald head gave him a certain resemblance to Lenin, addressed the group:

"During visits to the homes of their pupils, these three teachers have pestered parents with aggressive religious proselytizing, when they ought to have confined themselves strictly to school matters. The complaints filed by parents against them for this kind of unauthorized behavior are an embarrassment and disgrace. I think they need to be severely called down for injuring our prestige and honor as teachers."

It was true that the three young teachers had discussed religion and the power of the Gohonzon when they found people whose need of help was urgent. But they had never initiated such talks until after they had taken care of their professional duties as teacher-counselors. The good they had done was immeasurable because they had brought several desperate people to Nichiren Shoshu and the saving powers of faith. The volatile Katsu Kiyohara, who was always ready to defend what she believed against all comers, rose first to refute what the chairman had said.

"Let me explain what we do by asking you a question. If you visited a person and found him very sick, perhaps dying, and you knew a good doctor who could cure him, would you leave without letting him know about that doctor just because medical advice was not the purpose of your visit?"

"That's beside the point!" shouted the chairman. "The thing we're talking about now is the complaints we get from parents about your religious meddling. We teachers are responsible for the reputation of this school, and we have to take steps to clear up this situation."

"How?" asked Miss Kiyohara sharply.

"By demanding that you stop talking about religion when you visit pupils' homes. You must not impose your religion on others. We are all entitled to freedom of religion."

"We certainly are," replied Miss Kiyohara. "And that means us too. Anyway, we don't impose anything on anybody. We only recommend; we have the right to do that.

"People can't be forced to believe. Do you think people are stupid enough to put their trust in something just because they're told to? You are a teacher—and a socialist. Teachers are supposed to guide, and socialists are supposed to believe in the people. Stop and think. What you are saying in accusing us of forcing people to accept our religion is foolishness!"

Miss Kiyohara had worked herself into a rage. When she sat down after her outburst there were some derisive laughs in the room. Then a tall, slender teacher, rising, and brushing his long hair from his forehead, cleared his throat softly and said: "It is forbidden for teachers to propagandize any religious or political faith in the classroom."

Somewhat calmer than Miss Kiyohara but nonetheless upset by the unfair charges brought against them, Miss Irie replied: "Can you prove that we have ever propagandized in the classroom?"

The long-haired teacher said: "Home visits are an extension of the classroom. When one visits one's pupils' parents, one is obliged to speak only on educational topics."

"Oh, no," put in Miss Irie. "You're wrong there. Home is

home, and classroom is classroom. But I know that you and others like you never hesitate to speak up in favor of socialist ideas, and in the classroom too. What Miss Kiyohara said about helping someone who is sick is a good illustration of what we want to do. Why should you be allowed to preach communism when we are forbidden to offer help by showing people the religion that can give them real help now?"

"Well, then," added the slender man, "you must be in the wrong profession. Why not give up teaching and become evangelists?"

Miss Irie was by this time too angry to continue; sarcasm was a weapon against which she could not fight. But, in her new-found calm and dignity, Miss Oshima was a match for anything as she faced the gathering and said: "It is true that some of our teachers defend communism in the classroom in violation of all rules. I can give names if you like."

The tables were turned. What the young women had done outside school in the hope of helping people went against no ruling; teaching political ideas in school did. The many socialists present took great offense at becoming the accused when they had intended to be the accusers; and the heated discussion grew into an agitated uproar.

After a few minutes, the Lenin-like chairman was able to silence the group. He then said that Miss Oshima's accusation would have to be taken up by a higher authority. As the chairman glared at the three women, the tall, slender teacher, his long hair now thoroughly disheveled in his excitement, shrieked: "We cannot possibly allow these revolutionary elements to threaten the unity of our organization. They must be brought before a general board empowered to force them to see reason."

Miss Oshima, able to retain the same calm that had seen her through her almost disastrous domestic problem, presented the case for her group lucidly:

"To avoid misunderstanding let me make this clear. We are members in good standing of the union. We pay our dues and take part in demonstrations. No one has any right to criticize us as a disruptive element.

"The real reason for this embarrassing scene is that you dislike our religious activities. That's within your rights, but it is not within your rights to try to make us stop doing what we believe to be good. We teach our pupils to the best of our abilities. And if on top of that we try to help people in trouble, we are doing nothing wrong."

"How dare you try to make fun of us," sputtered the chairman.

"I'm not making fun of you or of the union. But I might say that the union can't solve everything. In fact, to date, all our union work and demonstrations haven't had much effect. Life is deep and involves many different kinds of problems. Let the union solve the things it can handle. But as members of Nichiren Shoshu and Soka Gakkai, we know that there are questions outside the power of unions. We believe that it is our duty to try to cope with these questions."

The blustering chairman and the willowy teacher immediately spoke up in objection. But things had clearly gotten out of hand. Announcing that matters of this kind would have to be referred to the union itself or to some kind of religious body, the principal hastened to adjourn the meeting.

Still, the issue was not yet closed. The union leaders lost no time in reporting the three young ladies to the general school inspector. There was, however, nothing that could be done. The women were excellent teachers, popular with their students. Their reputations were spotless, and more important, since the constitution explicitly guarantees freedom of religion, their activities in this field were matters for their own consciences.

Though tension continued to exist among the union leaders and the Misses Kiyohara, Irie, and Oshima, the three persisted with their good work in a spirit of unity and devotion strengthened by the antagonism of others. Eagerly waiting to seize on any mistake the women might make, some of the union leaders watched everything they did. In the end, however, the most violent opposers of their religious activities suffered severe retribution. One had a nervous breakdown and died in madness. Another quite mysteriously became permanently disabled as a result of an infection arising from an apparently mild injury.

But the Trio from Suginami persevered in their neighborhood, and it is largely thanks to their fervor and organizational talents that Suginami was later able to produce scores of top leaders in Soka Gakkai.

Hiroshi Izumida and the Trio from Suginami were only a few of the people that Toda trained and educated with great care. Some of the time he was severe and strict with his disciples; some of the time he was gentle and fatherly. But he regarded each as a precious jewel to be polished and brought to the full glory of its inherent luster in the warmth of his hands. Some of those he thought were to become treasures in the society slipped away from him, but those who remained were of inestimable value.

4. DRAWING CLOSER

SHIN'ICHI Yamamoto, who joined Nichiren Shoshu in 1947, was now twenty years old. He continued to attend meetings and lectures, but his physical condition was little improved. Since his family was not wealthy, he had to contribute to the household income in some way, in spite of his tuberculosis. Though the work was beyond his strength, he took a job in a printing plant in the busy Shimbashi district of Tokyo. He found that the long ride home in the evenings on trains packed with people aggravated his condition and sent his fever soaring. Upon arriving home, shivering with cold but with feverishly red cheeks, he rarely had an appetite. His sole pleasure was to retire to his room, after whatever skimpy meal he could force himself to eat, and to read the treasured books on which he spent the small amounts of money he saved. He passed most of his lonely nights either reading or thinking. Just as his physical condition varied from moderately good to very bad, depending on the time of day or the place where he found himself, so his outlook on the future ran the full gamut from enthusiasm to despondency. But some awesome power was being nurtured within Shin'ichi Yamamoto, though no one, not even he himself, was aware of it.

Toda had made so great a personal impression on Yamamoto that even when exhausted and unwell he attended the regular lectures on the Lotus Sutra. Gradually he came to regard the teachings of true Buddhism as a marvel, but deep in his mind a secret doubt nagged him. Would he be able to live up to what Soka Gakkai demanded and what Toda expected of him? His physical weakness might force him to drop out of Soka Gakkai. And if this was likely to happen anyway, why not give up now instead of waiting and suffering apprehension? His skepticism and pessimism about his future grew worse whenever he felt bad. But something would not let him quit. The more he learned, the more profoundly he perceived the greatness of Nichiren Daishonin's Buddhism and the magnitude of the task confronting Soka Gakkai. He continued to be inspired with the hope that through the glowing light of the truth of faith and the warm help of Josei Toda he would someday resolve both his personal problems and his philosophic doubts. Joining the Youth Division was one step Yamamoto took in striving to learn more about Soka Gakkai; but almost immediately afterward, he suffered a physical relapse that spared him the painful experience of witnessing an upheaval that soon split the Youth Division in half.

A rift between the senior and junior members of the Youth Division was the cause of the trouble. The senior members like Chuhei Yamadaira, Giichi Sakata, and Hideko Mikawa, who were already familiar with the power to be derived from faith, focused their attention on a particular way of converting new members to Nichiren Shoshu. They would often attend meetings of religious sects they knew to be foisting wrong doctrines on unwitting people and there initiate debates based on logic and sound religious thinking. When defenders of the false sects joined in the debate to attempt to refute the accusations brought against them by the Soka Gakkai groups, the result was inevitable. The Soka Gakkai members always proved the superiority and orthodoxy of Nichiren Shoshu. Many new converts were won in this way. The Youth Division members who found this kind of debate thrilling argued that it gave them a sense of accomplishment and heightened their awareness of the greatness of true Buddhism.

Recently converted members of the Youth Division, on the other hand, were searching for a philosophy to fill the spiritual vacuum in their lives. These sometimes poor, but always idealistic, young people looked on polemics and debates with other religious groups as egoistic display. To preserve harmony in the group, the younger members went along with this kind of activity for a while; but sooner or later the doubts they felt caused them to leave debating to those who had a taste for it. The new people stopped attending Youth Division meetings regularly, and their absence only strengthened the position of the senior members, who were in favor of continuing the polemic and debating campaigns.

Nevertheless, more and more new members joined the Youth Division, increasing the numerical strength of the antidebate faction. At a monthly discussion meeting on June 26, 1948, the issue came to a head. Now greatly outnumbering the senior members, the junior members voted to disband the Youth Division as it existed and to create a new Youth Division in which activities would not be determined by older members. Instead, everything was to be settled according to a democratic system ensuring that all members, senior and junior, had a say in the way the organization was run and equal opportunity to participate in all activities. Everyone present agreed that membership campaigns ought to be carried out on a wider scale and that displays of debating skill should be excluded from the methods employed. Solidarity was to be the byword of the new Youth Division, scheduled to be inaugurated on July 3, the third anniversary of Toda's release from prison.

Toda had been aware of the split in the Youth Division. It had grieved him because, as was true throughout much of his life, he placed the greatest hopes for the society in the young people. When a representative announced to him the unilateral, arbitrary decision of the Youth Division to disband and reform, Toda was irritated. It was not only that these young people had not bothered to consult the Soka Gakkai board of directors about taking this important step, it was also their attitude that upset Toda. They thought they could organize and dissolve the Youth Division as if it were a trade union. In other words, they seemed to have forgotten that Soka Gakkai and all its subdivisions are a religious organization dedicated to a sacred purpose.

The weakness of the young people, revealed in their failure to understand this, convinced Toda that a few more years were required to develop the kind of Youth Division that was needed. But they had made their decision, and though he feared that their new organization could not succeed, Toda was going to allow them to learn from their own mistake. After hearing what the representatives had to tell him, he said:

"You've made your decision; go ahead with your plan. But I want to give you a word of advice. You cannot make or un-make an organization that is part of Nichiren Shoshu. Our religious groups are created by the Buddha. They do not de-pend on human organizational skill to stay together or to run properly. They depend entirely on the grace of the Gohonzon. Now we are in a transitional phase of growth, and I am willing to let you try whatever you want. When you have matured in faith, you will understand the true character of the organiza-tion of our society and the gravity of our mission."

Toda let things go with these few remarks because he saw that, though mistaken, the young people were zealous and eager to work. In fact, the newly inaugurated Youth Division immediately launched a membership campaign that produced such good results that the number of people attending the sum-mer training course at Taiseki-ji that year was twice what it had been the year before.

Among the 188 members traveling to the foothills of Mount

Fuji for the summer course was Shin'ichi Yamamoto. It was his first pilgrimage to the head temple. At first, because of his poor health, he remained apart from the group except at lectures and meetings, but he found the place movingly beautiful with its clear sky and towering cedars. He was alive to the bustle of activity on the temple grounds. The scent of freshly felled cedar and the rapping of hammers filled the air as construction proceeded on the new Kyakuden. A celebration in honor of the completion of the framework of the building was scheduled to take place on August 22.

The natural setting of the temple, the friendliness of everyone he came in contact with, and the stirring content of the lectures and discussions exerted an exhilarating physical and spiritual influence on Yamamoto. Throughout the five-day course, he felt, if he did not always directly participate in, the vigorous purposefulness of the activities. Toda was largely responsible for this mood: he wanted to awaken in all the participants—and especially in the often gloomy Yamamoto—a sense of the joy of faith.

One of the highlights of the course was a talk delivered by Toda on the third day, when he explained one of the most important aspects of the role of Nichiren Shoshu believers and Soka Gakkai members.

"Have any of you ever thought why it should have been our fate to be born in this tumultuous Latter Day of the Law?" Toda asked the group. "If you know, then you have grasped the meaning of our role on earth; and the purpose of this summer course has been achieved.

"But if you know why we are here, do you understand why you know? Only those people who have been reverent and faithful in the presence of the Dai-Gohonzon are privileged to know that we have been born into this era to fulfill a grave mission and to perform the work of Bodhisattvas.

"I see doubt on some of your faces. Of course we are mortals, but in each of us is the seed of Buddhahood, planted in our beings since time immemorial. Because you have sincerely worshiped and believed in the Gohonzon, you have proved yourselves to be the inheritors of a task that only those partaking of Buddhahood can fulfill.

"All kinds of tasks exist. The politician, the businessman, the teacher, the artist, each has his own job to do. But their

work is ephemeral and ours is eternal. We are emissaries of the Buddha in our time, but we can realize our purpose only through active practice of faith. For that reason, in order to know what your task is and thus to know how to carry it out, each of you must dedicate his life to the protection of true Buddhism, to diligent chanting of the Daimoku, and to renewed efforts to bring as many new members as possible to an understanding of the meaning of our faith."

Some newcomers in the audience found it difficult to follow what Toda was saying about their being Bodhisattvas and emissaries of the Buddha. But Shin'ichi Yamamoto felt as if Toda had addressed the words directly to him. It was almost as if Toda were calling him to undertake a great work, the meaning of which, however, was still only vague.

The remainder of the summer course included two more lectures by Toda, and talks by priest Taiei Horigome, a short biography of Nichiren Daishonin, a graphically illustrated story about Nikko Shonin, the second high priest of Nichiren Shoshu, and the regular morning and evening Gongyo services. The young people found everything fascinating and rewarding but suffered physical discomfort from the Gongyo services, in which it was necessary to remain in the same kneeling position for an hour or two. After these ceremonies, legs were sometimes so numb that for a few painful minutes healthy men and women crawled about on the floor like cripples.

The five days were over too soon. The enriching experiences of late-night talk-sessions, the warm friendliness of meals enjoyed together, the meaningful lessons learned at discussions and lectures, and most of all, a renewed awareness of mission made this summer course a turning point in the lives of many of the participants. On the evening of departure, at the venerable two-story Sammon Gate in front of Taiseki-ji, Shin'ichi Yamamoto turned to take a last look at the now darkening temple against the deep violet shadows of Mount Fuji. He felt stronger in mind and body. It was almost as if he had discovered himself for the first time.

In October of 1948, high-placed politicians, financiers, government officials, bankers, and even prison officers became involved in a graft scandal linked with a chemical engineering firm called Showa Denko. So extensive were the ramifications of the ugly matter, that the deputy prime minister, Nishio Suehiro, was forced to resign while Prime Minister Hitoshi Ashida was brought to assume moral, though not political, responsibility for the arrests of those of his cabinet ministers suspected of shady activities.

The nation was shocked and indignant at the canker of corruption and bribery that contaminated even the loftiest government positions. People all over Japan talked often and long about the Showa Denko scandal. One evening at a lecture on the Lotus Sutra, Shin'ichi Yamamoto and some of his young fellow members questioned Toda about the existence of evil like the malignancy infesting Japanese society at the time. These earnest young people could not understand why efforts to stamp out evil seemed to make little headway, whereas wickedness seemed to thrive. Toda was glad to have the chance to talk on this subject because it gave him an opportunity to develop a very important train of thought and to give Soka Gakkai members a hint of what he had in mind for their future role in society.

"Social evils are nothing new. They have been a part of the world since civilization began. In spite of honest efforts by men of justice and good conscience to do something about such evil at various times in history, it has proved impossible to wipe out wickedness. Why is this?

"As you have already been taught, there are ten states of life, some of which are good and some evil. All ten states are, however, operative all the time. Therefore, if the good aspects of humanity—that is human life in good states—have made splendid cultural achievements, the evils—or the bad states of life—have not been idle. They too have made great strides. And this is the reason why human society always presents strongly contrasting merits and faults.

"But in saying that evil exists and in explaining its reason for being, I do not imply that we ought to resign ourselves to it. On the contrary, it is our duty to take concrete steps to eliminate evil. The ten states of life that manifest themselves in every human being are complicated, but it is possible to elevate the nature of a person from a bad state of life to a good one. As a matter of fact, the only way to make any progress in eradicating widespread social evil is for each individual human being to revolutionize his own inner nature.

"External revolutionary action has always failed to bring about basic human reforms, without which all civilizational, economic, and political reforms lack a basis. The essential foundation of our actions must result from an internal spiritual revolution taking place in the life of each human being. It is just such an inner revolution that is the basis of the life philosophy of Nichiren Daishonin. Until now, much of the world has refused to understand this; but it is our task to bring this all-important truth to the attention of mankind.

"The inner revolution must take place in everyone, and that includes prime ministers, cabinet ministers, and all other political leaders. When the people occupying these positions have effected their own personal spiritual revolutions, the danger of corruption, graft, and scandal—like that of the Showa Denko company—will vanish. Anarchists and terrorists in the past have sometimes quite honestly believed that the one way to bring about social reform is to destroy existing social systems. Assassination, they believed, could accomplish much by removing leaders and thus rendering systems powerless. Obviously, we cannot condone this method.

"According to our Buddhist beliefs, life—in its past, present, and future existences—is irreplaceably precious. To take life, then, is a heinous act against Buddhism. Consequently, assassins, who like all of us, are bound by the law of karma, inevitably suffer severe retribution. Anyone can criticize society and politics; they are both in a bad state and need criticizing. But this alone has no constructive effect. It is human beings who run society and politics, and the ten states of life are manifest in human hearts. Until people realize this and attempt to bring about fundamental individual revolutions, no policies for social and political improvement, no matter how promising, can be more than superficial. Throughout human history, people have believed in social revolutions and political revolutions, but no one has tried to believe in the human revolution as taught in the philosophy of Nichiren Daishonin. Failure to believe in this revolution is the greatest source of evil in the world today.

"Positions of leadership in society are the targets of revolutionary action—even the acts of our inner spiritual revolution. There are two ways in which we can ensure that the people in power in our society have experienced the spiritual metamorphosis that can enable them to create a better world. First, we can attempt to lead the men who are in political office now to true Buddhism. You need not think that your powers are too frail to confront government or financial leaders with ideas of spiritual revolution. We are all human beings. We are all subject to the law of karma; and whether we like it or not, we are all living in an age when spiritual revolution is inevitable. Approach powerful men as you would your own relatives, with the belief that you can and must convince them to see where they are wrong and that you can show them the right way.

"The second way we can provide society with political leaders of sound religious faith involves the future of Soka Gakkai. Because our age needs us, we are bound to grow strong. Each of you, if he maintains his faith, will grow into a valuable human being in our society and in our world. Undoubtedly, some of you are interested or talented in politics. When the time comes—and I don't think it is too far in the future—we will have to fill the pressing need for an altruistic political party devoted to the welfare of all people. The kind of party I have in mind will surpass conventional democratic principles because it will be based on profound religious truth.

"The teachings of Nichiren Daishonin prove that our age, the Latter Day of the Law, is the time when Bodhisattvas will rise up to save the world. We are those Bodhisattvas; and participating in a wide range of activities, including cultural pursuits, economics, and politics, will be one means of performing our saving task."

Inspired by the vital significance of his message, Toda had

talked longer than he had originally intended. Still, no one in the room allowed his mind to waver for so much as a second. To several of the young people listening, Toda's ideas of relating all phases of society to the universal propagation of the faith of Nichiren Daishonin seemed excessively idealistic. Shin'-ichi Yamamoto, however, caught the vision. Staring silently and intently at Toda's face, he had a glimpse of the vast edifice of faith that had to be built. It is clear that Yamamoto knew even then that he would have a role to play in the construction of that edifice. After the meeting that night, he took up his diary and wrote:

"What great fortune to know the infinitely profound and merciful canons of the Lotus Sutra. Mr. Toda I admire as a teacher for all mankind. The great conviction and faith with which he endeavors to bring mankind to supreme happiness, his burning passion for justice, and his patriotism. I am deeply moved by the great mercy of Nichiren Daishonin, who brought a radiant dawn into a dark, evil world in his struggle to enlighten all peoples. While we who enjoy the blessings of the Dai-Gohonzon are young, we must march boldly forward toward the eternal prosperity of Buddhism. All of our actions must be free from impure motives. Our minds must be free from doubt and delusion. Still we tend to hesitate. A religious revolution is a human revolution. It will lead to a true revolution in politics, education, and economics. But who will purify this chaotic world? The mission of our society is truly grave.

"Revolution means death. Through our deaths we return to the Myoho. Only through a truly great death shall we become the saviors of our nation and of the whole world.

"March forward with great mercy; march forward with a great philosophy. I, who am only twenty years old, have discovered the path to the highest glory."

One rainy autumn night Toda and Chuhei Yamadaira were hurrying to a meeting. They were already late because a damaged bridge had fallen to such a low level that the ferryboat they had to take could not pass under it. Finally, after a lengthy detour, they were approaching their destination, some two hours late for their appointment.

Yamadaira, who had come from a humble mountain village in the prewar days to work in Toda's school, Jishu Gakkan, had suffered much in the war. But he had persevered in his faith and for a while had worked in the editorial department of Toda's publishing company. Recently he had taken a job in a government office, though he continued to assume the initiative and participate in Soka Gakkai activities at night. He had become an important member of the Youth Division; every day of his life was amazingly busy. But his works of faith brought him good fortune of a magnitude difficult to attain in one lifetime. Yamadaira enjoyed Toda's confidence; and on the way to the meeting, the two were discussing something that both considered important.

"Will you bring Yamamoto to me soon, Yamadaira?" asked Toda.

"Yes, in a few days," Yamadaira replied as he helped the myopic Toda find his way around a puddle in the road.

"How is his health now? I should think he must be a good deal better."

"Yes, he's much better."

"Do you think he will be willing to work hard?"

"I'm sure he'll do well."

"Magazine editing is no easy task, as you know," said Toda. "The work hours are irregular, and you must be strong. You're always pressed to meet deadlines. I imagine you find your work at the government office lighter than what you had to do for me."

"Well, it's easier, but it's not as satisfying."

"I hope you're not complaining. You've finished college, you have a good job doing important work on labor problems, and you're married. What more do you want? Right now, though, I need someone intelligent for that editorial job. You're sure Yamamoto is the right man?"

"I think so. He reads a lot and he likes literature."

Yamadaira had been present at the initiation ceremonies a year earlier when Yamamoto joined Nichiren Shoshu. The two of them got along well, especially since Yamadaira willingly helped Yamamoto on matters of faith and religious thought. Though he did not have chances to meet Yamamoto often, Toda remembered that he had attended the summer course at Taiseki-ji and that he was regularly present at discussion meetings. He had been surprised, in fact, to observe the depth of the impression Nichiren Daishonin's philosophy was making on the young man. As they neared the house where the meeting was to be held, Toda reminded Yamadaira: "Tell Yamamoto to come to me as soon as possible."

Two days later, Shin'ichi Yamamoto arrived in Toda's office for an interview. But he had to wait his turn. Toda was dealing with a few of the many, varied personal problems brought to him almost every day. First, a young woman requested assistance in defining some difficult Buddhist terminology. Next, Toda spoke somewhat sharply to a middle-aged man for being foolish enough to allow himself to be swindled. Then, a gentlemanly individual of about forty poured out his unhappiness over his unfaithful wife.

"I hate this man from the bottom of my heart for what he has done to my wife and me. But I hear that he has recently become a member of Nichiren Shoshu. Now I worry that maybe in hating him I am taking a stand opposed to our faith," said the man unhappily.

Toda replied: "The late president Makiguchi would have called you a stupid fool for getting yourself into this position. In hating your rival and trying to get your wife back you won't necessarily be running against true Buddhism. But if you strengthen your own faith, you won't need to hate. Chant the Daimoku as often as you can, and you'll find a solution that doesn't call for hatred."

When the consoled and encouraged man had left, Toda turned to Yamamoto. After sitting down in a chair next to Toda's desk, Yamamoto submitted the résumé of his education and background that Yamadaira had told him would be re-

quired. Toda read the papers quickly, then said: "So you want a job. Are you willing to work?"

Yamamoto, who had been staring at his shoes, raised his eyes to meet Toda's gaze and said yes. When he had joined Nichiren Shoshu, he had tacitly accepted Toda as a religious and philosophical leader. But now that he was about to work in the same office with his teacher, he felt a slight insecurity about his own abilities. There was no turning back at this point, however. Recalling what he had written in his diary about the urgent need for inner revolution, the young man felt as if he was beginning on a path that would lead him to spiritual renovation through the power of the Myoho. Under no circumstances could he allow the opportunity to slip through his fingers.

Toda folded Yamamoto's papers and said: "Good. Resign from your present job as amicably as you can. Clear up all your unfinished duties there; then report to work here."

The time had at last come for this brief interview that was to decide so much in the future of the young man. One year ago, when friends insisted that he attend the discussion meeting where he met Toda, Yamamoto had sensed that something profoundly significant would be the outcome of the encounter. The inevitable results of it were beginning to unfold.

Toda beckoned the next visitor to come to his desk, indicating that Yamamoto's interview had ended. As he left, Yamamoto saw Toda reach out his hand to calm the crying infant of the woman who was asking him for some kind of help.

Immediately after his talk with Toda, Yamamoto returned to the offices of the Association for the Promotion of Medium and Small Industries, where he had been working since his poor health had made it imperative that he leave the printing plant. Though eager to begin at Toda's firm and to start editorial work, for which he believed he had aptitude, Yamamoto realized that he could not leave his present employment until a replacement had been found. After discussing the matter, Yamamoto and his employer decided that he would be free to leave on December 31 of that year.

5. RESULTS AND VERDICTS

IN THE informal atmosphere of the lectures on the Lotus Sutra, Toda had briefly discussed his thoughts about the role to be played by Soka Gakkai members in many aspects of the future of Japan. But at the society's third postwar general meeting, held on October 17, 1948, he had the opportunity to present his ideas to a wider audience. Attendance was large, indicating the forward strides the society had taken in the three years that had passed since reorganization. There were so many important topics to be discussed that the meeting was extraordinarily long, lasting from 9:40 in the morning until 4:30 in the afternoon and consisting of two sessions.

Experience had taught the society leaders that testimonials are both a good way to open meetings and the best way to prove the effectiveness and value of belief in Nichiren Shoshu. Consequently, the morning session of the general meeting began with eight deeply impressive personal tales of suffering and the relief brought by faith. Perhaps the most moving and dramatic of these testimonials was that of a young salesman named Kazuo Takahashi, who had joined Nichiren Shoshu in the prewar years.

Faith had not only given him strength to overcome a serious

83

case of tuberculosis, but had also inspired him to begin a vigorous membership campaign in token of his gratitude. But by the time he had converted sixteen households, governmental persecutions of Nichiren Shoshu accelerated. Soon twenty society leaders and President Makiguchi himself had been imprisoned. One of those leaders, however, procured his own release from prison by recanting his faith and burning his Gohonzon. He then convinced several other members that, as a temporary measure to escape mounting persecution, they too must burn their Gohonzons. Because the situation was indeed precarious at the time, young Takahashi fell into the trap set by this cowardly and wicked man. Though he never wavered in his faith, he burned his Gohonzon out of what he had been led to believe was expediency. Before long, he was to be made painfully aware of the gravity of his error.

Once, during an air raid on Tokyo, Takahashi and six other people had rushed to hide in a shelter. As the bombs whistled and destruction raged around them, Takahashi, quietly chanting the Daimoku, suddenly saw that in burning the Gohonzon he had committed a grave error. He had done so in ignorance it is true, but the mistake was serious nonetheless. Although he now found himself in great danger because of his foolishness, he knew that faith was his only hope of salvation. He continued to chant and to believe that somehow everything would turn out all right. Suddenly a bomb crashed through the shelter. Six people were killed instantly. Only Takahashi came out of the ruin alive. He was unconscious and near death, but he pulled through.

After regaining his health, he vowed that he would never again slight the Gohonzon or the faith in Nichiren Shoshu that had saved his life. He was convinced of the limitless merit of chanting the Daimoku. He knew that he had been spared to perform a part in the great mission of Soka Gakkai; and as he made his testimonial at the third general meeting, he vowed to all to do his utmost to change his own karma and to contribute to the wider propagation of Nichiren Shoshu.

After the testimonials, Yoshizo Mishima, a director of Soka Gakkai, made an annual progress report. He said that he was happy to announce a great increase in the number of chapters where discussion meetings were regularly held. Whereas at the preceding general meeting he had listed only twelve chapters, this year he reported twenty-five in Tokyo alone plus ten in outlying districts and six in rural areas. As he called out the name of each local chapter, representatives from the individual areas leaped to their feet and applauded. Mishima's good news inspired a general feeling of warmth and gratification.

Each of the three major speakers of the morning session had something very important to say on the nature of the task facing Nichiren Shoshu and Soka Gakkai. The first of the three, High Priest Nissho Mizutani, spoke on the topic "Good Omens." He said that in the midst of the darkness of scandal and corruption, inflation, and the spiritual apathy of the Japanese people, Nichiren Shoshu was already accomplishing several things that promised a brighter future. First, the Kyakuden of the head temple was nearing completion. Second, Soka Gakkai had already surpassed the size of the prewar organization.

Pointing out the ripeness of the time for a concerted effort on the parts of Nichiren Shoshu priesthood and laity, the high priest concluded with: "We must produce from among Nichiren Shoshu believers men of ability in the fields of industry, finance, literature, science, education, and politics. These men will influence the state and the whole world and in that way will become milestones in the march toward eternal peace. This was the wish of the Buddha of the Latter Day of the Law, Nichiren Daishonin; it must be our aspiration. Our age is the opening of a new epoch in the growth of Nichiren Shoshu. It is my earnest wish that, under the guidance and protection of the Three Treasures, clergy and laity will unite in body and spirit to work out and fulfill great plans for the good of our country and for the worldwide spreading of the saving faith."

Reverend Taiei Horigome, administrative director of the head temple, then spoke and touched on the problem of the democratic nature of Nichiren Shoshu efforts to convert people and win new members. The Trio from Suginami, Misses Kiyohara, Oshima, and Irie had already had occasion to deal with this issue when they encountered the opposition of socialist members of their teachers' union; and Horigome now gave formal expression to the doctrine these young ladies had used as informal proof of the goodness of their intents and the legitimacy of their methods. Like the young ladies, Horigome made it plain that freedom of religion, which applies to everyone, entails the right—indeed the duty—to try to help others who are in trouble. If bringing the word of faith to a man in sorrow can help lead that man back to the path of happiness, withholding advice and counsel amounts to a wrong. Horigome went so far as to show that democracy in the truest sense is to be realized only on the basis of Buddhist teachings. Therefore, attempting to win people to Nichiren Shoshu is taking a step toward the attainment of a democratic society infinitely more meaningful than European or American democracy, which are based on Christianity.

In closing his speech, Horigome said: "True democracy, which upholds individual liberty, cannot be achieved without perfection of the individual. Such perfection is possible only through a correct philosophy of life and a correct understanding of the universe. Since our faith is the only one that offers such a philosophy and such an understanding of the universe, it is the ultimate key to the perfection of man. By extension, then, it is the one key to the establishment of true democracy."

Reverend Seido Hosoi of Jozai-ji temple delivered an inspiring message on the superiority of the Lotus Sutra over all other scriptures. He stressed his conviction that, in the Latter Day of the Law, the universal law, Nam-myoho-renge-kyo, the quintessence of the Lotus Sutra, is the sole realistic way to enlightenment and Buddhahood. In conclusion he made illuminating comments on the nature of the lay organization: "As modern society becomes more complicated it becomes increasingly difficult for the priesthood to give daily-life guidance to the laity. Further, it is important for the laity to respect the priesthood. But if our faith ceases to be of help in daily matters and lapses into a religion for the sake of only the priests, whose virtual retainers the laity become, it will have abandoned the true meaning of the law. I am convinced that Soka Gakkai is acting to create an arrangement whereby the priesthood guards the law, the laity respects the priesthood, and the individual lay members offer each other assistance in leading lives of faith in the extreme difficulties of modern society."

As the morning session drew to a close, Josei Toda rose to deliver a brief message that was a preparation for the more important ideas he was reserving for later.

"We members of Nichiren Shoshu must be prepared to sacrifice our very lives for the sake of the Myoho. As Nichiren Daishonin says in the *Kaimoku Sho*: 'Though the heavens forsake me, though all persecutions assail me, unless my belief is refuted by a wiser man, I will not give up my faith, for I have consecrated my life.'

"In striving to achieve our goal, personal profit must never enter our minds. Our faith must overcome all greed. Our faith will help us accomplish a task of stupendous difficulty. To achieve our goal, however, we need the determination that enables us to face anything, even death and persecution.

"Nichiren Daishonin made it clear—and some of the testimonials we have heard today reinforce his teaching—that it is a sin to forsake the Lotus Sutra or the Gohonzon. If our devotion slackens and if we slight or harm the object of our faith, it may be hundreds of millions of years before we are given an opportunity to enjoy contact with the Gohonzon again. Still, for the faithful, the mercy of Nichiren Daishonin is infinite.

"No reward—not even a monarch's crown—and no punishment—not even the loss of those we love—should bring us to renounce a faith as exacting and as rewarding as this.

"As disciples of Nichiren Daishonin we must apply his philosophy to the solution of our personal problems. But on a wider scale, we must use that same philosophy in trying to rehabilitate our nation. The defeat of Japan in the war was divine retribution for a long history of disregard for the teachings of Nichiren Daishonin. We must now follow the example he set when he said: 'I shall never break my vow to be the pillar, the eye, and the great ship of Japan.' It is our duty now to serve the nation as a pillar of support, an eye of unclouded vision of the future, and a ship carrying us all to a brighter future."

Toda concluded his speech and, smiling, announced that contrary to custom the assembly would have to meet again in the afternoon to complete the unusually full agenda. A tea break in the corridors of the building provided a rest. A kind of picnic spirit was reflected in the laughter and chatter of people who drank cup after cup of hot tea to fill their empty stomachs. Not many could afford to provide packed lunches in those days.

The afternoon session of the assembly was informal. A number of people made testimonials, some funny enough to excite general mirth and others deeply moving. But the highlight of this part of the day and indeed of the entire meeting was Toda's address "The Way to the Restoration of the Nation."

"Philosophy must be the prerequisite of the restoration of a nation, but philosophy that is not backed up with practical action is no more than an intellectual game. Now that preoccupation with the erroneous ideas of Shinto has led to fiasco, where are we Japanese to seek a philosophy and a morality that can generate reconstructive action? Today, when misleading religious sects and biased communist ideas are running rampant throughout Japan, we of Soka Gakkai, acting in conformity with the great philosophy of Nichiren Shoshu, must make practical contributions to the rebuilding of our nation.

"Guided by that philosophy, many of us are already making efforts. But what we are doing is not enough. We must now begin a campaign to introduce the thought and mercy of Nichiren Daishonin into all phases of human activity. What we bring to the people must serve their needs; it must be compatible

with all the many levels of men's lives. But it must be based in the timeless principles of life force as taught by the founder of our faith, the Buddha of the Latter Day of the Law.

"In order to transform our defeated nation into a body of moral and peace-loving people, we must take it upon ourselves to remold politics, economics, and culture on the basis of the correct concepts of a correct religion. Only the Dai-Gohonzon and the philosophy of Nichiren Daishonin can be the foundation for the kind of nation Japan must become.

"The majority of Japanese people are still ignorant of the great mercy of the Dai-Gohonzon. In this chaotic and turbulent time, ours is the task to enlighten them and, in doing this, to begin bringing the light of faith to the whole world. Our work is prepared for us. It is difficult. Perhaps there are those among you who think that undertaking the total reformation of our whole civilization through religion is too great a job. To those people I say: 'Leave the society at once. We do not need you.' To those of you who are willing to suffer loss and deprivation if need be in order to achieve a goal of a magnificence unparalleled in the history of man I say: 'Prepare yourselves for the fight.' "

So fervent was Toda's address that a storm of applause burst from the congregation, who at last had a glimpse of the great social importance of their movement. This was Toda's first public expression of the concept of *obutsu myogo,* the harmonious blending of true religion with all aspects of human life. It was to be a subject of increasingly vital importance in the following years.

During the summer training course, Shin'ichi Yamamoto had been impressed by the activity surrounding the reconstruction of the Kyakuden, the important building where the Ushitora Gongyo ceremony—devoted to prayers for peace—is conducted every night. He and all Nichiren Shoshu members were gladdened when on November 12 and 13, 1948, services were held to officially open both the Kyakuden and the newly rebuilt Mutsubo, a special hall for the priests' ceremonies and practice of religious discipline.

Plans for reconstruction of the buildings had been completed and publicly announced in January, 1948. A building permit was obtained in March. At the same time, a budget of two million yen was forecast. On April 7, groups of fund-raisers dispatched throughout the nation gathered a total of three and a half million yen in donation pledges. Carpenters began the construction work in July. For the framework they used cypress logs from the forests of the temple compound. A ceremony to commemorate the completion of the framework was held on

August 22, and the Kyakuden was finished two months later. By that time, 2,037 workmen, including 1,181 carpenters, had participated in the project. Though the Kyakuden and Mutsubo were ready for use, further work remained to be done on the corridors and verandas and on small details.

The completion ceremony was held in the afternoon of the day of the annual Oeshiki memorial service commemorating the death and the eternal Buddhahood of Nichiren Daishonin. The great temple bell solemnly tolled the initiation of the ceremony at three in the afternoon of a bright, warm autumn day. Behind the temple, Mount Fuji, capped with immaculate snow, soared majestically into the blue sky. As if to join in the auspicious occasion, cherry trees bordering the approach to the main sanctuary had put out unseasonable, pearl-like blossoms.

In the new Kyakuden hall, filled with the sweet scent of new wood and the heavy fragrance of incense, two thousand priests and lay members, including six hundred pilgrims from various parts of the country, gathered for the opening.

After the booming of the ceremonial drum, silence reigned in the hall as High Priest Nissho Mizutani, attired in the rich regalia of his office, entered at the head of the procession of priests. The high priest began the observance by calling on the assembly to join him in reciting the sutra.

Toda, who, with fifty members of Soka Gakkai, was seated next to the high priest, glanced around the new building. He was filled with happiness at its beauty, especially when he remembered the burnt ruin he had seen on his visit to the temple after his release from prison. In 1945, a mysterious fire had consumed the building. High Priest Nikkyo had sacrificed himself in the flames. For Toda and many others, the destruction of this important building and the loss of an outstanding religious leader symbolized the depths to which the fortunes of Nichiren Shoshu had fallen as a result of unfair persecutions conducted by the wartime militarist government. The new building, however, symbolized something quite different: the upward surge

in Nichiren Shoshu activities and the growing duty of Soka
Gakkai to extend faith in true Buddhism to the whole world.

After the sutra recitation, the high priest delivered a welcoming address:

"On this beautiful day, blessed with fine autumn weather
and the matchless beauty of Mount Fuji, we are glad to announce the completion of the Kyakuden and the Mutsubo.
Perhaps equally as important as the completion ceremony itself is the fact that it is held on the six-hundred-sixty-sixth anniversary of the death of the founder of Nichiren Shoshu, Nichiren Daishonin, who as the eternal Buddha appeared on earth
to be the savior of the Latter Day of the Law."

After recounting the disastrous fire in which the two buildings
had been destroyed, the high priest continued: "It was the
government's refusal to rule the nation according to the teachings of true Buddhism and its brutal persecution of Nichiren
Shoshu that brought defeat on Japan. For nearly seven centuries, Japanese governments have pursued this fatal course,
which has brought our country to its present miserable state.
But there is a good lesson for us in this tragedy. To an extent,
we must all bear a share of the blame for our predicament.

"If the followers of Nichiren Shoshu had been more earnest
in their attempts to divert the rulers of the nation from the
path toward downfall, much misery might have been spared
Japan. For our part in what has happened to us and the world,
the priests of Nichiren Shoshu deserve death. Nikkyo, the sixty-
second high priest, may well have realized this. And it may
have been the torment of the enormity of the guilt of all of us
that drove him to immolate himself in the flames that destroyed
the Kyakuden. Shame and self-reproach would overcome us
in the face of our culpability if it were not that we now see the
path we must follow to make amends. We must now unite and
fulfill our destiny to bring help and faith to all men."

Following his stirring words, the high priest led the chanting of the Daimoku. Then the administrative director, Taiei Horigome, who would later be called Nichijun; Hiroyoshi Takano, chief of the reconstruction committee; and Seido Hosoi, chairman of the general affairs committee, delivered speeches outlining the history of the construction process and calling for assistance in raising the money still needed to carry out the remaining work. After congratulatory greetings from six more people, Toda rose to address the congregation as the representative of lay believers throughout the country.

"Especially now, when Japan is still in virtual ruins, the completion of the new Kyakuden is a good omen for our march toward universal faith in Nichiren Shoshu. Though our activities are still limited in scope and inexperienced in execution, viewed in light of the prophecy of Nichiren Daishonin, the time is ripe for the carrying out of our mission. As you know, the Three Disasters and Seven Calamities—including foreign occupation of Japan—have come to pass. Never in her history has Japan experienced tribulations like those she suffers today. Inflation, lack of ordinary necessities, increasing numbers of sick people, and political corruption are only some of the ills that plague us.

"But we must remember the lesson that history teaches. In the thirteenth century, when T'ien-t'ai Buddhism had declined, Nichiren Daishonin appeared to be the savior of the world. To all outward appearances, the war has brought about a decline in the fortunes of Nichiren Shoshu, but ours is the Buddhism of the Latter Day of the Law. And we are the Bodhisattvas prophesied to bring light to a dark age. The time to share our faith with all peoples has come. Our struggle will be fierce, but we will win. To that end, each of us must dedicate his entire loyalty to our cause. I hope that I am setting an example when publicly, now, in the presence of the high priest, I pledge myself to the achievement of our goal no matter what its personal cost to me."

The enthusiastic applause in the hall came mostly from Soka Gakkai members. Other followers of Nichiren Shoshu were not yet ready for the challenge Toda offered.

During the late lunch that followed the afternoon ceremony, each visitor to the temple was given as a souvenir a simple wooden mat on which to place a teapot. From scraps of the cypresses used to build the Kyakuden, the acolytes of Taiseki-ji had carved these mats, beautifully displaying the annual rings of the trees, some of them centuries old.

At seven o'clock in the evening of November 12, the temple bell tolled once again, this time to announce the beginning of the Oeshiki procession, led by the high priest. Each side of the pathway to the Mieido, where a life-size statue of Nichiren Daishonin is enshrined, was lined with seven symbolic bonfires. The entire priesthood took part in the procession, which was colorful and deeply impressive. The men moved with a slow, measured gait intended to recapture the walk of the Buddha as he expounded the law that brings enlightenment to the world.

The Oeshiki ceremony to commemorate the death and to celebrate the eternal Buddhahood of Nichiren Daishonin began on the evening of November 12 and continued through the night and into the following day. Unlike other Nichiren sects, which regard the Oeshiki as a mere memorial, Nichiren Shoshu stresses celebrations connected with Nichiren Daishonin's Buddhahood and his role as the savior of the Latter Day of the Law. During one of the several ceremonies connected with the celebration, Nichiren Daishonin himself is believed to appear to deliver a sermon. Although the Oeshiki has been observed since the fourteenth century, domestic wars and disturbances in Japan limited it to a modest ceremony until the eighteenth century. On the occasion of the completion of the Mieido in the mid-seventeenth century, the eighteenth high priest, Nissei, compiled the solemn and elaborate ritual as it is performed today.

At one o'clock in the morning, the Ushitora Gongyo service began. Afterward, the high priest received pilgrims in audience. On November 13, at eight in the morning, a series of rites was climaxed by the reading of ancient letters in which high priests of Nichiren Shoshu admonished Japanese governments for their abuse of true Buddhism. The most important document

read was *The Security of the Land Through the Establishment of True Buddhism,* written by Nichiren Daishonin himself. At ten in the morning, there was a lecture meeting for priests and laity; and at one in the afternoon, the splendid celebrations reached a peak when the Dai-Gohonzon was transferred from the Treasure Temple to the new Kyakuden, where worship services were held. Sermons and lectures, including one by retired high priest Nichiman, rounded out the two-day ceremonial.

Refreshed by the religious experience and by the serenity prevailing on the lower slopes of Mount Fuji, on the day after the conclusion of the Oeshiki ceremonies, Toda returned to Tokyo and to a world where things were anything but refreshing and serene.

On November 12, the very same day as the inspiring ceremonies at Taiseki-ji, the formal judgment of the Tokyo International War Tribunal for major Japanese war criminals was
handed down in a building that, ironically, had served as the
offices of the army division of Imperial General Headquarters
during World War II. The trials had dragged on for two and
a half years, and there were many conflicting opinions as to
their validity. They were, in fact, symptomatic of the confusion
that reigned in Japan and the world in the early postwar years.
Reading the full judgment, a massive English-language document of 1,212 pages, required five full days.

Electric tension gripped the courtroom as Sir William Webb,
president of the tribunal, pronounced the first sentence, that
of General Sadao Araki, who, reduced to no more than a shadow of a man, stood impassively in the dock.

"Imprisonment for life," said Sir William Webb. A murmur
ran through the courtroom.

Next, General Kenji Dohihara rose to face the court.

"Death by hanging."

Dohihara bowed ceremoniously and departed under guard.

One by one, the leaders of the wartime Japanese government
were sentenced: General Shunroku Hata and former prime
minister Kiichiro Hiranuma received life imprisonment. Former prime minister Koki Hirota, to the surprise of everyone
present, was sentenced to hanging. The sentencing continued
for hours, to reach its conclusion in the climactic appearance
of Hideki Tojo. Dressed in full uniform, he wore earphones over
which he heard a translation of the pronouncement of the judge.
Throughout the painful time, the only alteration in his facial
expression was a nervous grin that distorted his lips as the
words "death by hanging" were spoken.

In all, seven men were sentenced to death, including Tojo,
Hirota, generals Iwane Matsui and Akira Muto, and former
vice-minister of war Heitaro Kimura. Sixteen received life imprisonment, and several others shorter sentences.

Like the Nuremberg trials, the Tokyo tribunal was an un-precedented case of the victors' assumption of the right to try the leaders of vanquished nations for their alleged crimes against humanity. People in all countries entertained doubts as to the justness of both the European and the Far Eastern trials for many reasons. During the trials themselves, the very nature of killing in wartime had been discussed as pertinent to a defini-

tion of the nature of war crimes. An American lawyer, Ben Bruce Blakeney, who defended ex-general Yoshijiro Umezu, touched on this salient point when he compared killing with conventional weapons and the mass slaughter resulting from the atomic bombings of Hiroshima and Nagasaki.

Blakeney put this question to the court: if the killing of Admiral Kidd in the bombing of Pearl Harbor can be classified as murder, how must one define the killings caused by the atomic bombs? The name of the man who released the bombs over the two Japanese cities is known, as are the names of the chief of staff who planned the attack and the head of the state ultimately responsible for it. He asked whether these men had murder on their consciences and replied no to his own question.

His reason for adopting this stand was based not on the idea that victory had justified the acts of the Allies but on the definition of killing in war as an act perpetrated by states and hence different from murder in the usual sense. If this applies to the Allies, then, why does it not apply to the Japanese? If individuals cannot be held responsible for holocausts like those of Hiroshima and Nagasaki, why should it be considered just to try any individuals for their war responsibilities?

Nor was Blakeney the only person who questioned the justness of war tribunals or who feared that the judgments of the Tokyo tribunal could not be impartial. American Ambassador William Sebald, diplomatic adviser to the Supreme Commander for the Allied Powers, attended the opening session of the tribunal and later wrote:

"Although I was familiar with many of the sordid events covered in the indictment, my instinct told me that, on the whole, it was a mistake to hold the trial. I was not in sympathy with the theory that the victor should try the vanquished for deeds which, in the context of international law at that time, were not crimes, however abhorrent or deplorable they might have been from the viewpoint of philosophical concepts of right and wrong. Contrary arguments of considerable persuasiveness have been made, of course, and history may prove them correct. But my feelings on this point were strong; so strong in fact, that I felt uneasy throughout the first theatrical court session and never returned to the courtroom. I did, however, follow the course of the excessively long proceedings until the end."

The defense attorneys' application made to the United States Supreme Court for the right to file petitions for writs of *habeas corpus* was denied. And in the early hours of December 23, seven condemned prisoners mounted the thirteen steps to the execution platform. Present were Ambassador Sebald, official witnesses, and a Buddhist priest named Shinsho Hanayama.

Justices from the eleven council nations had failed to achieve unanimity in their verdicts. Representatives from India, the Netherlands, and France were opposed to death sentences. The minority opinion written by Dr. Radhabinod Pal, of India, showed uncommon perception and deep insight and included a criticism of modern civilization. Because of fears that his remarks would have what was called adverse effects on the Japanese people, they were withheld from the general public until their final publication in Calcutta, in 1957.

Dr. Pal's views deserve closer study and wider dissemination because of the light they shed on profound human issues. According to Dr. Pal, the radical changes and reshufflings in the cabinet during the war period proved that the war the Japanese waged differed essentially from the one conducted by the Nazis, who, over a long period, consistently and deliberately conspired for conquest of the world. He admitted the overwhelming evidence of atrocities committed by members of the Japanese armed forces but asserted that, unlike the Nazi leaders, the so-called Class-A Japanese war criminals had not been proved guilty of giving either permission or commands to commit acts of barbarity. Dr. Pal urged that, in light of the different natures of the two groups of leaders, all Japanese accused should be acquitted of the charges set forth in the indictment.

There is no reason to think that this famous judge and scholar was trying to justify the Pacific War waged by the Japanese. In the interests of universal justice, he was showing that the judgments of the tribunal were unfair. Perhaps one of the strongest points in his argument involved the nature of indiscriminate destruction in war. In discussing this, he quoted a notorious letter sent by Kaiser Wilhelm II to Emperor Franz Joseph of Austria:

"My soul is torn, but everything must be put to fire and sword: men, women and children, and old men must be slaughtered and not a tree or house left standing. With these methods of terrorism, which alone are capable of affecting a people as degenerate as the French, the war will be over in two months; whereas, if I admit considerations of humanity, it will be prolonged for years. In spite of my repugnance, I have therefore been obliged to choose the former system."

According to Dr. Pal, only one thing in the Pacific War reflected an attitude comparable to that of Wilhelm II:

"If in the Pacific War under our consideration, there was

anything approaching what is indicated in the above letter of the German emperor, it is the decision, coming from the Allied Powers, to use the atomic bomb. The future generations will judge this dire decision. It would be sufficient for my present purpose to say that if any indiscriminate destruction of civilian life and property is still illegitimate in warfare, then in the Pacific War, this decision to use the atomic bomb is the only near approach to the directives of the German emperor during the First World War and of the Nazi leaders during the Second World War. Nothing like this could be traced to the credit of the present accused."

Revealing the kind of wisdom and mercy characteristic of the greatest Oriental leaders, Dr. Pal said: "The name of justice should not be allowed to be invoked for the prolongation of the pursuit of vindictive retaliation. The world is really in need of generous magnanimity and understanding charity. The real question arising in a genuinely anxious mind is 'can mankind grow up quickly enough to win the race between civilization and disaster?' "

Even the president of the tribunal, Sir William Webb, expressed opinions that were very much in sympathy with those of Dr. Pal. In comparing the acts of the Japanese war criminals with those of the Nazis, he argued that the things of which the Germans were accused were more heinous, varied, and extensive than anything the Japanese had done. For this reason, he said, unless the Japanese were to be admittedly treated with less justice than the Germans, no Japanese accused should be sentenced to death for planning, initiating, conspiring to wage, or waging an aggressive war. Webb insisted that, instead of being put to death, Japanese convicted of crimes against peace and humanity should be banished to some remote island.

Although Toda could not at the time have known the contents of Dr. Pal's or Sir William Webb's discussions of the trials, his own opinions closely agreed with those of the two judges. Having been one of the victims of the fanaticism of the militarist regime, Toda knew their evil from firsthand experience. As a believer in the teachings of Nichiren Daishonin, he recognized punishment as the inevitable outcome of persecutions of true Buddhism. Still, the justness of convening the war-crimes tribunal at all and the validity of the sentences were issues about which he entertained profound doubts.

When friends who had been subjugated by the Japanese militarists vehemently supported the punishments as fitting the enormity of the crimes of the accused, Toda could not help disagreeing for two reasons. First, as a Buddhist he abhorred killing and therefore under no circumstances countenanced death sentences. Second, he, like others, recognized the unfairness of trying the Japanese for war killings while ignoring the guilt of the users of the atomic bomb. Since he believed that all killing is wrong, he insisted that anyone guilty of deliberate slaughter—no matter whether he was the winner or the loser in the conflict—ought to be held equally culpable. His analysis of the situation was based on a far-reaching moral attitude. When a man kills a neighbor, argued Toda, he is charged with murder, but when a man kills tens of thousands of people in war he is adored as a hero. With inexplicable irony, a righteous man can be branded a rebel and a criminal if he happens to be on the losing side in a war. Evil people should lose, but this does not justify unqualified judgment of the vanquished by the victors without considering the larger moral concepts of right and wrong.

The news of the trials and the subsequent executions confirmed Toda's belief that modern man had fallen into a grievous state. In the name of civilization, man turned justice into vengeance, vanity into power, fairness into menace, and triumph into brutality. But Toda held his peace, for he saw that conditions were far too turbulent for his pronouncements to have a constructive effect.

As a result of the political filth raked up in the early autumn by the Showa Denko scandal, Hitoshi Ashida's Democratic party cabinet fell. The redoubtable Shigeru Yoshida formed his second cabinet on October 19, 1948. With an eye to stability at all costs, he legislated a bill denying public employees the right to strike or to engage in collective bargaining. His next move was to bring all private trade-union disputes to the Central Labor Committee for arbitration. This committee, acting on a directive from occupation headquarters, imposed wage freezes on all areas affecting commodity costs.

But labor was not to be repressed without a fight. A wave of devastating strikes soon swept the nation. The seamen's union struck, thus paralyzing maritime transport. A later strike by the electrical workers' union temporarily plunged Japan into darkness. Nearly half a million coal miners refused to work for eight days. But all these reactions were piddling in scale in comparison with the virtual warfare ignited by—of all things—a strike at a large motion-picture studio. The United States cavalry, aircraft, and tanks, plus the Japanese police, encircled the studio until they coerced the workers to return to their cinematic labors. Obviously things had reached a sad state. Yoshida did not hesitate to attempt more forcible methods to bring labor into line; but his days in power were to end before much time had passed.

By December, 1948, matters had deteriorated still further. Hitoshi Ashida was arrested and later sentenced to imprisonment for complicity in bribery and graft scandals. In fact, the taint of corruption hung over not only the Democratic party, but the Socialist and People's Cooperative parties, as well. Furthermore, the road traveled by Yoshida's Liberal party was far from smooth. On December 23, the very day on which Tojo and the six other convicted war criminals were executed, the House of Representatives was dissolved after recording a vote of nonconfidence in the Yoshida government. The three discredited parties tried desperately to prevent this dissolution for fear that it might damage their chances in the coming elections. The occupation authorities intervened to save the House of Representatives. But all was to no avail. Elections for a new House were set for January 23, 1949. The Yoshida Liberals hoped, by capitalizing on the involvement of the three other parties in the Showa Denko disgrace, to win a majority.

On the international scene, the cold war got colder in the autumn as the United States and the Soviet Union sullenly confronted each other in Korea and Germany. In China, the Communists turned the tide in their favor when, after a series of offensives in Manchuria and in the north and central parts of the country, they succeeded in taking almost one-third of the whole nation. On December 15, they captured Peking and began to drive the Nationalist forces to the southern bank of the Yangtze River.

Alarmed by the extent of the incursions of communism in many parts of the world, the United States felt compelled to take a firm stand, especially in the Orient. This necessitated a sharp revision of the American attitude toward the industrial— and potential military—strength of Japan. Whereas earlier the United States had preached that Japan must never again have the strength to arm, on December 18, Washington ordered the occupation administration to enforce a nineteen-point economic stabilization program that later came to be called the Dodge Line. This program entailed sweeping reforms of the entire Japanese economy. Almost as a symbol of a new period of relations, on Christmas Eve the Supreme Commander for the Allied Powers released nineteen war-crimes suspects, including Nobusuke Kishi, who later became prime minister. With this, the punishment of the Japanese empire by the Allied forces came to a close.

All these confused developments combined with the continuing misery of most of the Japanese people to strengthen Toda's belief in the Buddhist teaching of ten states of life. According to this doctrine, life always exists in ten states whose simultaneous operations make possible completely contradictory desires and actions. Reflecting on this, Toda interpreted the condition of twentieth-century man as evolving from an inability to find liberation from karma. Failing to realize that the ideal and the actual are but two aspects of the same thing, man tends to regard ideals as so unattainable that he refuses even to try practical methods to realize them. Times were very dark in the fall and winter of 1948, but Toda and his fellow believers were in high spirits because for them the completion of the new Kyakuden of the head temple was more than just the successful rebuilding of a valued part of an important institution. It was above all physical proof of the progress their movement was making and a beacon of light promising guidance in troubled days.

6. A LONG PROCESS

THE RESULTS of the elections of January 23, 1949, reflected the doubt that the people of Japan had come to entertain about the democratic system and the government running it until that time. After the horrors of war and deprivations of living under a military regime, the Japanese greeted the idea of parliamentary democracy with joy and hopefulness. This system, they believed, would be the panacea to heal all their spiritual wounds and solve all their economic problems. Under the management of the governments that held office immediately after the war, however, the people had been treated to repressions and, still worse, disgusting scandals in the highest places. Though no one had expected the popular reaction to be as violent as it was, the Japanese people made their dissatisfaction felt in a dramatic way. All three parties that had been involved in the graft and bribery disgrace of 1948 suffered crushing defeats at the polls. The Socialist, Democratic, and People's Cooperative parties lost huge numbers of seats in the National Diet, whereas the Communists made considerable gains. The Democratic Liberals, headed by Shigeru Yoshida, were the true victors, for they took 264 seats in the lower house, enough to give them an absolute majority.

A combination of factors worked to strengthen the Communists' position. First, the implication of the Socialists in the ugly incidents of the preceding year meant that a number of people who would have voted for the Socialist ticket crossed over to the Communists. Second, the victories of the Communist Chinese, who had succeeded in driving the Nationalists out of the area north of the Yangtze and who had presented surrender terms to Chiang Kai-shek on January 14, influenced the emotions of many.

Realizing the source of the discontent, the Democratic Liberals directed their campaign to the heart of the desires of the people when they adopted the slogan "Bright Freedom or Dark Control?" The Japanese were fed up with the kinds of restrictions they had lived under during and after the war, and they were appalled by the contemptible behavior of politicians. Freedom from want, excess controls, and exploitation by the unscrupulous was what the people demanded. The politically adroit Democratic Liberals promised these things, and for their promises won a landslide victory in the elections.

Toda was perhaps one of the very few people in Japan not surprised by the election results. He understood that the people are wise, that they cannot be fooled for very long. They will always come to doubt and criticize what is basically wrong, no matter how cleverly those in power try to conceal their faults. Once doubt has been sown in the minds of the people, it will grow into open criticism and, given the right time and conditions, into practical action to correct abuse. Recognizing the critical doubting spirit as a wholesome part of the human psychological makeup, Toda also realized that it has its limitations. There are things that must be subjected to doubt and question, but there are others that are so fundamentally true and right that they transcend the realm of critical questioning. Indeed, the very act of criticizing these things can lead to malice and thus invite severe punishment. The first few weeks of 1949 saw some events that gave Toda an excellent chance to explain this important point to his followers, but the story that led up to these events began in the early days of the war.

Koji Morikawa was converted to Nichiren Shoshu in 1941. He and his wife were fond of children and had a large family of six boys and girls. But in October, 1942, one of their sons died quite unexpectedly. Because he was concerned over the welfare of all Nichiren Shoshu members, Tsunesaburo Makiguchi attended the child's funeral. At that time and in a number of subsequent discussions, Makiguchi said many things that influenced not only Koji but also his younger brother, who soon joined Nichiren Shoshu himself. Together the two brothers worked diligently for their faith and took active parts in membership campaigns conducted by Soka Kyoiku Gakkai, to which they both belonged.

In July, 1943, however, the militarists stepped up persecution of the society. At about the same time as the arrest of Makiguchi, Morikawa's brother was imprisoned. In the miserable conditions of a prison cell, doubts assailed him. Fear of what would happen to himself and to his family was greater than his faith. He renounced Nichiren Shoshu and in that way gained his own release. The same eagerness and persuasive personality that had inspired his activities for the society were now directed toward turning his family away from the society and vehemently criticizing the teachings of Nichiren Shoshu. Most of the family agreed with him. Only Koji Morikawa retained a degree of the old faithfulness to his religion, but even he refrained from associating with Soka Kyoiku Gakkai members. Gradually the entire group of people in the Morikawas' neighborhood, once a staunch band of loyal society members, stopped supporting Soka Kyoiku Gakkai and allowed their faith to lapse.

Koji Morikawa's oldest son, Kazumasa, was a serious and sensitive boy. Even as a child he had been impressed with the things he had heard Tsunesaburo Makiguchi say at the meetings that were often held in his father's home. When the war was over, like many young men of his generation, Kazumasa lost sight of all objectives in the turbulent social upheaval of the time. Education was sporadic at best, and he was eager to learn. Often he recalled how Makiguchi had castigated as rubbish the Imperial Rescript on Education. This document, which set forth the duties to the state of instructors and pupils, was regarded as sacrosanct in prewar Japan. With the fall of the military government, the collapse of everything the rescript stood for clearly substantiated Makiguchi's opinions and led Kazumasa to develop an interest in the religion and society to which the wise, elderly man had been devoted. His father, Koji Morikawa, still enshrined a Gohonzon in the house; and one day Kazumasa asked him about it and about Nichiren Shoshu.

Quite by coincidence, at that time word reached the family that Josei Toda, former director general of Soka Kyoiku Gakkai, had reestablished his publishing firm and was striving to rehabilitate the society under the new name Soka Gakkai. Unsatisfied with the life he was leading and filled with hope that the teachings of Makiguchi, the one man who had seen through the sham of the old educational system, might help him find something better, Kazumasa made up his mind to call on Toda.

It was early autumn, 1946, when Kazumasa decided to make his visit to Toda's publishing company. The Morikawa home was in Tsurumi, about forty minutes from Tokyo. The trains young Kazumasa had to take were crowded, and the weather was still very hot. By the time the young man arrived at Toda's company, he was soaked with sweat. The receptionist ushered him into the editorial room, where he found Toda, clad only in shorts, trying to cool himself with a paper fan. After a few cordial words of greeting, Toda invited the young man to make himself comfortable by removing his shirt. This first meeting, which was to have profound consequences for Kazumasa and for Soka Gakkai, took place under the most informal conditions of semiundress. But this was of no importance, for the two had many things to talk about.

Toda first asked the boy to tell him something of his background. Kazumasa explained that he worked for very low wages at a United States army tire-repair plant in the daytime and went to college at night. Then he revealed the emptiness of his life and mentioned his hopes of finding guidance and assistance from Soka Gakkai. Toda immediately sensed the young man's sincerity; and because he remembered Koji Morikawa from the early war days, he was happy to offer advice. He began by explaining something about the Nichiren Shoshu life philosophy and the Buddhist doctrines on which it is based. Kazumasa found the religious terminology hard to understand, but Toda's fervor conveyed a great deal more meaning than mere words. Soon the young man felt as if a new horizon was opening before him.

Time passed quickly for the men; but glancing at the clock on the wall, Toda noticed that he had to leave for an appointment. Before going, he asked Kazumasa if he often discussed religion with his friends. To the boy's negative reply, Toda suggested that he should try to do so more often and that perhaps Chuhei Yamadaira, who worked for Toda, would be willing to help him find people to talk to and guide him through the difficulties of Buddhist thought and terminology. Kazumasa was of course happy to take Toda's advice, but he had hoped that Toda himself would help him.

"I'll be glad to meet Mr. Yamadaira, but I was wondering if you wouldn't come to Tsurumi and talk to me and my family."

The minute he said this, Kazumasa regretted his forwardness. Toda was a busy man who had no time to spend on people like him. To his surprise and joy, however, Toda said: "Of course I'll come. Let me know when you can get several of your family and friends together and we'll have a meeting. Talk it over with your father."

Toda made it a point never to refuse requests of this kind from young people, even when granting them time meant extra effort and trouble. His generosity with his time won him many youthful friends, who sometimes became spoiled and tried to monopolize him. But he indulged them on this point because he knew that with time, care, and diligence he could develop these young men and women into the kind of members Soka Gakkai needed.

Just before leaving the office, Toda introduced Kazumasa to Yamadaira. The two settled down for a long discussion of such important issues as value, happiness, and goodness. Much of what was said remained vague in Kazumasa's mind. Yamadaira's way of explaining things lacked Toda's inspiration and warmth, but it did not matter. Already Kazumasa was filled with hope and a sense of warmth unlike anything he had ever known. This feeling stayed with him all the way home.

Arriving at their somewhat ramshackle two-story house in Tsurumi, Kazumasa hurried to his father's room to tell him about everything that had happened that day. Koji Morikawa was pleased and impressed to learn that his boy had taken it upon himself to meet and talk with Toda. But old doubts and memories lingered. He was concerned and dubious about the success of arranging a discussion meeting in their neighborhood, where all of the old faithful members had lost their spark of devotion to Nichiren Shoshu.

"If you want to hold a discussion meeting with a man as important in the society as Mr. Toda, you'll have to get together a lot of people," he said.

"I know," replied the glowingly enthusiastic Kazumasa. "I'll bring all my friends and plenty of others besides."

"They won't come," said Koji shaking his head slowly. "I've tried in the past. Times are bad. People are busy. You haven't got anything to entertain them with. I wish you hadn't promised to pull a meeting together," he sighed. "But I'll do what I can to help."

Father and son immediately began canvassing their neighborhood to find people who would be willing to attend a discussion meeting. Finally, in January, 1947, they thought the time was right. Kazumasa telephoned Toda's office to say that everything was ready and that he hoped Mr. Toda was free.

On the night of January 15, only a few minutes before Toda and his party of society members were to arrive, not a single one of the twenty people who had promised to attend had yet appeared. Koji Morikawa acted as if it was only what he had expected would happen. But Kazumasa refused to give in so easily. Rushing out to the homes of some of his friends, he rounded up two young men, both of whom were intelligent, but short-tempered.

As soon as Toda and his group arrived, the conversation immediately moved into realms of philosophy and religion that were too deep for the limited experience of Kazumasa's friends. They became uneasy because they failed to understand everything that was being said. The Soka Gakkai members, eager to help and guide, posed a number of questions. The young men did not answer because they could not. Toda remained oddly silent, but his companions tried to offer encouragement by rephrasing their questions. Their approach was completely wrong because the two already nervous young men interpreted attempts to draw them into the discussion as ridicule.

"What are you trying to do?" shouted one. "Are you making a fool of me? Look, I didn't come here to be made an idiot of. Morikawa, make them leave me alone."

Kazumasa stammered something incoherent, and one of the members of Soka Gakkai, a young man named Tanaka, had the temerity to laugh. That was all that was needed to send both of Morikawa's friends stalking from the room in a rage. Nor were they the only ones who had misinterpreted the innocent laugh of surprise and worry. Kazumasa himself hung his head as if embarrassed, though he was actually very angry. "So this is the great discussion meeting we have nearly killed ourselves to put together!" he thought. He was convinced that his father had been right in hesitating to agree to the meeting because, now that this one had turned out a fiasco, Toda was not likely to want to come to another one at the Morikawa house.

Just as he thought this, he heard Toda's gentle voice at his shoulder: "Don't let a thing like this discourage you, Kazumasa. This is what our work is often like. People who take the greatest offense at what we have to offer frequently grasp our profoundest meanings quicker than anyone else. I'll come again, and I want to see both those young men, too. When they've cooled off, they'll realize that no one here was trying to make them look like fools. Arrange another meeting for us soon."

Kazumasa nodded. Toda's words were soothing, but the sense of having failed at something he had wanted to be a wonderful success blocked all words of thanks. Besides, no matter how gentle Mr. Toda might be, if there were many people in Soka Gakkai who laughed at the embarrassment of others, he was not at all sure that he wanted to be a member.

As a matter of courtesy, Kazumasa and his father accompanied Toda's party to the train station. As they walked along, Kazumasa felt resentment grow stronger and stronger until he could no longer resist saying something to Tanaka, who had maliciously—or so Kazumasa thought—laughed at his friends.

"You know," said Kazumasa, "I don't know how you feel, but I think atmosphere is important at meetings. If some people laugh at newcomers and make fun of them, we can't expect to make much progress, can we?"

Tanaka was taken aback; his laugh had been a nervous expression of sympathy with the embarrassed men. He knew that the two angry friends who had stalked out of the room had misinterpreted his intentions, but he thought everyone else knew that he had meant no harm. Still, a glance at the overwrought face of Kazumasa told him that this was no time to offer explanations. He simply said: "Forgive me for saying this, but you are criticizing something that you must not

criticize. You don't understand now, but you'll learn soon."
As might be expected, this failed to calm Kazumasa's anger.
The remainder of the walk to the station was awkward and
silent.

Upon returning home, Kazumasa said good night to his
mother, father, grandmother, and brothers and sisters. Then
he climbed the dark, narrow staircase to his small room on the
second floor. After spreading his bedding on the tatami floor,
he undressed and prepared to sleep. Just as he was getting into
bed his mother appeared at the door with a small metal footwarmer filled with charcoal. "You'll need this tonight," she
said, "it's cold."

Kazumasa thanked her, put the footwarmer under the cover-
let, and tried to go to sleep. But he could not: the memory of
the painfully unpleasant evening filled his mind and drove
sleep away. He could not stop criticizing what he considered
to be Tanaka's callousness. And this thought cast doubt on
everything he had believed about Nichiren Shoshu. Once or
twice, however, he dozed off for a few moments. After one of
these fitful naps, he saw to his shock that the room was filled
with smoke. The quilt covering the footwarmer was smoldering
and on the verge of bursting into flame. Leaping from bed and
throwing open the sliding windows, Kazumasa hurled the
smoking quilt out into the night. He then dashed down the
steps, waking the whole house in the process, and rushed to the
side yard. Grabbing a bucket hanging at the side door and
filling it from an outdoor faucet, he doused the quilt, which
could have become the cause of a disastrous fire.

Shivering in the cold, wearing nothing but thin pajamas,
and looking at the black and now soggy remnants of his quilt,
Kazumasa suddenly realized what all this was about. There
was a reason for the fire: it was a punishment for his having
doubted and criticized Soka Gakkai and the faith of Nichiren
Shoshu simply because of a stupid mistake at one discussion
meeting. In a flash, Kazumasa saw that he was the one who

had been wrong. "Tanaka said I was criticizing something I ought not criticize," thought Kazumasa. "But how can I tell the difference between a correct opinion and criticism? I know one thing, I definitely felt resentment against the society. That must be it. I felt malice toward the society. I was wrong." He saw that he should have calmed his friends; he had been in charge of the meeting.

Now he understood it all, Toda's strange silence when a few words from him would have smoothed the issue over, the calm reprimand of Tanaka, whom he had accused of scoffing. All of it had been a test to see how strong Kazumasa was, and he had failed it. He had allowed himself to entertain malice against the faith, and that feeling had brought about the retribution that Nichiren Daishonin teaches is inevitable. The burning of the quilt and indeed the near disaster had been punishment.

Chastened, but resolved to try never to fail in this way again, Kazumasa returned to his room where the acrid stench of smoke still lingered. His mother had brought another quilt. Crawling into bed, he knew he would be able to sleep now because there was nothing on his mind to keep him awake. As he turned out the small lamp beside his pillow he thought: "Anyway, Tanaka probably didn't mean anything by laughing. My two friends did look pretty comical when you come to think of it."

Oddly enough the episode of the burned quilt was a turning point in the life of Koji Morikawa, as well as in that of his son. For him, more than a punishment for his son's sudden moment of doubt and criticism, the burned quilt was a manifestation of the will of the Gohonzon. It was an admonition to him to shake off his lethargy and to begin taking advantage of a faith that he had allowed to lapse. He accepted the lesson because he knew that if neglect of the Gohonzon brings punishment devotion to it brings reward.

Because of the diligent efforts of the two Morikawas, the Tsurumi discussion meetings were soon put on a monthly basis.

The formerly angry friends quickly recovered from their fit of temper and, as Toda had predicted, became regular and intelligent attendants at the meetings. Koji Morikawa increased the amount of time he spent on religious activities. As a result, he felt younger and stronger than he had for a long time. He was fifty-two; but his face was youthful, and his eyes clear and bright. In addition to the meetings held at his own home, Morikawa started going to Toda's lectures on the Lotus Sutra, which were held in Kanda. This meant that at exactly five o'clock on three days each week he had to leave the offices of the Yokohama Finance Association, where he was employed. But he never departed earlier than five, and he took great care to put in overtime whenever necessary to ensure that his work was always up to date and accurate.

Things were going well for Morikawa, until one day several months after the burning of the quilt, he fell into skeptical speculation about the intensity and depth of his own devotion to Nichiren Shoshu. "How true am I to what I believe? What is the measure of my faith?" he asked himself. But fearing to confide his self-doubt to anyone, he kept it in his own heart, where it continued to trouble him.

One night after a lecture meeting in Tokyo, Toda asked Morikawa to wait for a few minutes; he had something to discuss. The few minutes stretched into about thirty while Toda gave counsel to several people in trouble. Finally he finished and came to the side of the room where Morikawa sat patiently. After apologizing for keeping him waiting, Toda said: "I'm thinking of appointing you a director of the society, and I want to ask you whether you would accept."

Morikawa, stunned by the very idea and filled with doubt about himself, said nothing.

"You don't think much of the proposal?" asked Toda.

"No, it's not that. It's just that I have so little training in Buddhist philosophy. And, well to tell the truth, I do the best

I can; but lately I've been wondering if my faith is as deep as it ought to be. As long as I feel this way, I don't see how I could take on an important job like that."

"Do you think you can know how deep faith is, even your own?"

"Well, no. I guess not."

"Then don't worry. I believe in you, even if you doubt yourself. And I'll be at your side whenever you need me. Anyway, you don't have to say yes or no right now. Think it over. But if you agree, I'd like you to be ready to assume your duties in the near future."

Not until he had boarded the train bound for Tsurumi did Morikawa recover sufficiently from the surprise of what had happened to realize the full significance of Toda's offer. The knowledge that the leader of the entire Soka Gakkai considered Morikawa worthy to fill a position of great responsibility simultaneously revived his faith in himself and inspired him to make every effort to prove that Toda's trust was not misplaced. It was late when he arrived home; everyone in the family was asleep. Still, he performed his Gongyo before the Gohonzon. And as he got into bed, he experienced once again a feeling of happiness and responsibility over the offer Toda had made. But suddenly as he turned over to sleep there came to his mind the old saying that demons of danger lurk in moments of joy. "Perhaps I'm headed for trouble," he thought.

Just as Morikawa was taking his seat in the office the following morning, a messenger came to tell him that he was wanted in the director's office. Morikawa went promptly to the director, greeted him, and sat down in response to a wordless wave toward a chair. The director then said: "I know this is abrupt, but I am asking for your resignation." He shuffled some papers on his desk without looking at Morikawa, who for a moment was too shocked to speak. Finally Morikawa asked: "Why?"

"Believe me," answered the director, still pretending to examine something on his desk intently, "we have our reasons. They are good ones, and no discussion will help. We are prepared to give you the best severance terms possible under the present circumstances. Why not just leave without making a fuss?"

But Morikawa had regained enough composure to see that he was being duped, though he did not yet see quite how or why.

"Wait just a minute," he said. "I've been working in this office for seventeen years. Do you think I've been here just for my health? Now suddenly you ask me to resign and won't even explain why. This is important to me. We're not playing a game you know. Tell me what I've done wrong."

"Now calm down," said the director, at last raising his eyes to Morikawa's face. "I didn't want to explain our reasons because you'll be angry when you find out. But since you insist, it's this way. Lately you've been putting in a great deal of time with these religious activities of yours. You have a right to your own religion, but we feel that from the long-range viewpoint we'd rather have someone who put his work before everything else."

"Have I neglected my work? Have I skipped out early, even once? Have I in any way allowed my religious work to interfere with what I do here in the office?"

"Well, not exactly, but—"

"Then you've got some other reason you're hiding from me."

"As a matter of fact," murmured the director, "the truth is you're a little outspoken on some topics. Let's face it, you've been here for a long time; but we still don't see eye to eye on a lot of things. Times are hard now. We're short of capital, and a credit association can't run without operating funds. Do you see what I'm getting at?"

Suddenly Morikawa saw exactly what the director was getting at: he was being asked to resign because the company

could not fire him for any good reason. The source of dissatisfaction with Morikawa was almost certainly a rich landowner
and investor who held a large amount of stock in the credit association. Morikawa and this man had never agreed; and when
he felt it necessary for the good of the company, Morikawa had
often stood up against the wealthy stockholder. The company
was in financial straits because of the postwar devaluation of
Japanese currency. Obviously, the rich man had promised to
lend money but only on the condition that Morikawa be ousted.
The director of the firm, thinking of profit only, had plainly
conceded to the stockholder's demands.

"You think I'm a bad influence on the company then?" asked
Morikawa quietly.

"No, that's not what I mean. It's simply that the leadership
of the firm is going to have to change somewhat, and your
remaining here will be—shall we say, detrimental. I know I'm
not making much sense to you. But why not look at things this
way? Leave now as a personal favor to me. I'm sure I can find
a way to rehire you sometime in the future."

"Let me think it over," said Morikawa rising and turning
toward the door. As he left, the director called after him, but
Morikawa did not pause. Without stopping at his desk, he took
his briefcase from his locker and left to call on Josei Toda.

This time, however, he was not running for help. On the
train to Tokyo, Morikawa thought the whole matter over
calmly. Obviously he would have to leave the credit association. If he refused to resign, conditions would probably become
impossible in a matter of days or weeks. It was hard to give up
a job after seventeen years of devoted work, but that troubled
him less than the immediate future of his large family. Of
course, Kazumasa was working. Still, his wages were small, and
what little he could save went to pay his college tuition at
night school. Jobs were scarce, especially for people Morikawa's
age. But doubt was gone from his mind; he knew he would

manage somehow if he trusted completely in his faith in the Gohonzon. After all, Nichiren Daishonin had promised that great misfortunes are followed by great good fortune.

As Morikawa was shown into the office at Nihon Shogakkan, Toda said cheerfully: "Well, what brings you here so early? Business?"

"No. Actually I want your advice." And Morikawa told the

whole story from start to finish without pause. The smile had disappeared from Toda's face when he inquired: "How many people are there in your family?"

"Eight."

"Eight! You must be worried then. But you know, Morikawa, I'm not. A man of your faith will be all right. Fight it out and wait to see what happens. Call on me if you need me."

That short interview strengthened the resolution Morikawa had made before he arrived at Toda's office. The problem of breaking the news to his family, however, remained. It was evening when Morikawa arrived home. The children, his wife, and his elderly mother were sitting on cushions on the floor around the low Japanese-style table. The food was plain, but as usual, there was enough of it. Everyone was chattering and laughing when Morikawa joined them.

"Well, everybody, I've often talked with you about the divine rewards of faith, haven't I. Today I received a divine reward."

The chatter ceased. Everyone turned toward Morikawa in expectation of some exciting good news: a raise in salary, a promotion.

"I was asked to resign," Morikawa said with a weak smile.

"Some reward!" exclaimed his wife.

"We don't need rewards like that," chimed in the youngest girl.

"What did he say?" asked the grandmother, who thought for a moment that her ears must be going bad.

"No, I'm serious. It is a reward. I'm willing to quit. Times may be hard, but we have reached a stage where the Morikawa family needs to start afresh, to change our destiny, and to work toward something better than we've known up to now. You all know that Nichiren Daishonin has promised that good fortune inevitably follows bad for people who have faith. And we have that, so we'll be all right."

At just about that moment, Kazumasa returned from night school. As soon as he heard his father's news and his explanation of the way they would have to work to change their karma, he said with a grin: "Father, I'm really proud of you. I'm with you. Let's celebrate."

And celebrate they did. Mrs. Morikawa brought out some stale cakes that had been in the cupboard for a while. There was a little sakè and even a banana, a rare luxury in those days. Nibbling on these modest delicacies, the whole family enjoyed a feeling of warmth and unity that made even the uncertainty of their future seem less fearsome.

After one small cup of sakè, the grandmother worked up the courage to announce that she had an idea: "This old house is bigger than we need. Let's turn the downstairs into a restaurant. Nothing fancy, but lots of good, plain food at low prices. I can cook, Koji can handle the business end, and the children can run errands and wash dishes." The suggestion was approved unanimously.

Morikawa invested part of his severance pay in expanding the kitchen and remodeling the downstairs of their house into a simple, rather amateurish-looking restaurant that, after opening in the middle of January, 1949, promised to do well because it answered a pressing need of the poor people in the neighborhood.

Late in the afternoon of a cold, windy February day, Toda sat in his office trying to work out the schedule of discussion meetings for the night. It happened that he had a special reason for wanting to make a change in plans.

"Mishima, what meeting are you going to tonight?"

"The one at the Morikawas' in Tsurumi."

"Listen, you take my place at Suginami, and I'll go to Tsurumi."

Since the day in December, 1948, when Morikawa had called on him for advice on his resignation from the credit association, Toda had heard nothing directly from him, although word had reached the office that the family had opened a restaurant.

"Maybe that's a good idea. I've heard the Morikawas are in some trouble. But what's worse, something seems to be going wrong with the whole Tsurumi chapter," said Mishima.

Toda was not so much concerned about Morikawa, even though he was in financial trouble, because his faith was strong. But the effect Morikawa's apparent bad luck might be having on the new converts in Tsurumi troubled him. A few minutes before quitting time, a young man from Kamata called at the office. Toda inquired what his plans were for the evening and, on learning that the young man was free, asked him to go with him to Tsurumi. The two left the office together in that atmosphere of combined friendliness and teacher-pupil respect that characterized all of Toda's associations. Bracing themselves against the cutting, dry wind of the Tokyo winter, they talked about Soka Gakkai matters on the way to the train. The young man, too, was disturbed by rumors about Tsurumi and made his fears plain to Toda, who became even more concerned.

As the two hurried from the Tsurumi station through the shop-lined street leading to Morikawa's house and restaurant, Toda recalled the awkward silence of the walk to the station after the disappointing discussion meeting two years earlier. Young Kazumasa Morikawa had been very unsure of himself then. But he had grown in faith and had done much good work in his neighborhood. Toda hoped that the foundation of that work was solid and that misfortune had not shaken the faith of the new converts the Morikawa family had made.

Though it still stood on the edge of a wheat field by the bank of the Tsurumi River near the end of the local business district, the Morikawas' dilapidated old two-story house had taken on quite a bold new air. There was a sign out front advertising food and drink, and a huge paper lantern hung at the entrance. When he pulled the sliding door open, Toda was greeted with a burst of excitement. A smiling Koji Morikawa rushed from behind the counter and extended his hand in greeting. Mrs. Morikawa put down a tray and hurried to him, and the elderly grandmother bowed hello from the kitchen door. "No reason to worry about these people," thought Toda.

Morikawa guided Toda up the now familiar dark, narrow staircase to the room on the second floor where the meeting was to be held. None of the others had arrived yet, and the two men had a few minutes to talk. Toda was gladdened to learn that the restaurant was going well, but when the conversation turned to other Soka Gakkai members in the neighborhood, Morikawa became strangely reticent. There was no time to explain, however, because the first guests for the meeting began to arrive.

Koichi Harayama and Hisao Seki from the Kamata district came and sat next to Toda. About ten of the newer members drifted in, and the meeting began. Toda immediately saw evidence of insecurity in the faces of several of the people present. He decided to go directly to what he felt must be the source of the low spirits of the group.

"I suppose most of you think it's strange that a man with a strong religious faith like Mr. Morikawa should have lost his job."

A Mr. Sagawa, the owner of a small factory, spoke up at once: "Oh, yes, we do think it's strange. We've all gotten together to discuss it on several occasions. It's enough to make you question some of the things we've been taught about the rewards of devotion. I understand that we are told that if one professes and practices faith in true Buddhism, the Three Obstacles and Four Devils will plague us, but still—"

Toda interrupted: "You don't understand anything, obviously. If you really understood, you would never entertain the kind of skepticism that is evident in what you're saying.

"I'm not worried about Morikawa. He has too much faith to allow a temporary setback to upset him seriously. He has faced the Three Obstacles and Four Devils, and his faith has conquered them. But you are all new to Nichiren Shoshu, and there are a few points that I must make clear for you right now.

"The first thing is the nature of tribulation. You have some idea of what karma entails. You know that evil acts in past lives bring retribution at some time—maybe many centuries— after they were committed. Sooner or later, however, the debts must be settled. If you grasp this, can you see why Morikawa and all other people of true faith welcome the kind of hardship he is suffering now? It is because they regard it as a great good fortune to be able to accept the consequences of karma ahead of time and in a greatly attenuated form. Only people of deep devotion are capable of changing their karma in this way. They accept the task gladly because they know that firm faith turns everything into divine reward and brings closer the happy life of the future.

"But perhaps more important for you at this stage in your development is to understand the danger of doubt and criticism. Doubting is only too human; and it's wholesome in its way, as long as it is directed against things that can be doubted. Doubt of oneself can be constructive. To use the Morikawa family as an example again, some time ago, Koji Morikawa had entertained doubts about the strength and depth of his own faith. This doubt led him to come to me, and together we learned that a person cannot always accurately judge his own devotion. If Morikawa had not doubted himself, he might have fallen into complacency.

Toda glanced at Kazumasa, who sat thinking of discussion-meeting fiascos and smoldering quilts. Then Toda resumed: "Never doubt or criticize the teachings of Nichiren Daishonin or the Dai-Gohonzon because such criticism can lead to malicious slandering of the faith. This is one of the most grievous sins of which anyone can be guilty. Lack of wisdom does not make a fool. A fool, in the truest sense, is the man who regards his own misfortunes or those of others as a source of doubt or criticism of the infinite mercy of the Gohonzon.

"I'm willing to help you in time of trouble. So are all the other members of our organization. Strengthen your faith. Believe that you will be happy if you are true to Nichiren Daishonin's teaching. Then you will be happy in the richest way."

The future bore out what Toda said that cold February night. In less than a year, a large credit union in Kawasaki, not far from Tsurumi, heard of Morikawa's resignation and hastened to hire him because men of his experience and skill were scarce. A few years later, he was elected to the Yokohama city council with a large majority of the vote. Others present at that discussion meeting became successful and useful politicians, serving in the Tokyo metropolitan assembly and the House of Councilors of the National Diet. In addition, some of them were to become executive members of Soka Gakkai in later years.

When Morikawa found new, stable employment, he and his family gave up their homey restaurant with a mixture of regret and relief. Both Koji and Kazumasa continued to work for Nichiren Shoshu and Soka Gakkai with the result that before long the Tsurumi chapter was one of the strongest and largest in the nation.

BOOK FOUR

1. GARDEN OF LIFE

LATE ONE May night in 1949, Josei Toda, comfortable in a kimono, sat on the tatami floor of the upstairs study in his home. In front of him on his desk lay a sheaf of manuscript paper. He had written the words "The Philosophy of Life Force, by Josei Toda," but nothing else. He had been sitting there smoking cigarette after cigarette for hours; the words he wanted would not come to him. This was unusual for Toda, who generally devoted time and great care to the mental preparation of his writing but wrote very swiftly once his ideas had clearly formed themselves in his mind. Tonight, however, he was stymied because the topic he had chosen to write about was not only complex, but also immensely important to him, to Soka Gakkai, and ultimately to all mankind. The great significance of his task somehow made him hesitate.

As was his custom, however, he already had an idea of the general outline and development of the material. He intended to deal with the philosophy of life in its three existences: past, present, and future. To substantiate his own thoughts on the subject, he intended to quote from Nichiren Daishonin's *Kaimoku Sho* (On Awakening to True Buddhahood) and *Senji Sho* (On the Selection of Time), and from the Hiyuhon (Parable),

129

Kejoyuhon (Parable of a Transformed Castle), and Nyorai Juryohon (Fathoming Buddha's Blessings) chapters of the Lotus Sutra. Then he wanted to discuss the eternity of life. For this purpose he was going to summarize the Nyorai Juryo chapter of the Lotus Sutra and quote from several of Nichiren Daishonin's works, including *Totaigi Sho* (On the Substance of Nammyoho-renge-kyo), *Sanze Shobutsu Sokammon Sho* (On the Ultimate Enlightenment of the Buddhas of the Three Existences), *Ongi Kuden* (Oral Teachings), and *Jippokaiji* (Commentary on the Ten States of Life). Finally, he was going to give a full treatment of the continuity of life throughout the universe.

Set out in this systematic organization, the work he was contemplating seemed logical and relatively easy to handle. But the apparent ease was the very reason that he hesitated. He seriously doubted that the method of logical analysis alone could explain the substance of life force that lay at the core of his philosophy. In his heart he knew that unaided reason would fail because his own experience of enlightenment about the nature of universal life had come to him through sources outside the realm of logical thought.

Rising and walking to the open window, Toda paused for a moment to listen to a dog barking somewhere in the cool May darkness. Then, returning to the center of the room, he began to pace back and forth as he struggled mentally to find just the right way to give expression to his thoughts. While walking around the limited space of his small study, he remembered another room, darker and much smaller, where he had spent a long time as a prisoner arrested for what were called crimes of thought during World War II.

Toda's cell in the Tokyo Detention House was about five square yards in area. The door, about one yard wide and fitted with iron bars, could be opened only from the outside. Part of the room was floored with boards, but there were two tatami mats where Toda, and the inevitable prison lice, slept. In the west wall a small barred window provided the only view of the outside world that Toda was to have for a long time. In one corner was a wooden storage chest and a shelf for books and other small personal belongings. Between the chest and the window stood a board-covered wash basin that doubled as a kind of desk. Next to the basin-desk was a wooden chair, whose seat actually concealed a toilet. This tiny, compact cell was the circumscribed world in which Toda lived and meditated.

On New Year's Day, 1944, Toda made two resolutions: he would read the entire Lotus Sutra in the book containing Daishonin's writings; and he would chant the Daimoku ten thousand times a day. The compilation of the Lotus Sutra that Toda proposed to read had been drawn up by Nichiren Buddhist priests and scholars. Because it was an unpunctuated version in Chinese, it was extremely difficult to read. Giving it up as almost unintelligible, Toda had sent it back to his home on several occasions. Oddly enough, it was always returned to him in his cell. At first he thought that it kept coming back because the prison officials who handled the tasks of mailing and dispatching things either were maliciously teasing him or were negligent. Later, however, he sensed that there was a purpose in the persistent return of the book. It was this realization that inspired him to resolve to struggle through the difficult language, and he began to do so on New Year's Day immediately after making his two resolutions.

By March, he had read the Lotus Sutra three times and had carefully perused much of the writings of Nichiren Daishonin. In addition, he had chanted the Daimoku several hundred times at a sitting to make certain that he adhered to his vow of repeating it ten thousand times a day. One cold morning in March, he took the book from the shelf over the storage chest to begin reading the Lotus Sutra for the fourth time. He opened it to the first chapter of the introductory sutra of infinite meaning and read:

"Tokugyobon, or Virtuous Practice.

"Thus have I heard. Once upon a time the Lord was staying at Rājagṛha on Vulture Peak with a numerous assemblage of monks—two thousand monks, all of them Arhats, unstained, free from depravity, well-disciplined, thoroughly emancipated in thought and knowledge, of noble breed . . ."

Toda was already so familiar with this passage that in his mind's eye he could vividly see the Buddha teaching the Tokugyobon to the monks and sages. The next passage, however, is a series of verses—called *gāthā* in Sanskrit—that Toda had always found difficult to understand. The first eight lines, a panegyric on the Buddha and his supreme enlightenment, presented little difficulty: but the lines following those bewildered him. Once more he puzzled as he read:

"Its entity is neither being nor nonbeing;
Neither cause nor effect;
Neither itself nor another;
Neither square nor round; neither short nor long;
Neither rising nor falling; neither living nor dead;
Neither sitting nor lying; neither going nor staying;
Neither moving nor rolling, nor still;
Neither advancing nor retreating; neither safe nor
　　in danger;
Neither reasonable nor unreasonable; neither prof-
　　iting nor losing;
Neither this nor that, past nor future;
Neither blue nor yellow, red nor white;
Neither red nor purple, nor any other color."

This obscure passage is followed by one that begins: "It is the root of precept, concentration, wisdom, understanding, and perception . . ." The text continues, extolling the virtue and enlightenment of the Buddha in elaborate and repetitive phrases. After this comes a passage describing the physical existence of the Buddha. All this was relatively easy for Toda to grasp. The intriguing part of the opening section of the sutra was the verse passage with its twelve lines of negative statements.

Convinced that this heavy accumulation of "neithers" and "nors" is not mere literary device but a vehicle for a profound meaning concerning a very definite existence, Toda resolved to read no farther until he had solved what seemed to be a conundrum. How could existence be and yet not be? No matter how baffling, however, Toda knew that the something did exist and that riddles were the only way to explain its true nature. When he was tired of thinking, he would refresh himself by chanting the Daimoku, using homemade prayer beads of milk-bottle caps. But apart from these rest periods, he spent almost all his time contemplating the twelve obscure lines.

In the past, he had read some of the numerous commentaries on and interpretations of the Lotus Sutra. But now of course, because of prison regulations, he had none with him in his cell; and he could not remember much of what he had read in times gone by. He recalled clearly, however, that most of the commentaries with which he was familiar do not deal successfully with the twelve verse-lines that were at this time the central focus of his meditation. Some of the commentaries go so far as to ignore the verses entirely while giving prolix observations on preceding and following sentences. Even when the verses are discussed, the interpretations fail to satisfy. In a number of cases, the verses are explained as nothing more than a statement that the Buddha has no earthly existence or that, standing apart from material relations, the Buddha transcends all mundane things. But Toda already knew that this notion is absurd.

Some thirteen hundred years earlier, Chih-i, the founder of T'ien-t'ai Buddhism, though understanding the Lotus Sutra better than anyone of his day, had failed to give a clear interpretation of the verses. In Japan, Dengyo the Great, who inherited the orthodox T'ien-t'ai doctrines, attempted to give a verse-by-verse commentary in his *Interpretation of the Sutra of Infinite Meaning*. Once again, however, in saying that the entity of the opening section is the Buddha as the embodiment of enlightenment, he missed the heart of the matter.

It may be that, within the limitations of the teachings of Dengyo the Great, it was impossible to describe the entity more clearly than this. Later T'ien-t'ai scholars compounded the difficulty by taking Dengyo's definition of the entity in its literal sense and by regarding the negatives as abstract modifiers that in effect convert Buddhahood into something supernatural. If the entity is equated with the Buddha of supreme enlightenment and if the twelve verses are interpreted as no more than praise of the Buddha, then the Buddha becomes an idealized presence or image. But this seems unlikely, since the verses were offered to the Buddha by the Mahasattvas in unison.

Though the problem seemed to defy solution, Toda was positive of two things: the entity spoken of in the passage was a tangible existence, and it was the key to an understanding of the cryptic series of paradoxical verses. Determined to grasp this vital point before doing anything else, he first chanted the Daimoku without interruption for some time. He then went into deep meditation. In a kind of trance, he made strenuous efforts to visualize each of the negatively expressed attributes of the entity. Time and place gradually lost meaning for him, as he became completely absorbed in this baffling puzzle. But after a period, two words suddenly flashed into his mind: life force! And in that instant he deciphered the mystery of the verses:

"Life force is neither being nor nonbeing;
Neither cause nor effect;
Neither itself nor another;
Neither square nor round; neither short nor long; . . ."

The problem was not incomprehensible. The entity, the Buddha, is life force itself. For a brief time Toda was transported into a realm of pure joy. He understood that the Buddha is life force existing in the life of the individual and outside individual lives as the very essence of cosmic life force. The walls of his cell could not confine his happiness. A thrilling wave of rapture rose from deep within him and made him want to share this blessed knowledge and assurance with all mankind. He saw himself standing in a vast and infinite space filled with life force, and he wanted to bring everyone to that same plane of enlightenment. But the flaming rapture gradually subsided. Toda found himself once again in his cramped, barred cell; but somehow it all seemed insignificant in the face of the knowledge he had attained, a knowledge that nothing could take from him. In deep gratitude, he turned in the direction of Taiseki-ji and fervently chanted the Daimoku as dusk fell.

In a brief moment of enlightenment, Toda reached the threshold of a thought development that will someday revolutionize the philosophy of the world. The achievement was his, for no direct mention of life force as such is to be found in the Lotus Sutra. By uncovering the meaning of the twelve enigmatic verse-lines, Toda grasped the true substance of Buddhahood as life force existing in the cosmic life and in the phenomenal lives of human beings. This universal life force pervades all things in all three stages of existence—past, present, and future. By instilling into Buddhist thought a fresh interpretation, he proved two immensely significant things. First, he showed that the life-force philosophy of Buddhism is more than an equal for modern scientific thought. Second, he revealed the life-force philosophy set forth by Nichiren Daishonin is superior to all other philosophies of the ancient and modern worlds. In the process of doing these things, Toda himself caught a glimpse of life force in its purest, most exalted form.

Now that he had solved the most fundamental and most difficult problems in the Lotus Sutra, Toda continued to read the rest of the text. Armed with his new understanding, passages that had seemed obscure and puzzling he now found clear and easy to understand.

Spring and summer passed as he continued to study the Lotus Sutra. By autumn, he felt that he understood most of the great work as far as the individual parts were concerned, but he now faced the most important issue of all: what was Sakyamuni trying to teach in the twenty-eight chapters of the Lotus Sutra? Intellectually he knew that the essence of the work had been epitomized in Nam-myoho-renge-kyo and in the Gohonzon, the object of veneration for the Latter Day of the Law. Still, though this was a clear thought in his mind, he was forced to admit that he was unable to grasp it concretely as an incontrovertible truth.

Autumn set in. The days grew shorter and colder, but still Toda had no answer to this most pressing of all questions. Pacing back and forth across the floor of his dim cell, he mumbled to himself as he continued to cudgel his brains for an answer. Obviously the Lotus Sutra was no mere parable or tale of ancient India, because Nichiren Daishonin had repeatedly said in his *Gosho* that each of the 69,384 Chinese characters of the text is in itself a Buddha. This means that the work is the whole truth. It remained for Toda, the Daishonin's unworthy disciple, to find the essence of that truth and to bring it to mankind.

Though suffering from malnutrition, he continued faithfully to chant the Daimoku. By mid-November, he had repeated it nearly two million times since making his resolution on New Year's Day of that year.

One morning, as the weak light of a mild November day shone through his barred window, Toda sat chanting the Daimoku in a clear voice. He was thinking of nothing in particular. Somehow he was oblivious to everything going on around him, though he knew that outside, in the horrors of war, his family was in danger, his business enterprises were crumbling, and rains of death-dealing bombs were falling on the nation. More-

over, somewhere in that same prison was his respected and beloved teacher, Tsunesaburo Makiguchi. But on that November day, nothing existed for him but the Lotus Sutra. For some
time he had been reading and pondering the passages in the
fifteenth chapter where prophecy is made of Bodhisattvas issuing from the earth to bring aid to mankind in the Latter Day
of the Law. Toda sat in the weak sunlight. A springlike breeze
caressed his cheek. He felt an inexpressible happiness welling
up within him as reflected on the passage in that chapter that
begins:

"Upon hearing the sonorous voice of the Lord Sakyamuni,
a multitude of Bodhisattvas emerged from below the earth.
Each of the Bodhisattvas was the leader and teacher of a troop
and had a train of countless followers, equal to the sands of
sixty thousand Ganges rivers; some of the Bodhisattvas-in-the-
making, whose number was equal to the sands of fifty thousand,
forty thousand, thirty thousand, twenty thousand, and ten
thousand Ganges rivers. . . ."

Once again, the prison cell was no more. Toda found himself part of a multitude gathered to participate in the Ceremony
in the Air, in which the Buddha imparted to the world the
teachings of the Lotus Sutra. The ceremony took place in the
realm of the eternal Buddha, the dwelling place of all-pervasive
universal life. The number of the multitude taking part equaled
the sands of countless thousands of Ganges rivers. In the midst
of the throng stood a resplendent golden Dai-Gohonzon. And
Toda was there.

He was really there. It was no dream or illusion that he saw,
but a true, clear vision. Toda had no idea how long the vision
lasted. It may have been only seconds; it may have been minutes or hours. But it was vivid. Nothing in his whole life had
been so vivid. Just as a joyful shout—"I am here, a part of
this great multitude!"—rose to Toda's lips, he found himself
again sitting in the narrow strips of faint sunlight in his prison
cell. The vision was gone, but the inexpressible joy of it brought

tears to his eyes. Wiping the salty drops from his cheeks, he recalled, with all his being, another passage from the fifteenth chapter of the Lotus Sutra: "The numerous assemblage of monks, all of them Arhats, blameless, free from depravity, on Vulture Peak mountain, has not yet dispersed." And those words brought to his mind a few lines from Nichiren Daishonin's *Gosho:*

"Nichiren directly inherited the Three Great Secret Laws from the Lord Buddha as the Supreme Leader of all Bodhisattvas from below the earth two millennia ago."

In the past, when Toda had read of the transferral of the Three Great Secret Laws, the word "directly" had puzzled him. How could Nichiren Daishonin have received the laws directly from the Lord Buddha? Now he knew. He understood because he too had been part of the great gathering when the Daishonin, as the Buddha of Supreme Enlightenment, had stood at the head of the assemblage of Bodhisattvas and had received the laws from the Buddha Sakyamuni. Since he had been part of the assembly, Toda too was one of the Bodhisattvas from below the earth. How majestic and vivid was the eternal ceremony! Toda knew then that his role in bringing salvation to the people of the Latter Day of the Law was immense.

For a few minutes he walked rapidly around his small cell. Then picking up his copy of the Lotus Sutra, he turned to the fifteenth chapter, where he read the description of the Ceremony in the Air. "Yes," he shouted, "it was exactly that way; that is how I saw it." As if starved for more, he read on and on in the great book. But now, nothing was obscure. To his own amazement, the entire text was as clear to him as if he had understood it all his life.

Toda was forty-five at the time. As a man brought up during the early twentieth century, when such teachings were still popular, he was familiar with a Confucian quotation expressing the relation between age and maturity: "I was free from doubt and vacillation at forty and knew heaven's decree at fifty." Toda reflected that, although he had not been free of doubt until five years after the age specified in the quotation, he had understood heaven's decree five years earlier. "Now I know my mission in life," he said aloud. "I will devote my entire being to the propagation of this magnificent Buddhism. I will never forget this day." His loud and strangely joyful exclamations aroused suspicion in the guard at the cell door, who peeped through the window to find an enraptured Toda striding happily about his tiny room.

At that time, Tsunesaburo Makiguchi lay ill in a solitary room in a different wing of the same prison. During the year and a half of his stay there, malnutrition had seriously weakened the elderly man. On November 17, 1944, he agreed to be removed to a prison medical ward. The following day he died, ending a life that had been lofty in purpose and rich in meaning. He was seventy-three years old.

Not until January 8, 1945, fifty-one days later, did Toda hear, from a legal examiner, that his beloved teacher and leader had died. The blow was crushing. Toda wept until tears would no longer flow. Then he realized the weight of the burden that now lay on his shoulders. He vowed that he would exact retribution for the death of Makiguchi, not in a vindictive way but mercifully, by bringing to people of all lands the saving faith for which Makiguchi had given his life.

On that warm late-May night in 1949, Toda returned to the desk in his small study, took up his pen, and began to write. The recollection of the way in which his brilliantly vivid enlightenment had come to him in a bleak prison cell gave him the inspiration to express his thoughts in writing. He was convinced that he would have to approach his subject from the standpoint of his own experiences, though the written work itself would have to be a systematic explanation of the theory of Nichiren Daishonin's philosophy of life force. Its style would have to be appropriate to the loftiness of the theme, yet it would have to be persuasive and indicative of the universal validity of the philosophy. As an introductory paragraph he wrote:

"When Shinto was exploited and abused by the military for ultranationalistic and totalitarian purposes, which finally led Japan to wage a reckless war against the United States, our revered teacher Tsunesaburo Makiguchi, others among our colleagues, and I strongly denounced the government's religious policies. We pointed out the absurdity of forcing the Japanese people to worship at Shinto shrines. For our efforts, in 1943, we were arrested and imprisoned for two years."

As old memories pained his heart, Toda became indignant and angry. But he suddenly checked his emotions: "I must tell a greater truth than mere facts in this work; I cannot allow myself to be carried away by personal feelings." Slowly lighting a cigarette, he reflected for a few minutes then continued, writing:

"While living a life of prison loneliness and isolation, I meditated day after day, month after month on the ultimate nature of life. Is life eternal? What is life? Wise and holy men throughout the ages have pondered these great riddles, each attempting to solve them in his own way."

At this point, Toda was tempted to quote from the thoughts of Christ and Confucius, but he quickly abandoned the notion. The argument he was going to present must not be hampered by sophisticated playing with comparative philosophies. He had only to lay bare his own innermost thoughts to reveal the truth as it had been presented to him in his enlightenment. The writing must be clear and simple, free of difficult philosophical terms. No amount of talking about theories that neither the writer nor the reader understood clearly could convince the ordinary people. Once again, he knew what he must write next:

"If a person crushes a louse, where does the life that had animated the creature go? Does it disappear forever from this world? When one breaks a bough from a cherry tree and puts it in a vase of water, the buds on the branch burst into flower and leaf, though perhaps less richly than they would have if the bough had been allowed to remain on the tree. Is the life

of the severed branch in some way different from that of the parent tree?"

It was Toda's way always to approach abstract truths from the standpoint of concrete examples. For this reason, he had used the louse and the cherry bough to illustrate the ways in which he thought about the mysterious nature of life and death. Like all men, death had caused him great anxiety. He had experienced the agony of parting with loved ones. When he was a young man, his first wife and his daughter had died. Later his father had passed away. The shattering grief of these experiences and the innate fear of his own death had driven him to study Christianity and Buddhist teachings other than those centering on the Lotus Sutra in the hope of finding answers to this immense problem. Both had been disappointing because they had not convinced him.

"Interested in science, mathematics, and logical thought, I could not believe anything that was theoretically unconvincing. After trying several philosophical approaches to the issue, I began studying the Lotus Sutra and the *Gosho* of Nichiren Daishonin. One particular passage in the Lotus Sutra puzzled me. In an ardent desire to unravel its meaning, I chanted the Daimoku as Nichiren Daishonin taught us to do.

"After I had chanted the Daimoku nearly two million times over a period of several months, I had a mysterious vision that opened a new horizon for me. I trembled with joy as I stood among the Buddhas and Bodhisattvas of the whole universe. When my vision ended, I found myself back in the prison cell where I had lived for some time. But unmindful of my surroundings, I rose and declared aloud that I was free of doubt and knew heaven's decree. On the basis of these personal experiences—but more important, on the foundation of the Lotus of the Myoho—I will discuss here the essence of life force."

Thus Toda began writing a work that was to have the most profound meaning for Soka Gakkai and for all mankind; but he was too busy to devote himself entirely to literary and philosophical efforts. The events and needs of daily life pressed hard on him. On the first night of composition, he had worked until nearly dawn and had succeeded in laying a firm foundation for the entire article. It was to consist of the first section entitled "The Mystery of Life," a second section called "Life of the Three Existences," a third section on "Eternal Life," and a final section on "Continuity of Life." Now that the outline was ready, Toda felt certain that the actual writing would become easy. At any rate, he would have to work on it as hard as possible because it had to be ready for the initial issue of the new Soka Gakkai magazine *Daibyakurenge,* or Great White Lotus.

In 1946, Soka Gakkai had resumed publication of the small mimeographed magazine called *Kachi Sozo,* or Value Creation. Published at a time in the postwar period when materials were extremely scarce, *Kachi Sozo,* only about ten pages long, served as no more than a bulletin to disseminate a limited amount of information to society members in rural areas. As time passed and Soka Gakkai grew in strength, however, it became obvious that a more ambitious journal was needed. A meeting of the Soka Gakkai board of directors, held in December, 1948, voted to stop mimeographing the magazine and have it set in type. But Toda wanted to do more. He decided to convert the modest pamphlet into a full-scale religious monthly.

Since January, 1949, Takeo Konishi and Chuhei Yama-daira, appointed coeditors of the new *Daibyakurenge,* had been industriously working on editorial plans and policies. Their task was formidable, since they had to increase the amount of material in the old magazine by at least four or five times and they had to prepare for the introduction of serialized essays, critical biographies, and interesting testimonials of the powers of faith in Nichiren Shoshu. Toda had agreed to provide them with the article on life-force philosophy and had also promised to write an introduction to the first issue. They had planned to contact some other authors, but they were far from being ready to bring out a first issue. Since *Kachi Sozo* had already been discontinued, there was no Soka Gakkai publication for a while. Toda, finding this situation unsatisfactory, did something unusual for him.

Although under ordinary conditions he always respected the initiative of his staff members, seeing that in spite of the hard work put in by Yamadaira and Konishi nothing substantial was being done toward starting the new journal, Toda decided to intervene. One morning he asked the two young men to bring him their editorial plan. They did so. He read it and with a doleful smile pushed it aside, remarking: "You'll never publish a magazine with something like this. You provided for changing over from mimeographing to ordinary type; but aside from that, you are still thinking along the lines of a Soka Gakkai pamphlet. You can't succeed with a full-scale journal with articles by nobody but insiders. You've got to get things from well-known and competent scholars and critics whose names and abilities have drawing appeal. Remember, we're setting up a magazine for the general public, as well as for our society members."

Yamadaira, who was obviously excited by the nature of his work, spoke up: "Well, we thought we'd have the long essay you promised and then we'd go down the list of religious doctrines one by one and refute them all."

Toda interrupted at once: "Now, listen to me. I'll write for you, of course. But do you have any idea how much manuscript you'll need to fill up a thirty-two page monthly—a monthly I repeat? With the plan you've got here you wouldn't last beyond the first month. First, forget about the old magazine. It's impossible to start a new magazine if you're still tied to old ways. Unless you broaden and freshen your outlook, your magazine will be boring and unbought. A fresh idea for every issue each month—that's what you've got to have.

"All right, as a starter, let's get this first issue lined up. Then you'll see what I mean. It's a new magazine; you'll want an article of congratulation on the first pages. Why not ask High Priest Nissho Mizutani to write one? He will, I'm sure. Oh, yes, he's an excellent calligrapher. Ask him to design the lettering for the cover. You still want me to do an introductory preface? All right, but I'm working on the longer article too. Have you asked the retired high priest Nichiko Hori for an article?"

"Yes," replied Yamadaira. "He's been doing research on Nikko Shonin. I think he's about ready to start writing."

"Wonderful," said Toda. "Tell him to write as much as he likes. If necessary we'll make a serial of it. I'll bet his article will be difficult. We may not understand it ourselves."

Toda laughed and the two young men joined in. None of them suspected that Hori's article was to grow into a voluminous and definitive biography of Nikko Shonin, the second high priest of Nichiren Shoshu.

"Then we can round out the first month's contribution from the clergy by asking Taiei Horigome to write something for you. But what have you arranged in the way of works from general authors?"

"Well, our Yoshio Ishiyama has challenged Tomo Yamada of the Kokuchu-kai Nichiren sect to a debate by correspondence. Ishiyama went to Yamada's home in Kamakura to discuss the matter, and they have agreed to go through with the project," said Konishi.

"That's an excellent idea," said Toda. "Give them space for their argument. The more they write, the clearer it will become to the reader that Nichiren Shoshu, and not Yamada's Kokuchu-kai sect, is the truly orthodox Nichiren Buddhism. The Fivefold Comparison and the Threefold Secret outline the principle that in order to prove the truth of our beliefs we must allow them to be openly compared with the beliefs of others. The very greatness of Nichiren Daishonin's *Gosho* lies in the way it establishes its doctrines as absolute by means of comparisons.

"Of course, mere comparison and assertion of our superiority must not be our aim. We are launching *Daibyakurenge* to convince others of the truth of our beliefs. To do this, we must first point up the mistakes, weaknesses, and contradictions of others and then use all our persuasive powers to bring other people around to our way of thinking. Nichiren Daishonin himself is an extreme example of the power of persuasion fundamentally based on compassion. Perhaps we can't hope to do as well as he did, but we must try.

"The way to be convincing is to use language that the ordinary people will understand. That's why in this new magazine we must never talk as if we were limiting ourselves to religious

debate. We must now move on to a broader plane of operations where Nichiren Daishonin's great philosophy of life force
can confront and prove itself superior to all other philosophies.
The universal propagation of our faith is an unprecedented
ideological battle.

"What I'm saying is this: open your minds and expand the
scope of the magazine. Invite theology and philosophy professors from famous universities to contribute. Call on novelists
for articles. I understand that Hideo Motofune has recently
uncovered interesting historical material on Nichiji, one of the
six elder priests appointed by Nichiren Daishonin. Ask him to
write on Nichiji for us. He's a good writer, and his article might
develop into an interesting serial."

Konishi and Yamadaira were unconvinced that it would be
a good idea to ask university professors for work, since they
might say derogatory things about Nichiren Shoshu. But Toda
gave them further advice: "Don't worry about that. The important thing is to provide space for philosophical and religious
debate. Most of these conventional philosophy professors have
no profound knowledge of Buddhism, and all of them lack the
plain old guts to try to refute Nichiren Shoshu. Let them say
whatever they want, we know we are right. We have no one
and nothing to fear.

"Well, then, that should about take care of your editorial
policies for the first issue. Get to work."

With typical dispatch, Toda had solved the editorial problems that had been holding up publication of *Daibyakurenge* for
more than three months. Konishi and Yamadaira did get to
work, and things began to pick up in the editorial department.

This was the kind of activity that filled Toda's days. At night
he continued to work on his "Philosophy of Life Force," which
he felt was going to become a crystallization of the devotion
and belief of half a lifetime. The night after his meeting with
Konishi and Yamadaira he began the section entitled "Life

of the Three Existences." As a result of long and intensive study of Nichiren Daishonin's *Kaimoku Sho, Senji Sho,* and *Ongi Kuden,* Toda had a firm understanding and an unshakable faith in the three existences of life—past, present, and future. The Daishonin had given a deeper, more detailed, more fundamental treatment to the nature of life force than Sakyamuni. Toda adhered to Nichiren Daishonin's interpretation. He believed in a universal life that is not limited to the biological and medical definitions of the word, not tied to the present only, and not connected with ideas about an individualized soul.

The works that explain Nichiren Daishonin's interpretation of life are themselves complicated and difficult to teach. In presenting them to his classes on the Lotus Sutra, Toda often found that he had to repeat and repeat his explanations. Furthermore, he was aware that complacent intellectuals would probably sneer at the Buddhist concept of life. To silence any possible criticism from this quarter, he began by touching on the nature of the so-called intellectual approach.

"Many intellectuals may scoff at the Buddhist idea of life, but I am afraid that, in taking this attitude, they would only reveal their own thoughtless and basically unscientific approach. First, the law of causality is essential to science. All phenomena in the universe are governed by the law of cause and effect; therefore, to ignore this law by stating that life is no more than the result of the union of spermatozoon and ovum is superficial because it does not take cause into account. To assert that, whereas all other phenomena in the universe are ruled by cause and effect, life occurs fortuitously is to be amazingly insensitive to the nature of life itself.

"Natural science can explain much but has nothing valid to say about the nature of the phenomenon we call life. Man, cats, dogs, tigers, and trees are all alive. Science admits this but cannot tell us whether the lives of all these many phenomenal forms are identical or different." Toda was less concerned with modern man's ignorance of religion than with his ignorance and lack of interest in the nature of life itself. He devoted great thought to explaining life persisting through past, present, and future.

In the remainder of that section he outlined and illustrated the Buddhist concept of the greater life force existing throughout the universe and manifesting itself in individual phenomenal lives. In doing this, he took care to criticize intellectuals who ignore the value of religion to an understanding of life and prophesied that unless all mankind comes to realize the truth of the Buddhist interpretation of life the future of man and the planet would be in grave danger.

Before beginning the third section, called "Eternal Life," Toda meditated for a long time. The basis of the material in this part of his essay was to be taken from Nichiren Daishonin's *Sanze Shobutsu Sokammon Sho, Totaigi Sho, Jippokaiji, Ongi Kuden,* and the sixteenth chapter of the Lotus Sutra. Toda wanted to explain how the greater life force has no beginning and no end. In addition, he wanted to present in clearly understandable form the doctrine of Ichinen Sanzen, according to which the instant embodies three thousand existences or aspects of reality. Before taxing the reader with this complex issue, however, he decided to insert an introductory paragraph:

"Life has existed and does exist simultaneously with the entire universe. It did not come into being before the universe. It did not occur accidentally, nor was it created by some being. Since life and the universe are one, it is mistaken to believe that life is in any way limited to the planet earth. We faithful members of Nichiren Shoshu are endeavoring to grasp the reality of infinite life. In our efforts, we are aided by the boundless mercy of Nichiren Daishonin and by our devotion to the Dai-Gohonzon, which is both an embodiment of the meaning of the doctrine of Ichinen Sanzen and the source of immediate enlightenment and salvation."

Unlike many of the philosophers who have pondered the

meaning of life on the ideological level, Toda wanted to help every individual human being understand the eternity and dignity of life and its great force in daily activities. Before going further, however, he knew that he would have to clear up the misconception about life widely taught as modern biology.

"Of those who try to refute the idea of eternal life by saying that man and all the other animals evolved from unicellular creatures, I ask: 'Why did these creatures come into existence? When the raging heat of the young earth had cooled, whence came these unicellular creatures, then?' The answer is simple, but it is not found in biology textbooks. Amoebas, simple plants, and all other forms of life, high and low, come into being when the conditions for their manifestation and growth are right. This being the case, it should not seem surprising that various forms of life can appear anywhere in the universe. After appearing, they can develop; by this, I am saying that I do not refute the idea of evolution. But life is an eternal, all-pervading reality. Consequently, though man lives on this planet today, it is not inconceivable that billions of years ago he might have lived on some other planet. Furthermore, since life is eternal and coexistent with the universe, to argue that it originated from protein or some other matter at a certain time in the history of this one planet is nonsense."

Work continued on the important essay for about a week. If he had been able to devote all his time to it, Toda would probably have finished sooner, because once he had outlined the whole thing, he felt inspired to write quickly and persuasively. This could not be, however, because of the hectic nature of his schedule and the deteriorating economic conditions of the nation, which forbade his being absent from the office for so much as a single day.

In addition to working in his office, Toda continued his lectures on the Lotus Sutra three times a week. Usually he started his meetings at six in the evening and made it a point to conclude them by seven thirty. But there were always questions and discussions that held him until later. One evening, he found that he had to break off the meeting well before anyone else wanted to go home.

"Now, that really must be all for tonight. You must let me go now," Toda said with a note of pleading in his voice. "I'm not going home to have a few drinks, either. I'm writing an article for the new magazine *Daibyakurenge*. It's two days overdue, and the editors are hounding me for the manuscript. At this rate, I'll never finish it."

The people in the room laughed at Toda's urgency because they failed to understand the intense labor the article was costing him. Nevertheless, some of them had an idea of what he must be going through. As he hurried from the room and started down the steps he heard a loud burst of applause from behind him. "If they have that much faith in me," he thought, "I'll finish that article tonight if it's the last thing I do." When he sat down at his desk to continue the last section, "The Continuity of Life," it was already past nine.

Perhaps more than any of the other sections, this one required the deepest thought and the greatest care because it dealt with the immense question of what happens to life once the phenomenal form has died. By way of leading into the heart of the Buddhist concept of the continuity of life, Toda discussed some of the most popular concepts of afterlife. The easiest to counter was the notion of an individual soul that lives on eternally after the physical body perishes. Sakyamuni so flatly rejects this idea in his Nirvana Sutra that Toda saw no reason to go into it in any depth.

It is believed by some people that the continuity of life can be accounted for in terms of the progeny of the animal; that is, the parent lives on in the offspring. But suppose all the progeny die? What then happens to the life that they represented? If life is eternal, as Buddhist teachings insist, how can it come to an end merely because of the death of one or another generation of human beings or animals? Others have argued that the continuity of life is to be found in the works a man leaves. A great novelist or great philosopher produces works of merit that carry his name into other ages. But what about people who do so little of value that after their deaths they are completely forgotten. What about cats, dogs, other animals? All are alive —that is, all are manifestations of life. And this life has nothing to do with memories of the deceased.

Toda knew that even in Buddhism the problem of the after-life is extremely difficult, requiring great knowledge of meta-physics. Unless it is explained with care, people without such knowledge are likely to misunderstand. For this reason, he set aside his original plan to quote extensively from the Lotus Sutra and the *Gosho* and resolved to state the issue as clearly and intelligibly as possible:

"The sixteenth chapter of the Lotus Sutra treats death as an expedient. When a man is weary from great labor, it is expedient that he refresh himself with sleep. Similarly, when the human being is old, ill, and weary of his experiences on this earth, it is expedient that the life force within him be rejuvenated through death.

"To illustrate the way in which life is continuous throughout all time and space, I might draw illustrations from the workings of the human mind, which is itself an incontrovertible mani-festation of life force.

"At one instant a man feels joy. As time passes, the feeling of joy vanishes. Where does it go? Once again, after the passage of still more time, another feeling of joy may be experienced. Something very similar can be said about other emotions. The joy—or sorrow—felt at one time is clearly connected with the joy—or sorrow—felt later; but there is no joy—or sorrow—intermediate to the two experiences. Examine the nature of the mind in sleep. While man is asleep, his mind is nowhere. Upon waking, however, his mind begins to function again. Does it exist always or not? It exists, and it does not exist.

"These intermediary states in mind—and in life force itself—

are explainable in terms of the Buddhist theory of *ku,* or void. According to Western philosophy, life and all phenomena are classified as being or nonbeing; no provision is made for the intermediary void. But without understanding void, it is impossible to understand life, because void is ubiquitous and all-embracing. It is void that accounts for the marvelous continuity of life.

"As I said before, life force and the universe are one, they are *ku.* When the individual human being—the form or manifestation of life force—dies, his life is fused with the great universal life force. When in this state, life force cannot be experienced by means of our perceptions. In this respect it is like joy, sorrow, and the mind during sleep: it exists, yet it does not exist. After individualized life has fused with the universal life force, it is not always responsive—just as some people sleep without being troubled by dreams. But as study of the teachings of Nichiren Daishonin and reverence for the Dai-Gohonzon gradually make clear to all faithful people, the universal life force assumes individualized form once again as the result of activation by some karmic link. This might be compared to the way in which the mind takes up its ordinary functioning after apparent absence during sleep. And just as the mind after sleep retains its store of knowledge and memories of both good and evil, so the newly individualized life bears the effects of actions in former individualized manifestations. To round out the analogy, then, universal life, underlying all things, continues through an endless series of sleepings and wakings."

When Toda had finished this brief essay—it was little more than thirty pages—he was satisfied with the fruit of his efforts. Much that he had wanted to say had been omitted because some of it was too complicated to explain within the limits of style and space imposed by the nature of a magazine article. For instance, he later said that he had hoped to discuss in detail the ten states of life and the concept of Ichinen Sanzen; but he decided that he would have to put them aside until another time. He realized that there would be critics who would cavil that his explanation of afterlife was entirely hypothetical and insusceptible of scientific proof. Perhaps, at that moment, they were correct in a sense. Nonetheless, Toda had many years' experience of seeing how belief in this hypothesis had changed the karma of many people and had enabled them to attain Buddhahood. He was therefore convinced that the time would come when this Buddhist teaching would be proved correct. After all, though unaware of it, astronomers today are constantly discovering facts that substantiate the Buddhist cosmology, which was first evolved three thousand years ago. Today, so-called intellectuals all over the world ignore or refuse to believe Nichiren Daishonin's Buddhism, which is in fact an embodiment of life force and wisdom. Consequently, these people walk on the brink of a yawning abyss of spiritual debility and nihilism. But the day must come when they, too, will see the light-giving mercy of true Buddhism.

Toda's brief "Philosophy of Life Force" today enjoys a wide reading public, and a small number of intellectuals are at last coming to recognize its value. Though it is relatively short and plainly written, it contains a philosophy destined some day to sweep over the entire world. In a few centuries, "The Philosophy of Life Force" is certain to become the root from which will grow a flourishing tree of philosophy, just as *Discourse on Method* by René Descartes became the root for modern rational thought. The lucidity of the concepts and the use of everyday illustrations to bring to life philosophical ideas of a profundity and scope that one encounters only once in centuries are two of the more striking similarities between the two works. But perhaps most important is the nature of the effect both works have on all readers who are not prejudiced or biased. After reading either of them, one feels as if one's eyes have been opened to a fresh view of oneself and of the world.

Furthermore, both preface the major sections of their philosophies with personal experiences. Descartes' *cogito, ergo sum* appears in part four of his book. Before reaching this point, he filled three parts with a personal account of his intellectual and psychological development. Similarly, Toda felt it necessary to preface the main part of his "Philosophy of Life Force" with the section called "The Mystery of Life."

There are, of course, differences between the work of Toda and that of Descartes. Toda saw the reality of life force, existing through the three existences of all phenomenal life, as the basic element of the universe. Descartes, on the other hand, had unshakable belief in the operation in all men of the reasoning faculty. And he based his philosophy on that faculty. Toda, believing that the universal law of life force is the determining factor of all human happiness and unhappiness, taught that, applying this law, it is possible to save mankind from misery through actual religious practice. As a result of extensive study in many fields, Descartes came to the conclusion that the only way to truth is through reason. Viewing all existing knowledge with suspicion, he proceeded to develop a completely new philosophy on the basis of universal reason.

After many years of doubting, Descartes was able, at the age of forty, to proclaim that the one certain thing is one's own existence, which is provable on the basis of the fact that one thinks. The lucidity of the reasoning faculty, which Descartes places at the heart of all philosophy, is what still attracts modern thinkers to his system. Unlike Toda, Descartes was a speculative philosopher living in a time when the scientific revolution had just begun. Science fitted within the realm of the Cartesian concept of reason, but Descartes also found a way of dealing with religion. Starting from the thinking self, he realized that the human self is imperfect. This implies the existence of a perfect being, which he called God. He insisted that the thinking self did not willfully create God but that the concept of God arose because of the presence of the perfect being within the imperfect human thinking self. In short, his definition of God is based on the self. Descartes proved the existence of the self and, abandoning the elaborate diction of medieval academic philosophy, expressed his ideas with precision and clarity.

Toda went further because he perceived eternal life force as the fundamental aspect of the phenomenal thinking self—as it is the fundamental aspect of all things. After years of study and training, he attained enlightenment to the truth that Buddha and common mortals are in fact one. According to Descartes, the imperfect human self can never attain the level of God. Toda's arduous study of the teachings of Nichiren Daishonin, on the other hand, revealed that all life is one with the Buddha. Furthermore, Toda's study led to an understanding of the true nature of life. He realized that the knowledge he had gained was the one way to bring relief to the misery of the world. In practical terms, the application of this knowledge takes the form of bringing true Buddhism to all mankind. The movement to achieve this end is called the Kosen-rufu. The revelations Toda experienced and the way in which he put them into practice are the secrets behind the completely new image of mankind that he evolved as a modern thinker and man of religion.

Although the contents of their writings are different, both Descartes and Toda added new dimensions to philosophy. Descartes laid the foundations for modern thinking and the material progress that is based on it. But in our time, when this way of thinking and the outcome of this progress are proving more harmful than beneficial, the work of Cartesian philosophy has ended.

Since the middle of this century, men of science have displayed interest in the nature of the force called life. Many of them are striving to reproduce life artificially in test tubes or to examine it microscopically and discover its components. In itself, this interest is a fine thing, but it is misguided. No one can point out the true mystery of life in scientific ways. But Josei Toda has already explained what life is. His "Philosophy of Life Force" is a forerunner of the dawn of a new century, a century devoted to the forces of life. In the coming decades, scientists will continue to experiment and draw conclusions about life. They may even succeed in finding scientific proof for parts of what Toda said. Then "The Philosophy of Life Force" will begin to shed its full light. All people will know that when tired and confused they can return to Toda's philosophy as to a haven of rest and happiness.

Most members of Soka Gakkai were pleased with the first issue of *Daibyakurenge* and happy to see how different it was from the old *Kachi Sozo*. Reactions to Toda's "Philosophy of Life Force" varied. Suspecting that it was no more than a recapitulation of the Lotus Sutra lectures, which they had already attended, some people gave the work only a superficial reading. Those who read it with care and understanding, however, saw its depth and often became ashamed of their own shallow understanding of Buddhism. Numerous Soka Gakkai members used Toda's work as a kind of manual in winning new converts. But very few had an inkling of the monumental importance of the essay for their times and the inestimable philosophical effect it is certain to have on future generations.

One night, after returning to his home following a hard day in Toda's editorial offices, Shin'ichi Yamamoto, who was feeling lonely and tired, took out a copy of the first issue of *Daibyakurenge* and started to read "The Philosophy of Life Force." Once he began reading, the text put him in such a state of emotional excitement that he had to finish the whole thing. For some time, he lay in bed unable to sleep because of the thoughts and images that raced through his brain. Finally, he took out his notebook and pen. Compelled to try to express at least part of what he was thinking, he wrote:

> "Countless light flashes
> Hurtling through the dawn sky,
> As the radiant sun rises.
> The emotion of that instant,

The tremble of the wonder of life.
The leaping of the hearts of the young.
You, the young,
In this twentieth-century atomic age,
What can you save
With the philosophies of your hearts?
Nothing.
Will human happiness come
From lessons of plots, violence, or things?
No.
Can any believe in these things?
No. No.
To the teaching of Nichiren Daishonin,
The proof of the nature of life,
The revelation of the source of the universe,
I devote my life.
You who are young,
If you have wisdom, know.
If you have compassion for man, act.
Eternal peace
And the true faith for all.
You who are young,
Open your eyes.
You who are young,
Accept the one great teaching.
You have the passion and the power;
Move forward."

Closing his notebook, Yamamoto turned over and fell into a sound, peaceful sleep. His verses were printed in an inconspicuous corner in the second issue of *Daibyakurenge*.

2. SIGN OF THE TIMES

DURING the time when Toda was writing his "Philosophy of Life Force," the religious activities of Soka Gakkai continued to expand throughout Tokyo and the surrounding prefectures. Discussion meetings became too numerous for Toda to conduct personally, but fortunately, many of his disciples had now reached the stage where they were capable of handling the gatherings on their own. Before the war, Tsunesaburo Makiguchi had been in charge of almost all important meetings of Soka Kyoiku Gakkai; and Toda had followed this precedent in the early postwar years. But conditions in Japan in the late 1940s were very different from those of the late 1930s.

Taking advantage of the spiritual debility of the Japanese people, a great number of spurious and ill-founded religious sects had popped up and were gaining impressive followings. Toda was not overly concerned about such groups because he knew that the time for the universal propagation of the teachings of Nichiren Daishonin was at hand. Consequently, he concentrated on preparing each of his disciples to be able to lead the society in its vital role in the coming religious movement. Since he remembered how the old Soka Kyoiku Gakkai had disintegrated under pressure from the militarist government,

Toda was determined to train a core of diligent, faithful people who could hold the larger organization together no matter what happened.

One of his training methods involved taking his disciples with him to discussion meetings and on membership campaigns and allowing them to see how he worked under such conditions. In addition, he gave them doctrinal training through his lectures on the Lotus Sutra and afforded them personal guidance and instruction whenever necessary. In all of his training programs Toda combined just the right amount of severity with apparently inexhaustible mercy and patience.

Now that many of his trainees were taking charge of discussion meetings, Toda found it necessary to hold a briefing in the Kanda offices of his publishing company prior to each meeting so that he could give the leaders instructions and point out whatever mistakes he had observed in their past performances. The leaders came from many walks of life and represented many kinds of personalities. As was usual with him, Toda always understood the correct tack to take with each. At one of these briefings, for instance, to a senior leader of the Youth Division, who was about to depart for a discussion meeting in a nearby neighborhood, he said: "Don't let your enthusiasm run away with you so much that you get highhanded. I've heard that at some of your meetings you do solo performances."

Embarrassed by the reprimand, the young teacher stood tensely as he said: "Yes, I'll be careful tonight."

"And another thing," Toda went on, "don't get such a formidable look on your face. Remember, not everyone who comes to these meetings has the drive and energy you have. There are timid people and shy young girls who need to be encouraged, not frightened half to death. It's the teachings of Nichiren Daishonin that hold these meetings together. That means that they ought to be friendly, cheerful times, filled with a spirit of mercy and helpfulness. Things in Japan right now are bleak. Our meetings must be a ray of light for people. If you stand in front of the group with a threatening face like a demon, you'll defeat our purpose. Each person in our movement can become a Bodhisattva if he has the faith and if his faith is firm. You don't want to chase away a gathering of Bodhisattvas do you?"

"I understand," said the now smiling young man.

"I think you do, and I have faith in you. Go on to work now, and keep that smile on your face."

At that same meeting, Toda had occasion to talk to a stocky, middle-aged leader about a somewhat different matter.

"You know," said Toda, "you are a problem. How could you let a drunk pick a fight with you? And at a discussion meeting!"

"I tried to ignore him for a long time," the man said as he scratched his head nervously, "but he got worse and worse. Then he started making nasty remarks about Nichiren Shoshu. That was too much. I couldn't let him disgrace our religion. So I quarreled with him, and that led to the fight."

"What a thick head you've got. Don't you see that you're the one who disgraced Nichiren Shoshu? Of course, the drunk had no business coming to a meeting and starting a scene. But why did you have to go down to his level. Were you drunk too?"

"No, indeed!" the middle-aged man shot back at once. "But he made me angry," he added in a quieter voice.

Noticing the man's bandaged thumb, Toda said: "How's the wound?"

"Oh, it's nothing. It was just the broken windowpane."

"First of all," Toda went on, "you shouldn't have let the drunk in. But once he was in, you should have offered him a glass of water or something and let him go to sleep. Drunks always get sleepy if they sit quietly for a few minutes. When he woke up, he would have been bewildered. But if he didn't decide to run away at once, he might have stayed with you; and your discussion might have helped him. But no; that's not the way you handled it. You bungled the whole thing."

"It'll never happen again."

"It'd better not. One more blunder like that, and you'll never conduct another discussion meeting for me. Now go and apologize to the people who let you use their house for the meeting that turned into a brawl. And don't ever think that fighting drunks and courage are the same thing."

When Toda saw the dressing down had hit the man hard, he added: "Don't look so woebegone. Buck up and go on to your meeting."

Because Toda was smiling now, the middle-aged man smiled too and departed for his evening's work. Invariably these pre-meeting briefing talks had good effects on the group leaders. Although some of them were called down when they deserved it, Toda always managed to give them enough encouragement to send them on their ways in good spirits and with high hopes. For that reason, they all worked extremely hard in their efforts to be, as Toda called them, Bodhisattvas springing up from the earth.

Hiroshi Izumida, whose miraculous experiences in the South Pacific during World War II had inspired him to deepen his faith and work with boundless zeal for the advancement of Nichiren Shoshu, was a discussion-group leader in his neighborhood in the Koiwa district of Tokyo. Immediately before a meeting scheduled for the evening of July 12, 1949, he called on Toda for general instructions. Because of his concern for the development of the Soka Gakkai leadership, Toda had a few important remarks to make about the way things were going in Koiwa: "You're doing pretty well in your neighborhood, Izumida, but one thing worries me. So far no really promising and talented new members have come out of your group. The power of the Gohonzon is infinite, and I believe that it will help us find the kind of people we need for our mission. I wonder if maybe the reason why outstanding people have not yet turned up in Koiwa is your own complacent feeling that you are making achievements all on your own, without the power of the Gohonzon. If that's the case, you'd better do something about it. After all, you're in charge there."

Izumida immediately realized that Toda was right. No one who promised to be of great value to Soka Gakkai had emerged in Koiwa. He was deeply concerned that his own complacency might be at the heart of the situation. Since Toda had nothing more to say, Izumida hurried on his way. He was late for the meeting, and when he arrived at the Matsumura house, where the meeting was to be held, some members had already gathered. As they waited for Izumida, they talked briefly about the mysterious and perplexing events of recent weeks. For some reason, criminal acts, black-market activities, and all manner of shady dealings seemed to be growing in scale and intensity. The president of the Japan National Railways had been found dead on the train tracks between two busy stations. Foul play was suspected, though no evidence had been discovered so far. A crowd of hundreds of people, including some Communists, had seized a police station in nearby Taira. Killings and brawls upset many of the amusement quarters of Tokyo. A cloud of suspicion and fear enveloped much of the city.

Oddly enough, as Izumida reached the door of the Matsumura house he saw two decidedly suspicious-looking men lurking about the street corner next to the house. "I wonder who those guys are," he thought. But he had no time to worry about them. Wiping his now damp bald head of some of the sweat he had worked up in his haste, he entered the main room of the house to see, to his satisfaction, that attendance was exceptionally good.

Kneeling in front of the family altar, Izumida chanted the Daimoku. Then once again wiping his forehead, he greeted everyone: "Well, today has been a scorcher." Glancing about the room he saw some unfamiliar faces. Two or three men dressed in the loose-fitting shirts and baggy trousers that Japanese gangsters affect sat near the leader's desk. Izumida thought they looked like Koreans. But he was always glad to see new faces because he wanted to bring as many people to Nichiren Shoshu as possible.

Mrs. Hatsu Chitani, a small woman in her fifties, immediately approached Izumida and introduced one of the three men as the husband of Yuriko Kaneki. The man, who sat behind Yuriko, said nothing but glared at Izumida. Yuriko was pale, rigid, and obviously uneasy.

Before the war, Yuriko Kaneki had been a member of a faith-healing cult called the Church of the World Messiah, which combined religious observances with an odd massage therapy. Strange as the cult was, Yuriko needed it, or something else that would give her spiritual support, because her married life was unhappy. Her husband, a Korean laborer, was a habitual drinker with a violent temper. Their one child, a daughter, had been stricken with paralysis from birth. After attending meetings of the Church of the World Messiah, Yuriko frequently discussed her religion with Mrs. Hatsu Chitani, who was her next-door neighbor. In fact, she tried to convert Mrs. Chitani to the faith but without success.

During the war, the government ordered the Church of the World Messiah to disband. Yuriko was then left with nothing to help her in her times of trouble. Not long after the war, however, Mrs. Chitani, who had become a member of Nichiren Shoshu, introduced her to the Koiwa discussion group. Yuriko soon saw the difference between the true faith and spurious religions. She joined Nichiren Shoshu and Soka Gakkai and in doing so found a new lease on life through faith. Her husband, who had nothing to say for or against the Church of the World Messiah, became enraged as he watched his wife devote more and more of her time to her religious activities. In drunken fits, he beat her with his fists, dragged her around by the hair, and sometimes whipped her with his belt. Nothing he did, however, weakened Yuriko's faith, to which she clung tenaciously as the only thing worth preserving.

One night, when her husband's attack had been especially vicious, she suddenly asked him for a divorce, pleading that neither of them would ever be happy together. Astounded by this abrupt show of spirit in his ordinarily docile and meek wife, Kaneki said nothing for a few seconds. Then rising and lurching toward her with fist raised in preparation to strike, he happened to glance at the family altar in the corner of the room. Yuriko's eyes followed his. She saw in a flash that he intended to harm the sacred object of worship in the altar. Dashing past him, she quickly removed the Gohonzon, rolled it up, and hid it in the front of her dress. To Kaneki's fuddled mind, Yuriko's haste to preserve the Gohonzon seemed proof that this religious business was driving her from him. Uncertain what to do, he hurled himself from the room, uttering a string of coarse language as he went.

In the night air in front of his house, his drink-fogged brain was able to put together a few ill-formed ideas. If it was Nichiren Shoshu that made his wife want a divorce, that Chitani woman must be at the bottom of the whole thing. Staggering to the Chitani house, Kaneki burst in and forced his way into the first-floor room where Mrs. Chitani had already gone to sleep.

Bewildered by Kaneki's outrageous behavior and on the verge of tears from vexation and fear, Mrs. Chitani nonetheless composed herself to the extent of telling the drunken man what she thought. She insisted that she had never discussed divorce with Yuriko. Divorce and Yuriko's religion were two entirely unrelated things. Kaneki, however, would not, or could not, understand. He demanded that she arrange a meeting with the leader of the Koiwa group of Soka Gakkai so that he could bring the matter into the open. At the end of her patience with the irrational intruder and convinced that probably such a meeting would be the only solution, Mrs. Chitani told Kaneki where and when the next meeting was to be held. These were the circumstances that brought him and two of his rough friends to the discussion meeting that July evening.

Izumida, who knew nothing of the background of the issue, looked first at the dejected and sorrowful Yuriko and then at the flushed face of her sullen husband. Behind him sat his two friends. One of them had a nasty scar on the side of his neck; the other wore a look of sharp hostility. The whole trio, in fact, looked sinister enough to cause serious trouble. But Izumida, a former warrant officer with a degree in fencing and a powerful body, could not be bullied by violence. He extended a greeting to Mr. Kaneki, who answered the courtesy with a challenge: "Look, I want you to tell me just what this Nichiren Shoshu is." His Japanese was fluent, though marked with a slight Korean accent.

Izumida replied: "It is the only true Buddhism, and your wife is a firm and faithful believer."

"I know something about Buddhism. We have Buddhism in Korea too—Sakyamuni or something like that. But I've never heard anything about Nichiren. To tell the truth, I think you're probably not really Buddhists at all."

The people who had come to the meeting to discuss the teachings of Nichiren Daishonin were alarmed to see that the proceedings were likely to take an unexpected turn. Kaneki's anger was rising quickly. He sparked resentment as he said: "Right after she joined Nichiren Shoshu, my wife turned no good. To me that means Nichiren Shoshu must be no good."

Everyone could readily see that he was trying to stir up something. His two companions put their hands in their jacket pockets, which bulged most sinisterly. Izumida remained unperturbed as he said: "Wait just a minute. What is it you want? Just what is your problem?"

"Problem? I'll tell you my problem. This religion you preach is worse than no good. The minute my wife starts hanging around with your crowd, she starts asking me for a divorce. Some religion!"

"Slow down a minute. Face facts. Marital troubles are one thing. A sound, true religion is something else. Let's analyze this situation step by step." Izumida was trying to make Kaneki listen to reason. "You say our religion makes wives ask their husbands for divorces. But take my case. I've been married to my wife for well over ten years. Both of us are active members of Nichiren Shoshu. We don't want a divorce. Like most couples, we have our spats once in a while, but divorce has never crossed our minds. On the other hand, lots of couples who have no religious affiliation at all get divorced. Clearly then, the two things don't have any direct connection.

"In that case, we ought to try to find out why your wife wants a divorce. Could it be because the two of you just don't get along well?"

"No, no," shouted Kaneki. "We got along fine, until she started coming to your meetings. You told her she ought to ask me for a divorce. That must be what happened."

To give Kaneki support, his friend with the scarred neck roared out: "Yeah that's right! You religious busybodies mess around in other people's lives and cause a lot of trouble. Why don't you stick to your own business. Unless this religion of yours is some kind of money-making racket. That must be it. You can't fool us."

Izumida was fighting hard to control himself, and doing fairly well. He answered the provocations of Kaneki's vociferous friend by saying: "Calm down now. Let's solve this by asking Mrs. Kaneki if anyone in our group ever suggested the idea of a divorce to her. If your wife wants to leave Nichiren Shoshu, she is free to do so at any time. No one forces her to remain in our organization. Mrs. Kaneki, what do you say?"

Shaking her head firmly, Yuriko said: "Nobody suggested a divorce to me. I made up my mind by myself."

"You're a liar," Kaneki shouted menacingly.

Izumida turned to Mrs. Kaneki and said: "It's entirely up to you. If you want to save your marriage by leaving the faith, no one will stop you. You must do what you think is best."

In a very clear, steady voice, Yuriko Kaneki said: "I will not give up my religion."

"Do what I tell you," roared Kaneki.

"No," answered his wife.

"Then I'll kill you."

"I won't give up my faith, even if you do kill me."

"Why, you slut!" Kaneki spat the words through his teeth as he swung his heavy fist from his side and knocked his wife to the floor. Then standing towering over her, he started to strike her again; but his friends pinned his arms to his sides. "Stop it, Kaneki. We didn't come here so you could knock your wife around. We want a showdown with this bunch of religious troublemakers. They're the ones who put this stupid divorce idea in her head."

The men closed in on Izumida, who was trying to make a quick analysis of the situation. These three had already spoiled the meeting; there was nothing to be done about that. Of course, it was impossible to give way on matters of religious principle. Maybe he ought to call the police. No, the men were armed, at any rate from the look of the bulges in their jacket pockets. If the police came, there might be bloodshed. Still, the people who had come for the meeting must be protected. There was only one way: Izumida must handle the situation himself as best he could. Having made his decision, he was calm as he said in a loud, clear voice: "All right, we want to get on with our meeting. Your problems are a separate matter. I'll discuss them with you gladly but not now. You name the time and place."

"Backing down, eh?" sneered Kaneki.

"No one's backing down," Izumida shouted. "Remember you're not the only people here. We're trying to hold a discussion meeting. All I'm saying is that I'll talk this over with you later." It was the first time he had raised his voice in anger, and its power was felt by everyone. The room fell silent for a moment. Kaneki raised his fists as if ready to fight. His two friends brought their hands slowly, but deliberately, to their jacket pockets. Rising to her feet, Yuriko tried to put herself between her husband and Izumida. At last there seemed to be

no way to avoid a fight. Kaneki and his friends exchanged glances as if each of them was waiting for a signal from one of the others. The women were huddled in a corner terrified to move. Some of the young men were slowly preparing to leap on the ruffians.

For a moment no one made a sound, and then from the back of the room the voice of a middle-aged, gray-haired member of Soka Gakkai rose in the Daimoku chant. Then one by one, other voices joined in until ten or so people were chanting in chorus. Kaneki and his friends had in fact intended to do no more than bluff Izumida into submission, but the unity and harmony of the group chanting the Daimoku threw all of their plans into disorder. The three stood bewildered and perplexed, until that same middle-aged, gray-haired man, whose name was Hotta, stepped forward and said in an Osaka accent: "I'm sure you boys see that we're just trying to have a meeting here. We don't want any trouble, and you don't want any trouble. Now why don't you step over here to the next room. Young man, bring some cushions for the gentlemen to sit on."

Perhaps if Hotta had spoken in the ordinary standard Japanese dialect of Tokyo, Kaneki and his friends would not have acquiesced to his urgings. But the slightly humorous note of his Osaka accent destroyed the tension that had prevailed a few minutes earlier. Their attempts to force Izumida and Kaneki's wife to see things their way were in shambles, and all three were happy to follow Hotta to the neighboring room, through the window of which two figures could still be seen lurking on the street corner. Kaneki waved to them to move along. Obviously the men outside had been brought as reinforcements in case the bluffing tactic had turned into a full-scale fight. As a matter of fact, the house was surrounded by five armed members of Kaneki's gang. One of their duties was to make sure that no one from the meeting tried to contact the police.

Izumida excused himself from the meeting for a moment and joined the men in the next room. He was totally in control of himself. Kaneki demanded that Izumida force Mrs. Kaneki to renounce Nichiren Shoshu and that he be given a signed document to the effect that neither Izumida nor any of the members of his organization had tried to convince her to divorce her husband. Izumida was disgusted with the stupidity and pettiness of the demands. But he was astounded by the perseverance that foredrawn conclusions and ill-informed judgments of circumstances gave these men. He explained carefully that he and the members of Nichiren Shoshu did not force people to accept their beliefs and that they could not force people to renounce them. As far as the divorce was concerned, Izumida insisted that, since he was not running a marriage-counseling service, he did not see how he could possibly do anything to separate or bring the Kanekis together. Finally he said that if the three men were still not satisfied, he would, as he promised earlier, meet them when and where they specified. But he must return to his meeting. He therefore requested that the three leave quietly.

"No, you don't shake us that easily," said the man with the scar. "We want to settle this thing right here and now."

"I'm afraid that is out of the question," stated Izumida with absolute finality.

For all their wicked gesturing and show of brutality, none of the three was prepared for serious trouble. Izumida had pulled the foundations from under their bluffing, and now they had no recourse but to accept his proposal for a later discussion.

"You'll go anywhere we say anytime we say?" asked Kaneki.

"Yes."

"All right," said Kaneki with a grin. "Let's take the whole thing to the general headquarters of the occupation forces."

These three men felt no fear of the Japanese police; and though they realized the absurdity of taking a domestic problem to the general headquarters, like many Japanese of that time, they regarded the foreign authorities as the supreme source of authority. Of course they could not have appealed to the general headquarters, but they were trying to use the power of the occupation forces to frighten Izumida. Izumida was not easily upset.

"The general headquarters it is then," said Izumida in a cool and collected manner.

Now the roughnecks saw that they were dealing with a man whom they could neither scare nor beat. Stabbing a finger toward Izumida, Kaneki said: "Let's get serious. You be at the

Free Press Association—here's the address—at three in the afternoon on July nineteenth. You be there without fail."

Unable to leave without one more attempt to recoup his strategic losses, Kaneki said as he went out the door: "If you're not there, you're going to be very sorry."

Izumida shrugged and returned to the meeting, where everyone was eagerly awaiting the outcome of the brief talk in the next room. Throughout Izumida's absence, Yuriko Kaneki had been quietly crying. Izumida turned to Mrs. Chitani and asked her to be good enough to take Mrs. Kaneki home. He then said to his wife: "You'd better go with them, Tamè. The meeting is over anyway."

As the three women left, Mrs. Chitani experienced a moment of intense embarrassment. Since she had invited Yuriko to join the group and had told Kaneki where the meeting was held, she had been largely responsible for the meaningless violence of the evening. She felt that she had done what she thought was best, and she hoped the others would understand. But she vowed to herself that if there were any repercussions of the near brawl, she would do everything she could to bring about a peaceful settlement.

After the women were gone, Izumida turned to the remaining members and said: "I must apologize to you for what has happened here tonight. I'm sure you will agree that we had better call the meeting off for tonight and reschedule for a day in the near future. We'll let you know the time and place through your district leaders. Good night everybody."

Breathing a sigh of relief to know that they were safe at last, the group dispersed.

Later that night, when Izumida telephoned to tell him of the trouble at the meeting, Toda called an emergency meeting of the leaders and staff members of Soka Gakkai for early the following morning. After Toda hung up the telephone, his wife, Ikue, expressed worry about what might happen to Izumida.

Toda said with a laugh: "Izumida must have had the shock of his life. To come back safe and sound from the war only to be threatened at a discussion meeting! I wonder if that's karma expiation."

The meeting on the following morning was convened in a mood of tension and excitement. The leaders of Soka Gakkai and the people present at the meeting at which the trouble occurred, including Hotta and young Matsumura, the son of the family in whose home the meeting was held, were there. After hearing reports of the events, one young man said: "I should have gone to that meeting. I'll bet those three men were the Three Formidable Foes prophesied in the Lotus Sutra." Another young man, better versed in the theology of Nichiren Shoshu, said: "No, but I am convinced that they represent the third foe: *Sensho-zojoman,* or persecution by governments or other large groups. Did you see the way they tried to drag the occupation headquarters into the thing? That means they are trying to hide behind foreign strength. I smell some kind of big power in this. Mr. Izumida handled the whole affair very well."

Unaccustomed to such praise, Izumida blushed. But Toda's analysis of the significance of the evening was different from that of the young man. "No it's not serious persecution. It's too early in our development for that. It's a case of emotional entanglement and nothing more. Once we get the emotional problems settled, everything will be all right. This kind of incident proves how important honest leadership is in preventing problems like this and in helping us deal with them when they occur."

Though certain that one day its power for good would be great, Toda was well aware that at the present time the strength of Soka Gakkai was small. It was in light of this knowledge that he analyzed the nature and the significance of the incident at the discussion meeting the night before. The way to the universal propagation of the faith was constantly present in his mind. The way was still long, however, and Soka Gakkai was at that time too weak to contend with the great foes prophesied in the Lotus Sutra.

"Believe me, if what happened last night was all there is to the great enemy that we call Sensho-zojoman, I'd be the happiest man alive because it would mean that attaining the universal spreading of our faith would be easy. Unfortunately, such is not the case. Our mission is much harder than that; is a task on an unprecedented universal scale.

"Along the way to our goal we are bound to encounter the Three Formidable Foes, and we'll have to be ready for them when they come. But we're not in that phase yet. Before we face those enemies, we must carry our fight into all aspects of society. By this I mean that we will meet opposition everywhere, throughout all levels of politics, culture, education, and so on. No matter how great our enemies, we must never flinch. To give us the strength we need, we must maintain firm faith. With faith on our side, we'll win because we will fight together.

"I'd be happy if the time were close at hand for us to come to grips with the Three Formidable Foes because that would mean the universal spreading of our religion would be imminent. But the true battle is still a long way off. What we are encountering now is a small preview of *Zokushu-zojoman,* the first foe, involving prideful slander of the faith by an ignorant laity. It is true that even now some insignificant sects have been throwing mud at us, but that's nothing compared to what will come some day, when the second foe, *Domon-zojoman,* materializes. As far as Sensho-zojoman—the foe you mentioned earlier—is concerned, there is still no sign of it. But it, and Zokushu-zojoman and Domon-zojoman as well, will come. When they do, you must all be thoroughly disciplined to put up a good fight. I won't have any of you running away in the face of the real enemy. But Izumida, tell me, what are your plans for July nineteenth?"

"Well, I've promised to go. I suppose I'll get beaten up, but I'll go."

"Going to go to get beaten up? That's hard work for nothing. Neither side of the argument is very smart. What good will it do them to beat you to a pulp? Since you promised, you'd better go. But if I were in your shoes, I wouldn't resign myself to taking a beating."

Everyone smiled, but Toda interrupted them with a serious comment:

"Anyway, the outcome of the encounter between you and these men is already decided. It's just like a fight between the Buddha and devils. You can't lose. Remember, about seven hundred years ago, when Nichiren Daishonin was about to be beheaded at Tatsunokuchi, in Kamakura, a tremendous flash of light temporarily blinded and terrified the executioners. We are votaries of the Lotus Sutra and children of Nichiren Daishonin. He will protect us as long as our faith is strong. But we must be careful nonetheless.

"Still this doesn't mean that Izumida ought to go to a meeting like this unprepared and empty-handed. Some of the ruffians at that place may very well be armed. We have to work out careful measures to cope with them. Chanting the Daimoku alone is not enough at times like these. Don't forget what Nichiren Daishonin told Shijo Kingo, one of his faithful samurai followers who was in mortal danger: 'Everyone must be fully alert and careful.' "

In the next few minutes all manner of safety precautions were suggested. Izumida ought to go to the police instead of keeping his appointment with Kaneki. He ought to notify the occupation military police because the Japanese police were notoriously inefficient. Five or six strong members of the Youth Division, armed with pistols, must accompany him to the appointment and shoot if necessary: it would be self-defense. The longer the suggestions kept coming, the more improbable they grew. Finally Izumida himself interrupted:

"Enough of this. It's my responsibility. I'll go and I'll go alone. I don't want anything to happen to anyone else because of me."

Toda, who was gravely concerned for the safety of Izumida, one of his most devoted disciples, spoke up at last: "All right. Izumida, keep your appointment. But young Matsumura here will go with you."

"Yes, and if anything happens I'll shield him with my own body," burst in the youthful and most ardent Matsumura.

"No," said Toda, "that's not the idea. We don't want a fight, don't you see? If the situation seems to be getting dangerous, you slip out of the room, dash to a phone, and call us. Somebody will be standing by the phone here." He then gave detailed instructions to Izumida, Matsumura, and the others who were going to help. Before the meeting adjourned, Toda said: "Now everything is understood. Mishima, Harayama, you two take charge of all of the details. Matsumura, remember, the minute things look dangerous, run to a phone and call me at once."

Thrilled to be part of such a dramatic event, young Matsumura bought a new suit to wear for the occasion. He chanted the Daimoku furiously day and night. Izumida could not forget Toda's words: "The outcome of this fight is already decided." "If I fail in this," he thought, "it will be my karmic destiny." In the prewar days, when President Makiguchi was still alive, there was a popular song that went:

> "Though threatened at gunpoint,
> I won't retreat—not one step.
> A man can take only one way.
> Look up at the rosy eastern sky."

Humming the refrain, Izumida decided that he would not retreat either. He would stand firm for true Buddhism. In the confrontation with the Koreans he needed courage and faith, and he had them both.

On the night of the frightening experience at the discussion meeting, Mrs. Chitani had seen Yuriko home and had then gone to her own house, where for a long time she sat and mulled over her responsibility in all the unpleasantness that had occurred. Perhaps the others would understand, as she had hoped when leaving the Matsumura house. Still, she had been instrumental in bringing Yuriko into Soka Gakkai.

The next day she called on Izumida in the offices of the women's newspaper *Josei Shimbun,* where he worked. She apologized for what had happened and asked if there was anything she could do to be of assistance in clearing up the matter. Izumida then told of the appointment scheduled for July 19. This news upset Mrs. Chitani very much. She tried to force Izumida to tell her the place of the meeting; but he refused, saying that even if she went there was nothing she could do. He added: "It's no place for women; I'll settle it. You stay out of it entirely." Seeing that Izumida was determined not to divulge the information, Mrs. Chitani returned to her home.

But her anxiety continued to mount. When she became most restless, she found relief in chanting the Daimoku. For a while she almost resented Yuriko, but she soon reprimanded herself for this unworthy attitude and asked Yuriko to come to her house and join her in the Daimoku.

No matter what she did, however, she could not rid herself of worry and of a tremendous sense of responsibility. Finally, she resolved to settle the matter with the three men herself if she could only find out where the meeting was to take place. Yuriko would not tell her. Perhaps she did not know. Mrs. Chitani tried to find out from Mr. Kaneki, but he refused to speak to her. Neither Hotta nor Matsumura was of any help. Mustering her courage, she called on Izumida one more time. He still refused to tell her the location until she explained to him how serious the matter was for her personally. "I have to see these men and settle this thing," she said. "I must accept the consequences of my actions. I promise not to cause trouble. Your appointment is your affair. But I must know where the meeting will take place. I know I'm a stupid old woman, but I have my religious faith. And unless I abide by my duty, I cannot face the Gohonzon."

"Very well," replied Izumida. "I'll tell you the place but only on the condition that you make no attempt to interfere with our meeting. You may have your duty, but that meeting is my responsibility. I made the promise, and I must go through with it. If you want to see these men, go ahead. But don't let them think I sent you. And remember, you are acting now completely on your own initiative." He then gave her the name of the Free Press Association, which was located in Hitotsu-bashi, not far from Toda's Kanda offices.

This brief talk with Izumida took place on July 18. Mrs. Chitani returned to her home. She was frankly frightened, but she felt better because she saw her duty and now knew a way to carry it out. Anticipating the worst, she wrote a will and put out fresh underwear for the following day. Late that night she performed Gongyo services and chanted the Daimoku for a long time. Before going to bed herself, she went into the room where her two younger daughters were already asleep.

Kneeling beside their beds she thought over the many experiences she had had since the death of her husband in the war. She had worked hard as a peddler of various kinds of merchandise, but times had not been entirely dark. She had raised her two younger daughters alone. Her eldest daughter had married before the war. Her husband had been sent to the front but had come home safe and was now an artist and designer. They had two children of their own and lived in the upstairs part of Mrs. Chitani's house. All in all, she had managed well, she thought as she went quietly to her own room and went to bed. She felt prepared for whatever might happen on the following fateful day.

Arising early in the morning, she performed morning Gongyo, dressed, and went out. The morning was hot and humid. By the time she arrived at the Free Press Association building

in Hitotsubashi, she was bathed in sweat. Quietly pushing the door open, she started up a long, dark, but clean staircase. There seemed to be no one in the building. Doors opened left and right off the hall on the upper floors. Several of them were partly open, and Mrs. Chitani peeped in some, half hoping, half fearing to find the three dreadful Korean men. But after climbing to the third floor and looking around, she stopped to think a minute. The building was in altogether too good condition and too respectable looking to be the hangout of rascals like Kaneki and his pals. Bewildered and lost, she stopped for a minute to gather her thoughts. As she did so, an office girl came briskly up the steps. Mrs. Chitani stopped her and said: "Excuse me, but I'd like to see the president of the association."

"Yes, and what is your name please?" asked the polite young lady.

"My name is Chitani. But that makes no difference. He wouldn't know me anyway. Just tell him I want to see him about some—some of your countrymen."

"Just one moment please."

The girl disappeared into a room on the left side of the hall. The worried Mrs. Chitani chanted the Daimoku to herself.

It was some time before the young lady returned, but when she did, she said with a smile: "Please come this way, Mr. Fukuda will see you now." Mrs. Chitani followed on legs unsteady with apprehension. The office girl showed her into a bright, spacious office with a massive desk, behind which sat a large, broad-shouldered, gentle-looking man. He was speaking crisply into the telephone. Mrs. Chitani bowed and waited for him to finish his conversation. While waiting, she observed the man, trying not to stare. She was entirely unprepared for his pleasant, neat appearance. Already having too much experience with the likes of Kaneki, she had assumed that the president of the association would be the same kind of person. But here at the phone sat a gentleman with carefully groomed hair, wearing a fresh white shirt and a bow tie.

When he finished his phone call, Fukuda rose, greeted Mrs. Chitani courteously, and after conducting her to a sofa in one corner of the room, adjusted the electric fan so that it would cool her. "Now—Mrs. Chitani, isn't it?—what can I do for you?" His Japanese was impeccable. Confused, but determined, Mrs. Chitani blurted out her whole story in a fragmentary, disorderly, almost unintelligible way. Mr. Fukuda asked her to slow down so that he could piece the situation together.

"Is that the Kaneki who is involved in the black market?" he asked.

"Maybe. I think so. But doesn't he work for you?" inquired Mrs. Chitani, who was beginning to suspect that Kaneki and the other thugs had nothing directly to do with the Free Press Association.

"Oh, no, Mrs. Chitani. He is one of my fellow countrymen. He hangs around here a good bit, and I suppose I have met him on a few occasions."

"But he told Mr. Izumida to meet him here. So naturally I thought . . ."

"How did you get to know Kaneki?" asked Mr. Fukuda.

"He's my next-door neighbor. I converted his wife, Yuriko."

"Converted? What do you mean by that?"

"Oh, I told her about our religious faith and introduced her to our group. And that's how all of this started. That's why I feel to blame."

"Then you have come here to come to terms somehow with this Kaneki?" he asked.

"Yes. Can you help me please?" Mrs. Chitani now felt that she had an ally, someone who could perhaps bring the whole tangled situation to a peaceful conclusion. Wanting to make sure that Fukuda understood her position, she continued: "I hope you understand clearly that our religious teachings had nothing to do with Yuriko's wanting a divorce. I can't cause my fellow believers any more trouble. I'm to blame. So Mr. Kaneki can either try to understand that we have not influenced Yuriko, or he can take his anger out on me. I mean, if somebody's got to—be hurt, I'm the one because I caused the trouble."

"Now, now, calm down, Mrs. Chitani. There's not going to be any more trouble. Let's just get to the bottom of this," said Fukuda as he called his office girl and told her something in Korean. Soon, Kaneki's friend with the ugly scar on his neck came in the door; Mrs. Chitani almost fainted with fear. The man glared at her menacingly, but Fukuda immediately started a discussion in Korean. The exchange between the two was heated and obviously important to the man with the scar. Mrs. Chitani did not understand a word that was said, but she could see that Fukuda decidedly had the upper hand. Finally, he said a few words in a voice brooking no objections and sent the man with the scar skulking from the room. Mr. Fukuda turned to Mrs. Chitani with a satisfied look on his face. "I must say, Mrs. Chitani, I am glad you told me of this. If something hadn't been done promptly, those three men might have caused a lot of trouble. It's all settled now, though. You have nothing to worry about."

"Thank you so much," whispered Mrs. Chitani, on the verge of tears from relief.

"Please let me explain to you about these men," Mr. Fukuda said. "As you may or may not know, large numbers of Koreans were brought forcibly to Japan before and during the war to work as conscript labor. Now that the war is over, they have stayed here because many of them—like Kaneki—have married Japanese girls and have settled down. But now they are free. They don't have to take orders from anyone anymore, and unfortunately some of them don't know what to do with their freedom. Because I am Korean, I can offer a certain amount of help. Most of the men who come to me for assistance don't cause difficulties. But there are a few bad ones. I'm afraid Kaneki and his pals are among the bad ones."

"Aren't you afraid, Mr. Fukuda?" Mrs. Chitani asked in a low voice. "They look like such desperate characters. You must risk your life every day."

"Oh, no," chuckled Fukuda. "Do I look like a man who risks his life often? As a matter of fact, however, I would be willing to give my life if it would serve to help my countrymen. I graduated from a Japanese university, and I think I understand the good and bad points of both the Japanese and the

Korean peoples. Japanese, who have never known the kind of oppression that the Koreans have suffered, cannot understand our delirium with the freedom we have at last been granted. My fellow Koreans living in Japan, however, do not understand that freedom carries a heavy responsibility for personal conduct. Their wild—sometimes even criminal—behavior for the past few years has caused me and all other concerned Koreans great pain."

Mr. Fukuda fell silent for a few minutes. Mrs. Chitani, who had been attentive to his discussion, saw that she was dealing with not only a very considerate, but also a profoundly thoughtful man. How foolish her earlier fears for her life seemed. She was glad that she had made up her mind to come and happy that she had spoken her mind. She suddenly realized that when a person sees the need to do something, he ought to act with courage and good faith. To hold back and to procrastinate can invite great loss. There is no sense in spending a lifetime hesitating. This realization seemed to give her hope for a new way of life. But her job for the day was not yet finished. "I'm sure Mr. Fukuda will keep his word," she thought, "but perhaps I'd better ask him to give me a written statement, just in case." Turning to him she asked: "You're positive that my fellow believers have nothing to fear from Kaneki?"

"Absolutely nothing. I'll call them in today and give them orders to leave you and your group alone. I hope you will forgive them. As I said, they still don't know what to do with their freedom. And besides, I suspect that Kaneki is an ignorant and weak man who needs to find someone to blame for the mess he's made of his marriage. Obviously, Mrs. Kaneki's religious beliefs have little to do with the true problem. No one can tell her what to believe. On that score, she is as free as all the rest of us."

This put Mrs. Chitani's mind to rest, but she nonetheless thought a written statement would help the other Soka Gakkai members understand that the matter was settled peacefully.

"Please don't think me rude. But would you mind writing all of that down so that I can show it to the other members of our group. I'm sure it would calm their anxiety."

Fukuda was a little surprised at Mrs. Chitani's request, but he complied willingly. "Very well, here you are," he said as he handed her a written statement of the promise he had made to see that Kaneki and the others caused no further trouble to Soka Gakkai.

"Thank you, but you've forgotten to put your seal on it," said Mrs. Chitani.

"You are a stickler for formalities aren't you?" smiled Fukuda, affixing his seal to the paper.

As she folded the paper and carefully tucked it into her handbag, Mrs. Chitani thought: "I wonder if I couldn't convince Mr. Fukuda to join Nichiren Shoshu. But not today. Sometime in the future. Now I've got to hurry over to Mr. Izumida's."

Thanking Fukuda, then thanking him again, she departed from the Free Press Association. The young office girl guided her to the door and waved a friendly goodbye as Mrs. Chitani hastened down the street. The day was fine and bright. "My, I think it's not as hot as it was," mused Mrs. Chitani as she hurried along. At any rate, she was not perspiring as much as she had when she had made her frightened way to this part of town a few hours earlier.

Dashing into Izumida's office, Mrs. Chitani announced triumphantly: "I've fixed it all! Look, here's a paper promising that Kaneki won't give us any more trouble. You don't have to keep your appointment now Mr. Izumida."

Taking the paper from the excited woman, Izumida read it, folded it again, and said with a sigh: "In a way, I'm kind of sorry." Then he called Toda to give him the news.

In spite of the sultry weather, the meeting room upstairs at the Nihon Shogakkan offices in Kanda was full of people who had come to hear Toda's lecture on the Lotus Sutra held on the night of Mrs. Chitani's triumph at the Free Press Association. After concluding his talk on the scriptures, Toda referred to the Koiwa incident:

"Many things like this are bound to turn up during our work to spread our faith to all peoples," said Toda. "But we have nothing to fear. The Myoho cannot be stopped. One example of the power of the law is to be seen in the incident at Koiwa. The time has come for our teachings to spread from Japan to Korea and ultimately to all Asia and to the rest of the world. We have now entered a period, unlike the prewar years, when nothing can obstruct the progress of the Myoho. In the days before the war, the Koreans in Japan were too severely oppressed by the Japanese to stir up trouble. The time has come for the Koreans, too, to waken. And I take this as an indication that the Buddhism of Nichiren Daishonin will soon pass into Korea and later to all Asia. This kind of thing is prophesied in the *Kangyo Hachiman Sho*. Somebody find it and read the last part for us."

A young girl stood up and read in a clear voice: "India is called the Land of the Moon, which signifies the appearance of the Buddha Sakyamuni. Japan is named the Land of the Rising Sun, signifying the appearance of the true Buddha of the Latter Day of the Law. As the moon waxes from the west to the east, so the Buddhism of Sakyamuni traveled from India toward Japan. As the sun moves from the east to the west, the Buddhism of Nichiren Daishonin will travel back to India. The Latter Day of the Law will witness both the rising of Formidable Foes and the manifestation of the blessings of the Bodhisattva Fukyo. All disciples, therefore, be of good courage."

Toda interpreted the incident at Koiwa as a sign that the Buddhism of Nichiren Daishonin was beginning to turn toward Korea.

3. REPERCUSSIONS

VARIOUS steps taken by the occupation forces by 1949 had managed to save the Japanese people from starvation. The food-supply situation had improved enough that malnutrition was no longer a major concern, but living was still hard. Shortly after the general elections of January, 1949, Joseph Dodge, president of a bank in Detroit, came to Japan to examine financial conditions with an eye to curbing inflation, which had gotten out of hand. After five weeks, he described the Japanese economy as unstable, "like a man walking on stilts that are too long." As adviser to General MacArthur, he presented the Japanese government with a plan for the reform of the economic structure. This plan, later called the Dodge Line, consisted of nine points; but its salient features were: a balanced national budget, severe restrictions on investments and financing, wage stabilization—in effect, wage ceilings—and intensified control of commodity prices.

Dodge himself described his policy as castor oil that, however unpalatable, must be taken. In speaking of it, General MacArthur said that the Dodge policy would call for increased austerity in every phase of Japanese life and for the temporary surrender of some of the privileges inherent in a free society.

But he insisted that any attempt to hinder the implementation of the plan would be looked upon as a threat to public welfare. The irony of the situation was that, although the policy was intended to benefit Japan through economic stability, it had manifestly unpleasant effects. The Japanese people, only recently liberated from the oppression of a militarist government, were suddenly asked to give up part of their recognized privileges. The hardest hit by the austerity program were the working classes and small- and medium-size enterprises, which lacked capital to fall back on. In fact, it might be just to say that Japan's postwar economic recovery was accomplished at the expense of small business.

Oddly enough, virtually all political parties and labor organizations supported the new economic policy. After it won a sweeping majority in the February elections, Shigeru Yoshida's Democratic Liberal party—whose campaign platform had included promises to promote small and medium enterprises and to abolish restrictions on industrial financing—set about vigorously enforcing the Dodge Line. Even the Socialist party, the Communist party, and the Japan Federation of Labor Unions supported the economic stabilization program.

Blind to the fact that this economic plan truly stemmed from Washington's reevaluation of Japan as an industrial bulwark against the threat of Chinese Communism, people whose sworn duty was the protection and support of the laboring classes participated willingly in a policy that resulted in unprecedented layoffs of labor forces. Statistics show that between February and December, 1949, 10,546 small- and medium-size companies went bankrupt, putting more than 435,000 employees out of work. Big industry, too, dismissed laborers at an astonishing rate, and the government was busily concocting a preposterous plan to fire some 420,000 government workers and civil servants.

For a while, some elements in the laboring classes tried to resist management's wide-ranging dismissals of personnel. In

July, 1949, the Japan National Railways announced a plan to dismiss 92,700 workers, part on July 4 and the remainder on July 12. On the morning of July 6, the president of Japan National Railways was found dead on the train tracks between two busy stations. Murder was strongly suspected, but nothing was ever proved. Equally odd, one night an unmanned electric train in a car barn on the outskirts of Tokyo started rolling, apparently by itself. It crashed into private homes nearby, killing six people and injuring thirteen others. Ten railway workers from the suburban district—nine of them Communists —were arrested but were later released for lack of evidence. The most famous of these mysterious incidents was the so-called Matsukawa case.

At three in the morning on August 17, 1949, a train was derailed near Matsukawa Station on the Tohoku trunk line; three crewmen were killed. Investigation showed that the train had run off the track because someone had pulled out a number of rail spikes. Toshiba, that is to say, the Tokyo Shibaura Electric Co., had a plant in the Matsukawa district. At the time of the derailment, Toshiba workers all over Japan were disputing a planned mass personnel dismissal, and the labor union in the Matsukawa Toshiba plant was on a twenty-four-hour strike. Shortly after the incident, twenty railway and Toshiba workers were arrested. Their trials were to drag on for decades, but the immediate effect of the Matsukawa and other enigmatic incidents involving labor was a triumph for management.

By the end of August, large and small firms throughout the nation had successfully dismissed enormous numbers of workers. Labor unions were to a large extent a postwar development in Japan, and it is likely that immaturity was the reason for their failure to unite and work in close cooperation to oppose management. Be that as it may, however, by autumn Japanese labor unions throughout the country had suffered a crushing defeat.

The nation was flooded with unemployed people. Forced to

resort to day labor, or to make hopeless and frustrating tours
of employment agencies, many of these people turned to the
black market as their only hope of a livelihood. But generally,
the police made prompt raids on black-market peddlers, con-
fiscated their rice or other merchandise, and sent them back

again to roam the streets and railway stations. Nothing was
done to help the homeless and derelict as Japan became an
example of the misery political incompetence inflicts on the
ordinary people.

As one of the initial steps to implement the Dodge Line, all
new loans from the Financial Bank for Reconstruction were
halted. This dealt industry a crippling blow and caused a panic
in financial circles that had immediate repercussions in the
offices of Josei Toda's publishing firm.

Reopened after the war primarily to serve as a basis for the
rebuilding of Soka Gakkai, Toda's company, Nihon Shogak-

kan, had in that sense been a success, largely due to his efficient
and able management. But it was already financially shaky
when the Dodge Line, by stimulating a tight-money policy in
local banks, seriously reduced Toda's operational funds. It is
possible that he ought to have acted quickly to reduce business expenses by cutting back on the staff and effecting other
emergency methods. But he could not because he was fundamentally positive and humane in business. He could not find
it in his heart to fire people who had been loyal to him, the
company, and Soka Gakkai through very trying times. Perhaps he was not cold-blooded enough to succeed in modern
business.

A resourceful man, never at a loss for fresh ideas, especially
in time of trouble, Toda gave much thought to his predicament.
At last he decided that when money is tight the way to profit
is to open a credit association. A small moneylending business
would provide the operational funds so badly needed by his
publishing firm. As luck would have it, something promising
in this line turned up quite soon.

One morning in June, 1949, Toda received an unexpected
visit from Taro Kurikawa, an old acquaintance who had been
kind enough to lend office space to Toda when he first reopened the publishing business after the war. The two men
discussed many things, including the Dodge Line and the
menacing effect it was having on Toda's business. Kurikawa,
who had once been a member of the Tokyo metropolitan assembly, had many friends. When Toda told him of his idea
to start a small finance company, Kurikawa listened attentively. Then slapping his thigh, he suddenly said: "I've got it.
You're right that in times like these lending money is the only
way to survive, and I just got wind of some news that might
interest you. It's not definite yet, but I hear that an old acquaintance of mine—Toru Oi—is trying to convert his consumers'
guild into a credit cooperative. He used to be a high government official; but he's gotten old, and it would be dangerous

for him to assume management of a business. So far, he is having difficulties changing his guild into a credit company because he can't find the right partner. That's where you come in with your great knack for business. What do you think? I'll help too, if you need me. If you're interested, I could call on him today and check the matter out."

Toda knew too much about business to become overly enthusiastic over all offers presented. After thinking a minute he said: "It's not a bad idea, but it wouldn't be so easy to make a success of something like that. To be frank, if somebody else had come to me with the plan, I'd have turned it down."

"Oi is absolutely all right, except for his age. There will be some legal problems, but since the investor will be the same person, they shouldn't amount to much. It's not as if you were starting a new company from scratch; you'll just be changing an old one."

From what Kurikawa said, it appeared that the new firm could start operations immediately. Still Toda hesitated: "Are you sure this consumers' guild isn't in danger of going broke? I couldn't afford to take on anything unsound at this stage in the game."

"No. It's not making much, but I know for certain that it's not in the red either," said Kurikawa. "I'll talk to Oi, see what he says, and call you again. Maybe you could arrange a meeting in a few days."

"All right," said Toda. "We can meet first. I'll decide whether to get involved in this after we've met."

A few days later, Toda met Mr. Oi, who explained to him the legal procedures for changing the present status to that of a credit cooperative. He then outlined the running of the company, listed the board of directors, and briefly related their duties. Toda was appalled at the inefficiency with which Oi managed things. But the very challenge of taking on such a company, which was not in fact in desperate financial straits, whetted his appetite for business.

Toda accepted the offer of partnership that Oi made and set out immediately to take the necessary legal steps. Under postwar regulations, however, this kind of thing required a great deal of time because requests for conversion of companies had to be approved not only by the numerous bureaus of the Ministry of International Trade and Industry, but also by the Ministry of Finance. Months went by before everything was settled, but the new company, named the Toko Credit Cooperative, finally opened in the fall. The offices were on the first floor of Toda's Nihon Shogakkan, and most of the staff, too, came from the publishing company.

Though the business world was in an unsettled state, Soka Gakkai continued the advances that it had been making since its rebirth four years earlier. In 1949, though still not a large organization in comparison with the whole nation, Soka Gakkai had more than one hundred twenty-five district leaders. An average of more than seventy households was converted monthly. Thirty-eight discussion meetings and eighteen Youth Division discussion meetings were held in Tokyo and its vicinity every month. People who attended these meetings, the increasing numbers of participants in Toda's lectures on the Lotus Sutra, and the entire organization worked diligently and in harmony. They knew that, though their strength was still relatively small, they would succeed in their magnificent saving mission as long as they preserved unwavering faith.

On October 18, 1949, at the temple Kankiryo, in Nakano, Tokyo, eighty faithful society members attended ceremonies marking the anniversary of the death of Tsunesaburo Makiguchi. Although several of the people who had professed faithful adherence to Makiguchi's teachings in the past were conspicuously absent, a large number of new converts—people who had never met Makiguchi—attended. Toda was happy to see these new people because he knew that they would play important future roles in the society. Consequently, it was largely to them that he addressed part of his memorial speech when he said: "Do not forget that when you hear my lectures on the Lotus Sutra you automatically become the disciples of Tsunesaburo Makiguchi, a philosopher and leader of global importance. I hope that in the years to come each annual commemoration of the death of our founder will be held with greater numbers of people and more new converts. Even though you did not know him in his lifetime, I assure you that you are nonetheless his true disciples."

The fourth annual general convention of Soka Gakkai was held on October 23, in the auditorium of the Kanda Education Center in Tokyo. As Toda had once promised, the large hall, including all the seats on the first and second floors and much of the aisle space, was filled with people. High Priest Nissho Mizutani, retired high priest Nichiko Hori, and many priests from Taiseki-ji attended. Reverend Seido Hosoi smiled brightly at Toda as, during his speech, he said: "At the first postwar general meeting, Director General Toda predicted that in three years he would pack this auditorium. I am gratified to see that his prediction has come true." Hosoi's comment was symbolic of the brightness and hope that characterized all the proceedings at the conference.

Because the number of discussion meetings had increased so much that Toda was no longer able to attend them all, he decided to institute and conduct general discussion meetings in order to demonstrate good techniques to use in converting people to the faith and in order to prevent the development of a gap between the top leadership and the general membership of Soka Gakkai. The first of these general discussion meetings was held at the temple Myoko-ji, in Shinagawa, Tokyo. More than two hundred people—many of them new people who were not yet converts—attended.

In contrast to the rising trends in Soka Gakkai affairs, the Nihon Shogakkan publishing company pursued a steady downhill course. The tight-money policy, overproduction in the publishing business, and finally, the rebirth of many of the popular magazines that had been discontinued during the war defeated small publishing houses. Toda's magazines, *Ruby* and *Boys' Adventures*, had done well at first, even when book sales were dropping. But soon these two periodicals could no longer withstand competition from the big magazines. *Ruby* failed first, as large numbers of issues were returned unsold each month. *Boys' Adventures* managed somehow to stay in the black for a while. In August, 1949, Toda changed its name to *The Boy of Japan* in the hope of attracting buyers, but by autumn unsold copies had reached eighty percent of all issues printed.

One chilly, cloudy fall morning, Toda assembled his employees in the main office and had Okumura, the accountant, give a full statement of the financial status of the firm. The figures that Okumura read in a dispirited voice left no room for doubt: the company was facing a severe crisis, with a deficit of millions of yen each month. Until that moment, many of these people had not opened their eyes to the true significance of the returned books, the unsold magazines, the unpaid bills, and the complaints about arrears from the printing and paper companies. For one thing, the glow of happiness they had experienced at the wonderfully successful fourth general meeting of Soka Gakkai still lingered. But more important, no one who worked for Toda could believe that he would not somehow pull them out of any predicament. While realizing that the company was in trouble they nevertheless continued to trust that Toda would fix it all.

"I have thrown this open to you because I trust you and need your suggestions," Toda said, addressing everyone present.

"Those figures must be wrong," came a voice from the back of the room.

"Figures don't lie," retorted Toda. "And Okumura arrived at these figures after long and very careful calculations. Human beings—especially people who lack strength—interpret things the way they want them to be. When it is convenient, they can convince themselves that black is white. But cold, hard figures can't be treated that way: you can't make a credit out of a debit. Figures do nothing but illuminate the incontrovertible facts, and recognizing them frankly for what they are takes courage. The way a person acts on the basis of these frightening figures shows what kind of stuff he is made of. Facing the facts and using them is what is meant by true human strength."

The employees believed for a moment that this remark was another one of Toda's introductions to a splendid solution. But from his solemn look and from what he said next they saw that the situation was grave.

"I'm serious. If any of you have any ideas to offer, please speak up. These figures are not just correct, I suspect they are optimistic. They are still incomplete, for one thing. The number of returned magazines covers only the period ending three months ago. We can be fairly sure that when the rest of the figures are in the picture will be still darker. Since the situation is certain to get worse, we've got to put our minds to it now. Don't misunderstand me; I'm not blaming you. I only want your ideas and opinions."

Bewildered by the gloomy outlook of the company and by Toda's complete lack of his usual wit and humor, no one had anything to suggest.

"Well," said Toda, "it's not surprising that you have nothing to say on such short notice. I've been thinking about this for a long time, and I have only one idea. We must stop publishing. It may be that in the near future we can start again, but examining the pluses and minuses has convinced me that we must stop right now. If we do not, we will only be adding to our deficit, no matter how hard we work.

"Of course, I shall expect all of you to do your best in cleaning up the remaining affairs of the publishing company. We'll gradually start thinking about what future steps to take at the proper time. I hope you'll all take this bravely. Try not to be discouraged. Remember that I expect a lot from my disciples. Stopping publication is hard on us, but we won't be causing anyone else any trouble."

As they drifted aimlessly back to their desks, the employees of Nihon Shogakkan were in a state of semishock. The publishing company was going to close down. Toda's words of encouragement had little effect. Many of the people thought most seriously about what they would do for a living if the company closed permanently. Still, all of them cared enough about Toda not to betray such feelings by so much as a look, let alone a word.

The news of the cessation of publishing activities came as a deep shock to Shin'ichi Yamamoto. Since joining Toda's firm in January, 1949, he had devoted himself to the magazine *Boys' Adventures,* which had gained some popularity. In May he had been appointed editor-in-chief of the magazine. Toda was severe with Yamamoto and scolded him when he made foolish mistakes, but his guidance was careful and sound. A sense of accomplishment and happiness at his promotion inspired Yamamoto to devote all his time to the magazine, of which he was proud. His work brought him into closer contact with many small children. He watched them fondly as they played pranks, laughed, cried over quarrels, or chewed their pencils as they puzzled over difficult problems in their textbooks. Often he felt an impulse to hold them in his arms. He felt that he would be willing to do anything for them.

His devotion to his young readers inspired him to work hard and to try to improve the quality of the magazine. He made closer acquaintanceships with the artists and writers working with him. His enthusiasm conveyed itself to them with the result that the stories they wrote and the illustrations they drew became more attractive and appealing. Yamamoto's personality and his ardor for his magazine won him friends among the artists and their families. From time to time, when writers or painters were out of sorts, the charm of Yamamoto's way triumphed over their bad humor and enabled them to finish on time tasks that otherwise might have been late. For the most thorny personal problems, Yamamoto called on the intercession of wives and other family members. He always made a good impression and won the affection and confidence of everyone with whom he came into contact. As he learned the many aspects of his work, day by day Yamamoto found it more interesting and worthwhile. Gradually, as he became proficient in his tasks, his self-confidence grew and fed his aspirations for the future.

In the fall of 1949, he started working on ambitious plans for a special New Year issue of *The Boy of Japan,* as the magazine was by then called. He carefully selected the writers and artists, who, by the middle of October, were already working on several interesting new children's stories and on illustrations that were promising to be better than anything that had appeared in the magazine so far. Coaxing and guiding other people and at the same time carefully carrying out his own editorial tasks, Yamamoto was dreaming of a brilliant New Year's magazine that would be popular enough to stimulate sales and help remedy the company's deteriorating financial condition.

Because his hopes were high, the announcement of plans to halt publication came as an especially great blow to Yamamoto. It was almost as if an airplane that he had been piloting had suddenly lost power and started hurtling earthward. He saw with painful clarity that he could do nothing but resign himself to the collapse of his beloved boys' magazine. After the meeting in Toda's office, he returned to his desk and sat staring blankly ahead for a few minutes.

Fortunately, a messenger boy from a printing company came in with the galley proofs of the December issue of the magazine. Remembering what Toda had said about not letting the halt of publications interfere with outstanding business, Yamamoto started thumbing through the pages of proof. As the smell of fresh printer's ink filled his nostrils, Yamamoto quickly became absorbed in his task, aware all the while that perhaps this was the last work he would ever do on the magazine to which he had devoted so much love and care. When he finished his proof, he looked at his watch and saw that he had read through the lunch hour. He was hungry. Deciding to go out for some-

thing to eat, he rose and moved toward the front door of the office.

As Yamamoto passed the reception area, he caught a glimpse of Toda laughing happily over a game of Japanese chess that he was playing with a frequent visitor to the company. "What a man!" thought Yamamoto. There he sat playing a game as if nothing was wrong, when only this morning he had announced that the company was about to collapse. For a few seconds as he walked along the street, Yamamoto could not understand how a man could seem so carefree in the face of such difficulties. Then he remembered something that Toda had said a few days earlier while the two of them had been walking along the same street together. "Shin'ichi, in our lives we sometimes fail. But life is long, and a few failures don't mean that everything has gone wrong." When Yamamoto had heard these words, he understood them with only part of his mind. After having seen the way Toda took a defeat that must have cost him immense personal pain, he realized the invincibility of spirit of his teacher and guide. No matter what happened, Toda remained resourceful and unperturbed.

When word got out about the condition the company was in, Toda's associates in the publishing field were certain to react in different ways. Some would sympathize, others would laugh, and perhaps some would make derogatory comments about Toda's abilities in business. But none of this would alter him. Let the publishing firm stop operations, let it go bankrupt, Josei Toda was and would remain a man with a great mission. Storms might buffet him, waves of trouble might sweep over him. But he would always rise to the top again. That was the kind of man he was, and Yamamoto was certain that some day the whole world would come to understand and respect this great personality.

Noticing that it had started to drizzle, Yamamoto ducked quickly into a small Chinese restaurant for a bowl of noodles. Throughout his modest meal and all during the walk back to the office, he thought about Toda and about himself. He saw that he, like his teacher Toda, must remain unchanged in the essence of his being. To the people around him, he might seem to change with the passing of time, but inside he knew that he would remain the same basic personality. Given this mental and psychological stability, he was positive that he could find strength to go on with his work with complete devotion and with a sense of deep responsibility no matter what the world might say about him. He realized that both the criticism and the praise of the world are unreliable and worthless and that it is foolish to fear the one or seek the other. When he arrived back at his desk in the office, he was calm and prepared to work at his ordinary pace. While the rest of Toda's employees suffered under the paralyzing effects of the bad news, Yamamoto set briskly about his afternoon errands. First, he had to call on an artist to pay for some work. Then he had to pick up the plate for an ink drawing for the December issue of *The Boy of Japan*.

The rain was falling steadily when Yamamoto left the office. He had no overcoat—in light of the financial status of the company, it did not seem likely that he would be buying one soon. The home of the painter to whom he was to deliver a fee was in a distant suburb and took some time to reach by train. But this was less a burden than a treat to Yamamoto, who always read while traveling. He believed that books are food for the young, recreation for the elderly, ornaments to the rich, and consolation to those in trouble. The knowledge gained through reading remained with him and gave him encouragement and help in practical affairs.

The artist's house was cold, bleak, and disorderly; but the man had apparently been eagerly awaiting Yamamoto's visit. He had stirred up the few bits of charcoal in the brazier and had put the kettle on for tea. When the painter smiled, an extraordinarily clear light shone in his eyes, and deep wrinkles developed in his pale, haggard cheeks. As the wind and rain lashed the rattling windows of the room, the two sat together over cups of imported tea—a rare luxury—and discussed things in a mood of friendliness.

Almost before he was aware of it, Yamamoto was talking about Nichiren Shoshu and the philosophy of Nichiren Daishonin. He had not intended to try to convert the artist. In fact, he was still not actually talking with that aim in mind. But the painter became very interested. Though he had no knowledge of Buddhism, what Yamamoto told him fired his imagination. Before they parted, the painter said he would like to discuss the matter more fully some other time. Yamamoto, after promising to contact him again soon, went out into the twilight.

The rain had not slackened. The muddy road was full of puddles into which Yamamoto stumbled in the thickening darkness. By the time he reached the station, his secondhand, badly worn shoes were soaked, and he was thoroughly drenched. But there was still the errand to the printer. This took him to the downtown Ginza district, which, because of the rain, was strangely deserted. After going to the printer and picking up the plate of the line drawing, Yamamoto started for Kanda and the publishing offices. But gradually he realized that he was extremely tired and slightly feverish. He was wet and cold and his feet were nearly numb. "I'd better rest a while," he thought. He happened to see the gaudy neon signs of a motion-picture house flashing in the rainy darkness and making garish reflections in the puddles of the street.

Yamamoto bought a ticket, went into the theater, and immediately removed his shoes and stockings, which he hastily wrung out. A sour smell assailed his nostrils. Putting his soggy footwear on again was not pleasant, but when it was done, he sat back in the dark theater and tried to follow the plot of the American movie flashing on the screen. Weariness and physical exhaustion, however, overcame him. Just as the heroine was calling on the hero in a hospital ward, Yamamoto fell asleep.

When he awakened, he had completely lost the thread of the story, which was nearly over at any rate. But worse, a glance at his watch told him that he had slept through a discussion meeting that he ought to have attended, especially on a day that had started as badly as this one. For some reason, his failure to attend this meeting preyed on his mind and made him feel extremely guilty. "It's all the fault of these wet shoes," he thought. "I really must have them fixed. But are they worth it?" Another discussion meeting was planned for two days later, and he vowed that nothing would keep him from it.

The weather did everything possible, however, to make attending the meeting difficult. A typhoon struck the Tokyo area on the scheduled day. Though many people in the offices of Nihon Shogakkan were still confused by the announcement to halt operations and were uncertain about their futures, Yamamoto worked as if nothing had changed. When time came to leave for the discussion meeting, he found that he had accomplished a great deal. But the storm had not abated. If anything, it had grown more violent.

Still, he and Yoshizo Mishima braved the weather and the crowded trains to go all the way to Yokohama, where the meeting was to be held. Upon arriving they were delighted to see that more than fifty people had come out in spite of the howling winds and cutting rains. The vestibule of the meeting place was filled with umbrellas and raincoats. Although the elements raged around them outside, the meeting itself was exciting and hope-inspiring. When it ended, at about ten o'clock, Yamamoto made his way alone to the train station. Drenched to the skin and almost bowled over by the force of the wind, he reflected: "Even when the weather is violent and the world around us is in turmoil, Soka Gakkai does not weaken, Josei Toda does not weaken, and I too must not weaken."

The day that the last issue of *The Boy of Japan*—the December issue—came off the press, the weather was clear and bright outside the Kanda offices of Nihon Shogakkan. Inside, a gloomy silence reigned. As Shin'ichi Yamamoto sat caressingly reading the final product of his work, others in the office were whispering among themselves about where they would go to work and what they would do when the company finally collapsed, which it was certain to do within a matter of days.

As a matter of fact, on the very next day, Toda called his staff together to announce the closing of the publishing company and, on a more hopeful note, to explain the nature and policies of the new credit cooperative. All members of the publishing staff who wished to remain were automatically put on the payroll of the credit company as soon as Shogakkan was officially declared closed. Toda had sensed the dissatisfaction and insecurity of his staff members and he held this meeting of explanation in an attempt to calm fears. While relating stories of his many years of management experience and the successes and failures he had lived through, he illustrated his points by referring to the basic principles of both communism and capitalism. He explained what a credit cooperative is and went on to relate why he had decided to undertake this kind of enterprise, showing wherein he saw hope for its future development and growth.

Yamamoto realized that much of what Toda said was not being sympathetically received by members of the organization who were already planning to quit at the earliest chance. Nonetheless, he was deeply moved by the speech, especially when Toda concluded with: "All business enterprises are subject to rises and falls. Economics, like all other things, has its own rules, which cannot be ignored. Once those rules are understood, it is effort, enthusiasm, and patience that determine the success or failure of a company. Hard work is the same in all companies, big and small. As far as my experience teaches, as long as people are not afraid of hard work, even though things may sometimes seem desperate, a way will always be found."

Before adjourning the meeting, Toda instructed Okumura to divide all cash on hand equally and to distribute it among his employees as part of their salaries. None of them ever knew how valuable that money could have been to the firm itself.

As 1949 drew to a close, the domestic and international scenes were upset and clouded by important events. The Dodge Line controls continued to cause acute suffering in large segments of the Japanese population. In September of that year, the Soviet Union reminded the world that she had been in possession of nuclear weapons for two years. After a brief period in which they established an interim capital in Chungking, the Chinese Nationalists were finally driven from the mainland by the Communist army. On December 7, 1949, Chiang Kai-shek and his followers set up a Nationalist capital in Taipei, on Taiwan. As the cold war between the East and the West intensified, the United States, hoping that Japan would take the place of Nationalist China as an important Asian ally, announced preparations for the drafting of a peace treaty.

On New Year's Eve, Shin'ichi Yamamoto was studying the *Gosho* at Toda's house. When the study session came to an end, Toda treated his young disciple to a simple meal and a few relaxed minutes in a peaceful, warm atmosphere. At the end of the meal, Toda's face became stern as he said: "The whole world is in turmoil. Now is certainly the time when you young people must study as hard as you can. I'll prepare the stage so that later you—the new champions of peace—will have a place to carry out your mission."

4. BUFFETING WINDS

GENERAL Douglas MacArthur's annual message was rather unusual on New Year's Day 1950. It began: "To the people of Japan. On this fifth New Year's Day following hostilities' end, one fact inescapably stands out—although Japan is still technically at war, there are few places on earth more completely at peace."

This was of course an allusion to Japan's demilitarized state. The end of the message, however, contained a surprising twist, something that was possibly MacArthur's newest interpretation of the famous no-war clause in the Japanese constitution.

"While by no sophistry of reasoning can it be interpreted as complete negation of the inalienable right of self-defense against unprovoked attack, it is a ringing affirmation, by a people laid prostrate by the sword, of faith in the ultimate triumph of international morality and justice without resort to the sword. It must be understood, however, that so long as predatory international banditry is permitted to roam the earth to crush human freedom under its avarice and violence, the high concept to which you are pledged will be slow in finding universal acceptance."

By "predatory international banditry" MacArthur apparently meant the victory of the People's Republic of China over the Nationalist Chinese forces. This altered view of the no-war stipulation in the constitution reflected a new evaluation of Japan's international role in the face of mounting tensions between the free and Communist camps. But how were the people of Japan to know who was right? It is true that the Americans repeatedly emphasized the importance of justice, but then, so did the Communists. The definitions of justice of the two sides differed, but there was nothing to indicate that either was intrinsically more just than the other.

The most consequential point of MacArthur's address and of the attitudes it symbolized was certainly the new approach to the no-war clause. When the constitution was promulgated, MacArthur had nothing but praise for the Japanese renunciation not only of military establishments, but also of the right of belligerence. Now when it seemed possible that Japanese assistance might be needed against the forces of communism, the Americans were changing their tune. According to the new posture, the no-war clause does not deny the inalienable right of self-defense.

Shigeru Yoshida, the prime minister at the time, adjusted his stance to that of the Americans. Four years earlier, at a plenary session of the lower house of the Diet, a Communist leader named Sanzo Nosaka had put a question to Yoshida about the nature of the constitutional renunciation of war and had asked how it affects self-defense. To that question Yoshida had replied: "As regards the clause on renunciation of war in the draft of the new constitution, you think that war for the purpose of self-defense ought to be recognized. But I feel strongly that such thinking is dangerous and harmful. . . . It is a well-known historical fact that many recent wars have been waged in the name of self-defense. For us to approve war for the purpose of self-defense would be dangerous and might lead to hostilities and run counter to the spirit of an international peace organization, when such an organization is established."

On January 23, 1950, following MacArthur's New Year address in the newspapers, Yoshida, in an administrative policy speech before the Diet, had a very different comment to make: "Quite naturally, grave concern has been voiced regarding the future security of Japan. Let me say that the key to our security lies in the very determination on our part to abide fully by the constitution, which renounces war and armaments, and to devote ourselves to the cause of world peace, civilization, and prosperity. . . . Renunciation of war does not mean abandonment of the right of self-defense."

As was only to be expected, the statements by MacArthur and Yoshida touched off controversy throughout the country about the true meaning of the no-war clause and about the related issue of possible rearmament. But these were only the forerunners of much more serious developments.

On January 31, 1950, a whole array of top American military leaders—including General Omar Bradley, chairman of the Joint Chiefs of Staff; General Joseph Collins, chief of staff of the United States Army; Admiral Forrest Sherman, chief of naval operations; General Hoyt Vandenberg, chief of staff of the United States Air Force; and others—arrived in Japan to inspect eight American air bases and two naval bases and to confer with General MacArthur. Patently, the main purpose of the visit was to assess the strategic value of Japan in connection with the growing tension between the East and the West.

Granted that Japan had the right to defend herself in case of unprovoked attack, outlining how she was to effect this defense within the framework of the peace constitution remained a controversial issue. Without some kind of defense mechanism, Japan could not protect herself at all. Obviously, then, the problem boiled down to defining the degree of armament she might possess. This issue was complicated by the nature of modern warfare, which has now come to rely on at least the threat of nuclear weaponry. No amount of self-defense preparedness that fails to include nuclear weapons can be effective.

At the time, there were people who argued that Japan must become completely neutral, like Switzerland and Sweden. But neither the East nor the West was likely to endorse the neutrality of a nation that, though recently defeated in a major war, nonetheless possessed the greatest industrial capability in Asia. For many years to come, the self-defense dilemma was to plague Japan. A variety of solutions was to be suggested —for instance, ensuring Japan's neutrality by stationing United Nations troops on her soil—but most of them were too visionary and idealistic to be of practical value.

Nuclear weaponry was at that time rapidly becoming a matter of grave concern for peoples everywhere, especially as the American and Soviet stockpiles of nuclear weapons threatened to grow. Japan, the only nation in the world ever to have suffered nuclear attack, was naturally most apprehensive about these weapons and the menace they posed to the survival of mankind. In 1949, a peace movement directed against nuclear weapons was born in Hiroshima. A petition signed by 107,854 objectors to such methods of warfare was sent to President Harry S. Truman, who refused to accept it. But Truman's refusal in no way slowed down an antinuclear-weapons tide that was beginning to sweep the whole world.

In 1948, groups of intellectuals and scholars in a number of countries began postwar peace movements against nuclear weapons. In 1949, world congresses for the defense of peace were held in Prague and in Paris. A total of three thousand representatives from sixty-four nations attended the meetings, resulting in the formation of an executive committee with the aim of preventing both the spread of nuclear weapons and the rearming of Germany and Japan. In March, 1950 the first global conference against nuclear arms was held in Stockholm; and it adopted what is called the Stockholm Appeal, urging immediate bans on all nuclear weapons. This appeal, which was the crystallization of a longer movement, declared that any nation making use of nuclear arms would be regarded as a war criminal perpetrating crimes against mankind. In a period of eight months the Stockholm Appeal was signed by five hundred million people from all parts of the globe. Even in Japan, six and a half million signatures were obtained in spite of censorship, which screened out all news items about the appeal and about the operations of the executive committee formed at the world conferences for the defense of peace. In number of signatures on the Stockholm Appeal, Japan came third after Italy and France.

In 1950, people everywhere began to give serious consideration to the enormity of the threat presented by nuclear arms. They were gradually coming to see that this is an issue that cannot be solved by single nations or blocs of allies. The immense destructive power of modern nuclear weapons has removed warfare from the realm of old-fashioned military common sense. The fact that a disagreement between nations with nuclear stockpiles might suddenly trigger attacks that could annihilate all mankind makes nonsense of the notion of war for the sake of national defense, since in such combat no one would survive. On the stage of international events, many complicated problems arise. All of them obviously deserve attention, but none is so pressing as devising a way to eliminate the danger of nuclear war because until that question has been safely and satisfactorily resolved solutions of all other issues are ultimately meaningless. A global nuclear catastrophe is not necessarily inevitably preordained. Mankind has created the monster weapon; therefore, it is within mankind's capability to control it.

The top leaders of nations in the modern world are like Damocles, over whose head a sword was suspended by a single hair. But their responsibility is infinitely greater. In front of each of them is the button that could launch a nuclear attack. In light of the threat of destruction posed by the atomic weapons of the potential enemy, if the likelihood of a nuclear attack from without should arise, no leader would have time to convene national assemblies for the sake of asking for formal declarations of war. He would feel compelled to push the button immediately and thus start what could become the end of everything.

But all these leaders are human beings. They all have loved ones and homes that they want to protect. If all top-echelon leaders were to meet with the express aim of banning nuclear weapons and giving to humanity the blessing of lasting peace, it is entirely likely that they would reach an agreement. The time has come to stop sending powerless government representatives to nuclear disarmament conferences and to insist that the men with the power assume the responsibility for making such meetings meaningful. When problems concerning international finance develop, the men holding real power in finance ministries and banks assemble to discuss the issues in person. Is it sensible, then, to send only second- or third-level representatives to deal with issues that directly affect the survival of mankind?

At a large meeting of the Youth Division held some years later, Josei Toda expressed his courageous and bold views of the nuclear-weapons issue: "I should like to take this opportunity to state clearly my opinions of the experimentations with nuclear weapons and hydrogen bombs that are currently stirring up a great deal of controversy. It is true that movements have been instigated to halt this kind of testing, but I feel we must make nuclear experiments completely harmless. The one way to do this is to decree the death penalty for anyone proposing to use nuclear weapons, no matter what his nation and no matter whether he is on the winning or losing side of a conflict.

"I feel this way because all of us, the ordinary people of this world, have the right to live. Anyone who attempts to deprive us of that right is a demon, a monster. People who would use nuclear weapons in war and in that way rob vast numbers of people of their lives deserve death. Should it ever happen that one nation conquers the whole world by means of nuclear weapons, it would be the duty of you, the young men and women of Japan, to spread throughout the globe the idea that such conquerors are diabolic fiends."

Toda was aware that, at the time, he and the society he represented were too small and powerless to make their opinions felt on a large scale. He was nonetheless convinced that the time would come when *obutsu myogo*—the harmonious blending of Buddhism and all aspects of human society—would take place, and to that end he continued to train his faithful followers.

Many things made his task difficult. Among them was the rapidly worsening social condition of the Japanese people. In an article he wrote for *Daibyakurenge* Toda said: "The nation is filled with sorrow and suffering. Many people are out of work. Even those with jobs are unhappy; and without peace, happiness, and hope, human beings are truly miserable. The leaders of the nation tell us that we must lead a life of austerity. This may sound heroic, but in fact it spells only tragedy for the people. If politicians in power see nothing but austerity as a way out of our dilemma, perhaps the people must resign themselves to their lot. But there are limits to what the people will endure. They will not tolerate bad government forever."

By "bad government" Toda meant the Dodge Line nine-point stabilization program, which was wreaking havoc on the national economy. Big enterprises were forced to close large numbers of plants. They were lucky to be able to trim their sails. Small- and medium-size industries could not afford to cut back; they had to go bankrupt. Almost every day the newspapers carried stories of whole families who committed suicide because of financial disasters, sometimes aggravated by heavy taxes. On one occasion, Hayato Ikeda, minister of finance and later prime minister, made a statement that was incredibly callous: "An investigation would have to be made of the extent to which bankruptcy and heavy taxes have caused the suicides. But in times like these, when the nation has lost a war and when we are trying to control inflation, some sacrifices are inevitable. It cannot be helped if five or ten people commit suicide." A remark of this kind from the finance minister incensed the people, but times were so difficult that they could do nothing to make their anger felt.

Toda and his new credit cooperative were faring no better than other small businesses of the time. Money was very scarce. Consequently, though there were countless people eager to borrow, Toda found it impossible to acquire the needed capital to operate. As if this were not bad enough, the failure of his publishing company dissuaded prospective investors from putting into the company the money that was so desperately needed. Week by week, funds dwindled. The shortage became more acute when, as often happened, it proved impossible to collect loans that had fallen due. In addition to the trials of the new company, Toda faced the liquidation of the publishing firm. Salaries to his employees were paid in installments and were behind schedule. After a while, several people left the company, and he would do nothing to try to stop them.

As director general of Soka Gakkai, Toda never allowed his business worries to hinder him in carrying out his duties as leader and teacher. Though his daytime work taxed his mental and physical strength, he continued to hold discussion meetings and to offer counsel and help with his usual seriousness and compassion. But one thing about Soka Gakkai began to trouble him.

A number of old acquaintances, former disciples of Tsunesaburo Makiguchi who no longer took any active part in the work of Nichiren Shoshu or of Soka Gakkai, had begun to frequent Toda's offices. For a long time, none of them had shown his face except for so-called honorary staff appearances at general Soka Gakkai conventions. Their exact purposes in calling on Toda now often were not clear, but desire for profit seems to have motivated them. They brought dubious investors and many loan seekers. All of this traffic contributed to bustle in the offices that gave people the erroneous impression that the credit cooperative was thriving. Toda knew better and was fully aware that the faithless old members of Soka Gakkai and their loan-seeking cohorts were not contributing to an improvement in conditions. This became manifestly clear whenever old acquaintances and customers disappeared without a trace when time came to collect an outstanding loan.

Toda was disgusted with these people and let his feelings be known when he talked with the younger, faithful members of Soka Gakkai: "We are an active, practicing organization. We don't need people like these men who have long since given up practicing their faith. They are worse than deadwood because they can be a source of real harm in the future. You young people must be reliable. You must grow quickly into fine members, because without you the future of Soka Gakkai will be unsteady."

Old dropouts may have given Toda discouraging moments, but some of the younger members of the organization provided him with assistance in work and moral support. For instance, throughout the company's dark times, Shin'ichi Yamamoto worked ceaselessly at tasks that he genuinely disliked and at which he was not very good. Since the opening of the credit cooperative, Yamamoto had been in charge of obtaining endorsements or support from creditors and of collecting— or trying to collect—outstanding loans. Because he was by

nature timid and serious, the psychological demands of convincing and cajoling people left him exhausted at the end of
every day. But he never sloughed his duties.

About a year earlier he had left his parents' home and had
rented a small, unheated apartment in Omori. Work kept
him late at the office more often than not. And when the
innocent young man, who was only twenty-two, returned to
his cheerless room, he found that after chanting the Daimoku
he had insufficient energy to do anything but go to bed. From
time to time, physical weariness and loneliness made him want
to rush home to his parents and never leave them again. But
one thing kept him from taking that step: if his family could
see how much damage overwork and long hours had done
to his body, they would blame Toda. Because his devotion
to his teacher was too great to allow him to hurt him in any
way, Yamamoto resolved to bear his loneliness.

A longing to cry out for help often filled his heart, but rather
than give in to grief he chanted the Daimoku, which gave him
spiritual strength. If only his health had been better, he would
have been able to stand the strain of work. But at the time, his
body and his spirits had plunged to new depths.

As a self-discipline and to gain knowledge and courage,
Yamamoto made it a rule to read one passage from the *Gosho*
each night before going to sleep. After reading, he commented
on the contents of the passage in his diary. Both the text and
the act of thinking about it brightened the dark and lonely
hours.

One night, as he was thumbing through the *Kaimoku Sho*,
his eye was caught by: "One leaves home and enters the priesthood as an infallible way to save one's parents."

Reading this, Yamamoto felt as if Nichiren Daishonin were
in a way endorsing the kind of life he had chosen for himself.
It was true that he was not a priest, but he had left his home
in order to devote himself to the great task of a religious revolution. All of the sufferings he endured seemed to augur

well both for his own inner revolution and for the welfare of his parents. As he reflected on this situation, Yamamoto thought: "I must be strong now in the face of suffering. I can do it; I am still young. All I have to do is allow courage and happiness to well up from within me and keep moving forward. The Dai-Gohonzon is watching everything I do. I don't have to worry about people who scoff or laugh."

Lying on his back in his cold, narrow room, he thought deeply about the present crisis in the company and the effects it would have on his future. His throat was clogged with phlegm—a painful reminder that his tuberculosis was far from cured—but the willpower and sense of purpose filling his heart would enable him to go on with courage and determination.

Though Yamamoto found courage to help him stand firm in the winds of trouble buffeting him, Toda, and their business concerns, the Japanese nation was about to be thrust into much more violent gales of unrest. On May 30, at a mass meeting of leftist workers and students held at the Imperial Plaza, an incident occurred that proved indicative of future political trends. The meeting, in fact an anti-American demonstration, turned into a melee of fighting and shouting. Students spotted and surrounded a Japanese plainclothes policeman taking notes on the proceedings. An American military officer became involved in the fracas, which did not halt until eight leftist workers and students had been arrested. These people were tried before a provost court and were sentenced to unduly severe terms of imprisonment, the maximum of which was ten years at hard labor.

The next development in the course of social upset was to be a general strike on June 3, but the Japanese authorities mobilized the police and the fire brigades and placed them on alert against leftist activities. Rallies and demonstrations were banned, and Tokyo was placed under what almost amounted to martial law.

On July 6, two days after elections for the upper house of

the Diet, General MacArthur surprised the nation by ordering
the twenty-four members of the Japan Communist party central committee purged. In his directive to Prime Minister
Yoshida, MacArthur revealed a completely new stand on the
definition and use of the purge. His note read in part:

"The guiding philosophy of this phase of the Occupation
has been protective, not punitive. . . . The area of its application for the most part has embraced those persons who because
of position and influence bear responsibility for Japan's totalitarian policies, which led to adventure in conquest and exploitation.

"Recently, however, a new and no less sinister group has
injected itself into the Japanese political scene which has
sought through perversion of truth and incitation to mass violence to transform this peaceful and tranquil land into an
arena of disorder and strife as the means of stemming Japan's
notable progress along the road of representative democracy
and subvert the rapidly growing democratic tendencies among
the Japanese people. . . . Their coercive methods bear striking
parallels to those by which the militaristic leaders of the past
deceived and misled the Japanese people."

Until this announcement, the purge had been limited in application to militarists in political and financial circles. Now,
aimed at the Communists as well, it was to have double-edged
power.

On June 7, the seventeen editors of the Communist party
organ *Akahata,* or Red Banner, were ordered purged. The situation grew extremely tense for people of communist persuasion,
although the purge never went so far as to bring about the
outlawing of the party itself. Nevertheless, most of the top
leadership went underground. Ten days before the purge of the
newspaper editors, as if sensing that something untoward was
in the wind, Lieutenant General Kuzma Derevyanko and
the forty-nine-member Soviet delegation to the Allied Council
for Japan suddenly left for home.

But the tension between the capitalist and communist worlds was headed for a more serious outburst. On Sunday, June 25, all regular noon-hour radio broadcasts in Japan were interrupted with the startling news that North Korean troops had invaded South Korea across the thirty-eighth parallel. Only recently launched on a road of recovery after the hell of World

War II, the Japanese people saw in this eruption of hostilities a forerunner of their most dreaded nightmare, another global war.

Of course, the Korean conflict would have remained no more than a civil war if it had not been for the fact that the Soviet Union and the United States operated behind North and South Korea and in this way gave international significance to the fighting.

On June 26, President Truman promised aid to the South Koreans and asked the United Nations Security Council to discuss the Korean conflict at once. The Security Council met on June 28 and passed an American-sponsored resolution branding North Korea as the aggressor and requiring immediate United Nations military sanctions. The Soviet Union was absent from this Security Council meeting.

United States forces went into action at once. Under the direction of MacArthur, as commander in chief of the United Nations troops in Korea, they began air raids and coastal bombardment of North Korea.

The North Koreans met the American attacks with strength and force. They drove the South Korean government out of Seoul and made such serious advances that the United States appealed to United Nations members to dispatch ground forces to Korea as quickly as possible. While the Korean people suffered the agony of war, Japan was being transformed into the major logistics and supply base for the United States forces participating in the fighting.

As soon as the fighting broke out in Korea, strict security measures went into effect throughout the islands of the Japanese archipelago. The Communist newspaper *Akahata* was first suspended for thirty days; then, on July 18, it was suspended indefinitely. Rallies and demonstrations were forbidden. On July 28, a sweeping purge was conducted of all leftists engaged in newspaper and other communications business. This was ostensibly done to maintain peace and security. By mid-November, 10,869 such people had been removed from their jobs. In August, the Federation of Labor Ministry Workers was ordered disbanded. These are some of the steps that the occupation authorities took in what can only be described as direct intervention in Japanese domestic affairs. This intervention was, of course, counter to the Japanese constitution.

The apprehension the Japanese people felt about these measures naturally grew, but it was to reach a peak when to their surprise they found themselves put on a virtual war footing by the establishment of a 7,000-man, so-called national police reserve force and by personnel increases in the Maritime Safety Agency. Like a fire in a neighbor's house, the war raged in

Korea and kept the Japanese in constant fear that it might spread to their land.

There can be no lasting peace on earth and no progress toward the resolution of differences between capitalism and communism as long as the two persist in confronting each other with antagonism and narrow-minded prejudice. Furthermore, large countries must not be allowed to sacrifice weaker nations to their own selfish ends, for such an act is inimical to all mankind. What was needed in the time of the Korean war and is still needed is a moderate third party that, with the guiding principles of a profound philosophy, can reconcile the two opposing groups by rising above them. The true Buddhism of Nichiren Daishonin meets these requirements.

5. A STORMY SUMMER

ALL OF Tokyo sweltered throughout the summer of 1950, but August 22 was the hottest day of the year. Oddly enough, however, when the sun began to set, cool breezes started blowing into the open windows of the second-floor of Josei Toda's offices in Kanda. Though the fresh, cool air brought relief from the oppressive heat, it could do nothing to relieve the gloom and dejection of the group of people gathered in the room. Toda, whose mouth was drawn tense and whose eyes betrayed anxiety, fatigue, and a hint of forlornness, addressed his employees:

"I am very sorry to have to tell you that tomorrow the Toko Credit Cooperative will cease operations. The responsibility is all mine. You have worked well and faithfully. But in spite of your efforts, this is the only way out of our present crisis. I want you to know that I am grateful for your loyalty and for all that you have done for the company and for me."

The news of the company's failure hit all of the employees very hard, especially since it so quickly followed the collapse of the publishing firm. The atmosphere in the room after Toda's brief statement of the situation was oppressively tense. No one said anything; no one cried. It might have helped if some tears could have been shed, but weeping was a luxury that could not be afforded. The people around Toda on that unhappy day were the ones who had stayed with him through his dark times, confident that he would resolve all difficulties. Now the company was finished. Failure was all they had to show for their faithfulness and hard work.

The meeting had lasted for some time, and it was already eight thirty in the evening when Toda concluded with: "I may have failed in the management of our economic endeavors, but I do not admit defeat either for my life or for the religious faith my life rests on. I am as determined as ever to dedicate myself to spreading our faith to the entire world. Nichiren Daishonin's true Buddhism will never be defeated, and that means there is no defeat for Toda's faith.

"Naturally, I have given the present situation a lot of thought. To be frank, at first I could not understand why this happened, but I think I am beginning to see the meaning of our predicament. No matter what happens, I know that Nichiren Daishonin will save me as long as I remain faithful. I may not be able to make you see what I mean, but I want to try. I suspect that for some reason I am being reprimanded by Nichiren Daishonin. From your standpoint, the outcome of my reprimand is extremely trying. But I am glad that it is happening to me. The time is not ripe to tell you everything that I now understand, but remember this: it is good that Buddhism is severe because its very severity helps prevent a great deal of misfortune in the world. What is happening to me is no accident. As you all know, everything is governed by the law of cause and effect. Of one thing I am certain: I have not failed in my faith.

"Believe me, I am deeply pained to have caused you such trouble and to know that all of your difficulties are by no means over. What's more, it is a great sorrow to know that I must cause our creditors and depositors inconvenience and delay. But under no circumstances will I take the cowardly way out. I intend to settle all accounts no matter how long it takes. This is my responsibility.

"In the coming few days, we must all busy ourselves with the hard and thankless task of liquidation. I want you to understand my attitude toward my responsibility in this last difficult stage because there must be no attempts to slough our financial duties. We must, however, try to convince our depositors and creditors to understand our position and to wait until we are in a position to repay. The only way to do this is to give them a clear and accurate picture of our standing and to ask them to believe in our sincerity. I am resolved to pay back all debts, but I need time. If our creditors decide they can trust me, they will wait. In the meantime, I will be trying my hardest to think of a way to make a comeback.

"In rounding out the affairs of the credit cooperative and in trying to get on our feet again, we will have to put all of our past experience to maximum use. But more important, we will have to have intense faith. Be prepared. We are likely to be covered with slander and abuse from all sides. If we flinch in the face of the misunderstandings and false accusations of others, we are all lost. Courage and faith are what we must have if we are to recover."

There was no doubting the gravity of their situation; but though some failed to understand Toda's full meaning, everyone in the room was both moved and inspired by his profound faith and determination. For several minutes, there was complete silence. The office girls quietly wiped away tears with their handkerchiefs. Then Toda broke the silence: "All right, everybody. Let's have a drink together. We've made up our minds now, and we know what we have to do." Cups were brought out, and Toda filled them with sakè. For some, the ensuing toast was a drink of parting, since several of the people present were soon to leave the office to find work elsewhere.

But the truly faithful were to remain with Toda; and from their standpoint, the sakè was a symbol of determination to face the formidable tasks that lay ahead.

For weeks before the general announcement of failure, Toda had made every effort to save the company. He had long realized that operating funds were dwindling and that the directors were less interested in the welfare of the firm than in protecting their own investments in it. After much thought, Toda decided that the one way to save the company was a merger with another credit cooperative. The board of directors empowered him to do as he saw fit in locating a partner for the merger. But no matter how hard he searched, he could find no suitable company. When he asked the Ministry of Finance, which supervised credit organizations, to help him find a merger partner, they sent inspectors to investigate the state of his firm. After two full days of combing through a vast amount of documents, the inspectors announced that they were finished with their study. One of them asked Toda: "What do you intend to do with your company?"

"The only thing I can think of is merging with another dependable credit cooperative," he replied.

"With a balance sheet like yours, a merger with another firm is going to be very difficult to bring off," said the inspector, looking sadly at Toda. "Unless you own a lot of real estate, I think it would be better to give up the idea of merger."

"We have no real estate. Merger is our only hope."

Shaking his head, the inspector said: "Well, I'll go back to the ministry and report our findings to our superior and ask him to consider your request for permission to merge. But don't expect much. If I were you, Mr. Toda, I'd try to find another way out."

"Another way?"

"I think you know what I mean."

"Give up entirely? Close the credit cooperative?"

"I'm afraid that's what it amounts to." The finance investigator was cool and dispassionate. He knew the condition of the firm. Toda thought: "I would have said the same thing if I were in his shoes."

Somewhat later, at a meeting of the board of directors, Toda presented the issue as the inspectors from the Ministry of Finance had explained it to him. In the following few days, his partner, the aging Mr. Oi, made several trips to the Ministry of Finance in hopes of obtaining permission to merge, but to no avail. When word got out that the situation verged on hopeless, the depositors in the credit cooperative immediately began withdrawing their investments. Then, on August 22, the Ministry of Finance ordered the Toko Credit Cooperative to cease operations.

On August 23, as Toda and Shin'ichi Yamamoto were returning from lunch, they came upon their office boy standing at a gasoline station around the corner from the company. The boy's presence in this strange place made Yamamoto suspect that something unusual was happening. Then when he noticed a newspaper-company automobile parked nearby he realized what it was. Running up to them, the office boy said breathlessly: "There's a newspaper reporter at the office. He wouldn't go away even when I told him you were out."

"All right," Toda said and began to walk toward the company.

"Wait, Mr. Toda," called the office boy. "You don't understand. This man's heard about the closing. I eavesdropped on his telephone conversation to his office. He said he had a scoop. He's come to interview you. He told them to wait till the last minute. He's going to phone in the story."

Looking at Yamamoto, Toda said: "Well, they got wind of it pretty fast. They are a nuisance. I don't have much time to deal with him. I've got a meeting of the board of directors in less than fifteen minutes. What do you think I ought to do, Shin'ichi?"

"Why not let me see him first. I'll tell him you are still out."

"Good. You do that, then. The thing to find out is exactly how much he knows. Try to get that out of the reporter without giving away too much information, will you?"

Toda went to his meeting, which was to be held in another part of town, and Yamamoto returned to the office to face the journalist.

Entering the front office, he saw a man in his thirties standing in one corner scribbling away on a pad. Yamamoto introduced himself, and the reporter said that he wanted to meet the person responsible for the credit cooperative. In reply, Yamamoto said: "I'm sorry but both the chairman of the board and the executive director are out and won't be back till very late. Is there anything that I can do for you?"

The reporter handed Yamamoto his calling card, which identified him as Yasuo Tanaka and stated that he was a reporter for a leading newspaper. He then said: "I happened to hear that your organization closed down, and I wanted to get the exact information. It must be a terrible blow for you. I'm very sorry to hear of it. Now, I would like to know the number of your depositors and the amount of your liabilities."

Obviously well-versed in his trade, the reporter asked a string of questions that covered all essential points. He was clearly in a hurry to make his deadline, however; and this gave Yamamoto a hint as to the best way to treat the situation. He realized that he must try to gain time. He had to talk the matter over at some length and prevent the reporter from going away with hastily gathered, hence inaccurate, information. Caution and discretion were of the greatest importance.

"Well, Mr. Tanaka, I believe the liabilities come to a considerable amount. But I don't have reliable figures to give you. After all, we only ceased operation yesterday."

"Yes, I see," said the reporter with an understanding air. His next question, however, betrayed what he was really after: "Of course I do want accurate figures; but since you say you don't have them now, why not give me just a rough estimate of your financial situation? I'm sure you won't be too far off."

But Yamamoto was not to be taken in by this. "Newspapers are most concerned with accuracy, aren't they?" he asked.

"Right, but you say you don't have accurate figures. That means I have to use what I can get. As you probably know, I'm pressed for time. So just let me have your estimates. After all, I'm not going to write anything bad about your company."

"I hope not. But tell me something. How did you find out so fast? No other newspapermen have been to see us yet. You must have a pretty good ear for news. Let me in on your secret. You know, I always wanted to be a newspaper reporter. And I admire people who are first with information."

The reporter, who was always happy to tell about his skill at his job, began explaining how he had managed to get this scoop and then went on to tell a number of stories about past successes. When he looked at his wristwatch next, it was already too late for his deadline. With an exclamation of disgust, Tanaka asked if he could use the telephone. When he returned from calling his office to say that the story was off for that day, he asked if he might call back the next day to get the detailed information from the executive director of the company.

Feeling that sincerity would be the best approach with this pleasant but garrulous man, Yamamoto said: "Look, we are confident that we can save our depositors and creditors from inconvenience and damage if we have the time to complete the measures we have already started. But an untruthful or biased newspaper article about our company might ruin everything. We welcome fair coverage. And if you promise to give the facts in a truthful way, I will provide you with accurate materials."

"OK, but promise not to give the information to any other newspaper."

"I give my word if you give me your word to write a factual and truthful account."

"You can count on me. I believe in social justice, too."

The reporter relaxed as soon as he was convinced that his

scoop was safe. Yamamoto, who felt better because he had prevented the publication of a hasty and possibly misleading article, arranged for a meeting between the reporter and Toda. He selected a coffee shop as the scene of the interview to make it as inconspicuous as possible. Even after the meeting was arranged, however, the reporter stayed around the office asking questions and listening casually to telephone conversations. Yamamoto filled him in on the personality and activities of Josei Toda, and the information aroused the reporter's interest and curiosity.

On the following day, at eleven in the morning, Toda and Yamamoto, bearing a large sheaf of documents, arrived at the nearly empty coffee shop, where Tanaka was already waiting for them. After he went through the documents, Tanaka asked several probing questions to which Toda gave open and manifestly honest replies. Toda's forthright attitude impressed the reporter. When the explanations had been made, Tanaka said: "With the amount of uncollected outstanding loans you have, you could easily cover your debts if you could call in your money."

"Yes," replied Toda, "but right now we can't call it in. We need time. We want to protect all our depositors. That's why we asked the Ministry of Finance to allow us to merge with another company. But instead of helping us find a partner, they ordered us to close down. The decision was unexpected and has caused a great deal of confusion."

The surprised reporter said: "But that's a coldblooded way to treat you, especially after you had already turned yourselves in."

"Turned ourselves in? That's not exactly the way I'd put it," Toda said with a wry smile. The reporter laughed slightly at Toda's reaction, and this gave Yamamoto a chance to say what was on his mind: "The problem is this. The true facts about our ability to repay in time and about the order from

the Ministry of Finance are unknown. An irresponsible newspaper article at this point would cause our creditors to panic
and rush on us. It could also give the people who owe us money
an excuse for not repaying. If these two things happen, we will
have no way of settling with our depositors. This is what we

must prevent because, as I have said, if we are given a little
more time we can settle accounts without causing anyone trouble. Our firm would not have been ordered to suspend operations if we had not—as you put it—turned ourselves in. Even
if the Ministry of Finance had someday got around to issuing
such an order, it would have come much later. Since we've been
working on liquidation for the past two months, by the time
the order was handed down, we would already have settled
everything."

"I see," the reporter said in a low voice.

Yamamoto decided that plain language was in order: "It

never rains, but it pours, as the saying goes. And if you write us up now, you'll spoil everything we have been trying to do. We'll be branded as swindlers, when in fact we're doing everything in our power to make sure that none of our depositors takes any loss at all. As you can see, we are in a very delicate position. Now, of course I wouldn't do anything to limit the freedom of the press. But if you could hold off on your story for two or three months, until we have settled our problems—"

Yamamoto was too proud to plead. He merely put the facts to the reporter, made a straightforward request, and left the matter in the other man's hands. The reporter listened with his head tilted to one side. Perhaps he was thinking about matters of the freedom and influence of the press. Perhaps, having seen that his scoop could bring disaster to many people, he regretted that he had become so involved in this story. After a while he said: "You put me on the spot. This story could do me a lot of good at the office."

At last Toda put in a few words: "You are in a position to destroy or to save those of us connected with the credit cooperative. Of course, the decision is yours, but please remember that our fate depends on you."

"Well, it hurts to give up a good story. The news value will drop if I wait to publish, but that can't be helped. All right, you let me know when I can release the story."

Yamamoto smiled as he said: "You make us very happy. This will give us time to fulfill our obligations. As soon as we have done that I promise we'll let you know."

Toda said nothing, but stared up at the ceiling as he puffed on a cigarette. Then the three men left the coffee shop. After parting with the reporter, Toda and Yamamoto began to walk along the street. It was already noon on a very hot, sultry day. The sky was overcast. It would probably rain soon. For a few minutes neither said anything. Yamamoto was relieved that near disaster had been averted by the postponement of the article. Before long, Toda said: "Shin'ichi, newspapers are very influential. I admit they can be a nuisance, but they can be useful too. I wonder if Soka Gakkai ought not to start a newspaper in the near future. Think about it."

As the two hailed a taxi and started for the offices in Kanda, Yamamoto gave some serious thought to the idea of a Soka Gakkai newspaper. Without doubt, general financial conditions at that time gave little encouragement for the kind of expansion needed to undertake such a project. Still the idea was not all that farfetched.

When the two men reached their destination, Toda went directly to a small Japanese-style room on the mezzanine level, where Yoshizo Mishima, a director of Soka Gakkai, had been waiting for him. Yamamoto, who remained downstairs, did not know what the topic of the conversation was, but he was puzzled and disturbed by the great length of time the men spent shut in the upstairs room. In fact, the talk continued so long that it was necessary for one of the office girls to go to a nearby restaurant and to bring in something for dinner. When she left the Japanese-style room, the girl announced in a low voice that whatever Toda and Mishima were talking about must be very serious because they both wore intent expressions.

Soon it was six in the evening and time for the regular lecture on the Lotus Sutra. Among the large group gathered for the meeting were numerous young men and women who kept up an animated and cheerful discussion of passages in the sutra and of other issues related to their religion. The mood in the second-floor meeting room contrasted sharply with the quiet of the mezzanine room, where Toda and Mishima were still in conference. After a few minutes, however, both men came into the meeting room; and Toda began another of his witty, yet profoundly moving, discussions of the sacred text. The lecture ended at eight o'clock; and as the members of the group began gathering their notebooks and materials, Toda said in a calm, strong voice: "Would you mind waiting for a few minutes more? I have an announcement to make."

The group settled themselves again to hear what Toda had to say.

"Although the state of the Toko Credit Cooperative is in no way directly related to you or to these meetings, I must tell you that, as of yesterday, we have closed down our organization. And after giving the matter a great deal of thought, I have decided that in light of many important issues it would be better if I resigned from my post as director general of the society."

Shock registered on the faces of everyone present. Toda continued: "I have asked Mr. Mishima to take over my duties. I trust that you will show him the same kind of support that you have always given me.

"Of course, my resignation does not indicate any change in my faith or in my determination to work with utmost strength for the universal propagation of Nichiren Daishonin's Buddhism. No matter what I do, no matter what happens to me, Soka Gakkai will go on because it is under the absolute protection of the Dai-Gohonzon. For that reason, my resignation should not cause you to be disturbed.

"But I want you to know that I am taking this step as a result of a deep resolution in my own heart. Anyone who casts doubt on my move or who criticizes or attempts to take unfair advantage of it will make himself an enemy of Buddhism. Each of you must carefully understand this and must strive not to commit indiscretions connected with the step I am taking. Now let me present Mr. Mishima to you, and let me ask that, under his leadership, you and the rest of Soka Gakkai continue to strive for the attainment of our great goal."

The faces of Izumida, Harayama, Konishi, and other staff members of the organization revealed the greatest perplexity. Katsu Kiyohara was openly in tears. Everyone was too disturbed and too bewildered to pay much attention to Mishima's words. Although Toda had asked them to understand his action and not to be upset by it, they could not resign themselves to the idea of Soka Gakkai without their leader. Toda's resignation would drain the society of its major strength.

When Mishima concluded his brief remarks, everyone was still too shocked to ask questions. As the meeting broke up, several people whispered among themselves expressing their concern. Mishima himself was not the least upset because Toda had virtually forced him to assume a position that he did not want. Toda stepped quickly into the Japanese-style room on the mezzanine and shut the door.

Like most of Toda's other close disciples, Shin'ichi Yamamoto felt that Soka Gakkai without Toda would lack all of its spirit and vitality. For him, Toda was Soka Gakkai. Still, what Toda had said about taking this step because of a deep resolution in his heart gave young Yamamoto a measure of hope. Nonetheless, one very important doubt was upsetting him; and as soon as he could, he slipped away from the group gathered around Mishima and followed Toda into the small room. Toda smiled gently upon seeing Yamamoto's gloomy face and asked him in a soft voice: "What's the matter Shin'-ichi?"

For a moment Yamamoto said nothing; then kneeling on the tatami in front of Toda he asked: "Now that Mr. Mishima is the director of the society, will he become my personal teacher and leader as well?"

"No, of course not," said Toda quickly. "I will remain with you as long as you need me, though I seem to bring you nothing but trouble."

In these simple words, Toda gave Yamamoto the answer he had longed for with all his being. In the heart of the innocent young man there opened a happiness that was like a light in a dark sea of misery or a spring of cool water in a desert. The collapse of the publishing company and of the credit coopera-

tive, even the resignation from the post of director of Soka
Gakkai, could be tolerated as long as Toda remained his teacher. Though he seemed relaxed and carefree, Toda too had
moist eyes when he asked: "Is anything else troubling you?"

"No," replied Yamamoto with a smile. "Everything's all
right, now." Rising and bowing to Toda, Yamamoto left the
room. Downstairs, he put on his tattered shoes and, with
bounding, joyous strides, went out into the warm night. He
whistled a favorite tune as he told himself over and over again:
"He will be my teacher for all of my life. That is all I need to
know." Three years had passed since Shin'ichi Yamamoto had
become a believer in Nichiren Shoshu.

Toda had known for some time that he might have to resign
from his post in Soka Gakkai; and he had been fully prepared
to do so, though he had not thought the necessity would arise
as quickly as it did. But after he met the newspaper reporter
in the coffee shop, he saw that there could be no postponing
this decisive step. True, he and Yamamoto had managed to
convince one newspaperman to wait, but there were other
newspapers, many of which would almost certainly get wind
of the credit cooperative's failure and be hot in pursuit of Toda
for information. Furthermore, now that the government—in
the form of the Ministry of Finance—had intervened, there was
no way to know how the situation would develop.

Toda's most serious worry was connected with his fear that
the news of his financial troubles would reflect discredit on
Soka Gakkai. He was prepared to take the blame for the business collapse, but he could not see the good name of the society
damaged as a result. Consequently, when he realized that the
outbreak of news coverage of the business failure and of possible
disparagement of Soka Gakkai because of its connections with
him were probably only matters of time, he decided that he
must resign at once. He knew that his followers would be grieved
by his action, but the honor of the society outweighed all other
considerations.

In spite of his resignation from Soka Gakkai, Toda had an immense amount of hard work to do in concluding the liquidation of the affairs of the credit cooperative. Each day he sent his office staff out to negotiate with creditors and to attempt to make them understand that Toda was sincerely committed to the repayment of all his debts. Negotiations and protestations of sincerity, however, usually failed to produce results. The office personnel had to make trip after trip to discuss each small point. The work was so exhausting physically and emotionally that before long most of the old office members had given up and left Toda. Shin'ichi Yamamoto, of course, remained by his teacher's side with a few of the most faithful workers. As the staff grew smaller, the workload for the remaining people became heavier.

At about ten o'clock one Saturday night, Yamamoto returned to the office after a gruelling day of largely fruitless talks and negotiations. His back ached and there was the old nagging tubercular pain in his chest. The downstairs office was deserted when he arrived, but Toda was upstairs in the meeting room waiting for him to return.

"Well, it's been a hard day. I'm sorry to be late. Where's everybody?" asked Yamamoto.

"They all had a rough day too, so I sent them home early. How did your work go?"

Yamamoto's description of his failures, combined with what Toda had heard from everyone else in the office, convinced him that sincerity alone was insufficient to convince creditors that they ought to wait until Toda had a chance to pay back what he owed. Some other strategy was needed, and it was this that he and Yamamoto sat discussing until much later that night. At about one in the morning, they decided to go home. Yamamoto saw Toda to his house. Ikue, Toda's wife, was waiting on the porch and invited Yamamoto to come in.

"Thank you so much for working so late, Shin'ichi," she said as the three entered the house.

"Come on up, Shin'ichi," said Toda as he mounted the steps to his upstairs study. "It's long past midnight, but let's perform our midnight Gongyo together."

The two men knelt in front of the family altar and chanted the Daimoku in unison until they felt refreshed and invigorated. Presently Ikue came in with a bottle of sakè for her husband and a soft drink for Yamamoto. As she filled the sakè cup and the glass, she asked: "How did work go today?"

"Not so well, I'm afraid," replied Toda. "But don't worry. Fretting won't help. Why don't you go on to bed now? Shin'ichi and I are going to play a quiet game of *shogi*. How about it Shin'ichi?"

"Oh, but it's so late," said Ikue with a frown of disapproval.

"No, you go to bed. I'll be along in a while. We both have to work tomorrow, but tonight we need the relaxation of a couple of games. Shin'ichi, bring the board."

With childish excitement in his heart, Yamamoto brought the Japanese-chess board from the alcove, and the two men began arranging the *shogi* pieces. Resigned, but not pleased, Ikue left the room for bed. Soon Toda and Yamamoto were halfway through a game. In spite of the fact that all of Toda's days were agonizing rounds of exhausting and often futile work, here he sat late at night serene and deeply absorbed in a game. It seemed to Yamamoto that this calm must be Toda's true self, while the hectic turmoil of daily work was only an illusion. "If that is true," thought Yamamoto, "I must preserve my own calm just as he does."

Yamamoto had become too absorbed in his thoughts to pay complete attention to the game, and Toda won easily. But during the second game, both men were intent. Yamamoto won by a very close margin. When the second game was over, they were too tired to go on. Saying good night to Toda, Yamamoto went downstairs to sleep in the room with Toda's son, Kyoichi.

During their late breakfast the following morning, Yamamoto noticed that by daylight Mrs. Toda looked very haggard
and worried. At first, Toda sat drinking his tea in a relaxed
fashion, but gradually he became irritated with his wife for
her glumness.

"Ikue, stop worrying, I tell you. It will not do us any good."

"I know, but I can't help it."

"Look, I've had hard times before, and I've always managed
to make a comeback. A business failure or two doesn't mean
that everything's over. From now on I've got a very important
job to do. All you will do by worrying is ruin your own health.
Don't give up on me so easily."

"I'm not giving up. But you made all those other comebacks
when you were young."

"Well, I'm only fifty now. That's the time in life when a

businessman is just getting mellow. Stop talking like an old woman."

Toda realized that he ought to be more understanding of his wife, and this very realization ruffled his spirits all the more. Without making amends, he and Yamamoto left for a busy, if less than entirely productive, Sunday at the office.

It was ironic that just as Toda's firm reached the lowest point in its fortunes the Japanese economy in general was beginning to experience an upsurge as a result of the boost supplied by the needs of the military forces fighting in Korea. On the surface of things, it might seem that Toda could have made a success of his credit business if he had managed to hold out for a few months until the Korean war had given new impetus to the Japanese economy. But in Toda's eyes, this was impossible. He could not profit by the tragedy of the people of Korea.

When he thought of the strange fate of the Korean people, caught between rival Eastern and Western powers, he felt only profound compassion. Korea at that time lacked true Buddhism and was suffering in the darkness of the Latter Day of the Law. Toda saw all too clearly that something must be done to bring that true Buddhism to the Japanese as quickly as possible for two reasons. First, without the saving strength of a true faith, the Japanese might be forced to undergo a tragic fate like that of the Koreans. Second, as soon as the true Buddhism is established firmly in Japan, it will travel westward to bring light to Korea just as, many centuries ago, the Buddhism of Sakyamuni moved from west to east to illuminate China, Korea, and finally Japan. Helping to bring true Buddhism to Japan and then to the world was Toda's true mission. The financial failure of the credit cooperative was a secondary matter. It was a bitter dose that Toda had to take before he could sense to the fullest the immensity of his great task of bringing to benighted mankind the light of salvation.

6. A COLD AUTUMN

TODA FOUND himself attacked from all sides. At the height of the trouble, almost all the creditors of the Toko Credit Cooperative refused to trust him. They wanted their money back at once and were prepared to go to any lengths to get it. Some of them hired unscrupulous lawyers to try to force Toda to pay, even though he did not have the money. Others threatened to take the matter to the Ministry of Finance. Often, creditors intruded on the privacy of Toda's home. Though he would not discuss matters with them there, he always agreed to talk as long as necessary if the creditors would go with him to his office. Sometimes, as he led them from his home to Kanda, where the company was located, he was forced to submit to the embarrassment of derogatory comments about his financial dealings uttered in voices loud enough for all the neighbors to hear.

Toda was fully prepared to withstand this barrage of abuse. Regarding the failure of the business as his own responsibility, he wanted to return everyone's money as quickly as possible. He and Shin'ichi Yamamoto worked very hard trying to convince creditors to wait. After a while, they achieved a certain degree of success. Some people signed contracts stating that they would not press for immediate payment if Toda would accept personal responsibility. All of this was extremely painful to Toda, but it was not the main cause of his worry.

Financial damages suffered by believers in Nichiren Shoshu naturally struck home most bitterly in his mind for an important reason. The small number of such people who had invested in his company of their own free will were shocked when the credit cooperative failed. They mistakenly believed that they were being victimized by the man who was the leader of the lay society of Nichiren Shoshu. Some of them, in doubting Toda, entertained questions about the power of the Gohonzon itself. Even worse, a fraction of them abandoned their faith in Nichiren Shoshu because of the financial crisis of Toda's company. Word of such cases grieved Toda deeply because he knew that in giving up faith in true Buddhism, they were shutting the door on the sole way to happiness.

Still other people fell into even greater danger because of the collapse of the Toko Credit Cooperative. This was a very small group of individuals who whispered maliciously about Toda and the company to new Nichiren Shoshu believers who were totally unconnected with the issue. These backbiting people attempted to stir up trouble within the society itself. Knowing that in Buddhist doctrine this kind of treachery— called *hawagoso,* or disturbing the unity of believers—is one of the five cardinal sins, Toda prayed fervently to the Gohonzon for the protection and enlightenment of people foolish enough to commit such a wicked act.

The fact is that Toda's business failure and Nichiren Shoshu were two entirely separate things. It obviously hurt him to know that some people, by trying to establish a connection between the two, cast aspersions on the true faith. It was especially unfair of the faultfinding minority to use Toda's business troubles to accuse him of harming the faith and Soka Gakkai when the amount of good he had done for both was immense.

Of course, anyone who finds salvation does so through the grace and power of the Dai-Gohonzon. Still, without the guidance and care of Josei Toda, thousands of unhappy people would never have been brought to the saving light because they would never have heard of its existence.

The mental anguish of his situation impaired Toda's health. Though the heat of the summer had passed and the nights were cool, he broke out in feverish sweats. In the morning, as she took up the Japanese-style bedding, his wife, Ikue, often found large sweat-drenched spots on the sheets. Longing to help, she knew in her heart that she was powerless to be of any assistance; and she kept her sorrow to herself.

Yamamoto too noticed his teacher's physical weakness, but to his surprise, Toda was more concerned about the conditions of others than about his own health. For instance, Yamamoto was especially moved once when a worn, haggard Toda said to him: "Shin'ichi, what is the matter with you? You look as pale as a ghost. Come here. We'll perform Gongyo services together so that you'll recover some of the strength you'll need if we're ever going to find our way out of our troubles." Unmindful of his own physical weakness, Toda applied all the great strength of his soul to prayers for the health and strength of his beloved disciple. Yamamoto could hardly hold back his tears.

Still profoundly moved by the experience, when Yamamoto returned to his room that night he wrote a poem:

> "Still serving an old and mystic fate,
> Though others change,
> I alter not."

Before going to sleep, Yamamoto made a clean copy of the poem. Folding it carefully, he put it in the breast pocket of his coat. At the office on the following morning, after exchanging greetings and expressions of concern over each other's health, Yamamoto shyly handed the poem to Toda. For a few minutes after he read it, Toda looked severe, but then he burst into a smile as he said: "All right, I'll write a poem in reply to yours. Give me a piece of paper." Toda thought for a few minutes, then with bold strokes of the pen wrote:

> "Whenever I stand on fields of war,
> Unfailing at my side,
> You are my sword."

Handing the poem to Yamamoto, Toda said: "There, that's for you." As the overjoyed Yamamoto reached out to take the paper Toda stopped him. "Wait, I have another poem to go with that." He quickly added:

> "Fading, failing,
> At death, I the king leave to you
> My crown."

Satisfied at last, Toda remarked: "Now, that should about say it," as a look of mingled sadness and joy came over his face. Barely able to murmur his thanks for the emotion welling up inside him, Yamamoto looked up to find Toda's affectionate, merciful eyes gazing into his with penetrating brilliance that seemed to enter the young man's heart to remain forever. Though two physical bodies, the older and the younger man were one eternal life force.

Even after Toda's resignation as director general, the course of Soka Gakkai activities continued much as before. Discussion meetings were held as usual, and Mishima was taking over the three weekly lectures on the Lotus Sutra. New converts continued to be made in steadily increasing numbers. Toda attended as many society functions as his schedule allowed.

But the small number of members who tried to take advantage of the failure of his business did not cease their undermining activities. For instance, in a town on the Izu Peninsula there was a man who had invested in the Toko Credit Cooperative. As a result of this business connection, he heard about Soka Gakkai and later joined Nichiren Shoshu. When he got wind of the failure of Toda's company, he immediately took severe measures to try to get his money. Failing in this, he set out to incite other society members to make personal attacks on Toda's character. The sixty families who made up the Soka Gakkai membership in the town were naive and easily deluded. The agitator therefore had little trouble convincing most of them that Soka Gakkai was dishonest and deceitful.

Many local members were on the verge of withdrawing from the organization when Ume Iida and Kiyo Yamanishi, the two women who were the driving force in the chapter, reported the situation to the headquarters in Tokyo. As it turned out, Katsu Kiyohara was in charge of the Izu district. Upon hearing of the crisis, she hurried to Izu and called a discussion meeting. In spite of the very short notice on which the meeting was called, attendance was large; but most of the people present were glum and manifestly distrustful. Miss Kiyohara sensed the air of suspicion in the room and realized at once that great care was required in dealing with the situation.

"Well, ladies and gentlemen," she began, "I know what you have on your minds. I have already heard something about your problems. But I should like to ask what you think would happen if the suspicions you are entertaining in your hearts right now should be wrong in terms of the Buddhism of Nichiren Daishonin. Because Buddhism is a demanding religion, basic errors in connection with it cause you to forfeit your claims to happiness."

Someone in the room spoke up: "We're not going back on

our faith. We believe in Nichiren Shoshu. Only we don't want to have anything to do with Soka Gakkai. After all, who wants to get cheated?"

"What do you mean?" retorted Miss Kiyohara. "When did anyone in Soka Gakkai ever cheat any of you?"

"Well, look at Josei Toda and the credit union that folded and left lots of people without their money. Any organization headed by a man like that can't be trustworthy."

Miss Kiyohara then refuted everything they had to say about Toda. She explained that his activities and his religious work with Soka Gakkai were two entirely different things. She also made it clear that if they unjustly criticized the lay organization devoted to the Buddhism of Nichiren Daishonin they would be committing one of the cardinal sins: slandering true Buddhism. Finally, after carefully showing that Toda's business failure in no way affected the reputation of Soka Gakkai, she warned them not to stray from the path of happiness by abandoning the society. She then cited a number of testimonials in substantiation of her argument and said she would be happy to answer all questions that people might put to her.

The audience, however, was unconvinced and insisted that they were going to leave Soka Gakkai and form their own lay society in association with Nichiren Shoshu. The volatile but now bitterly disappointed Miss Kiyohara closed the meeting by repeating her conviction that they would be wrong to follow such a course. She added: "True Buddhism is always victorious. You'll see before long whether I am right or wrong. And I'll tell you one thing: if you prove me mistaken, Mrs. Iida here and I will walk up the main street of this town on our hands." Everyone in the room greeted Miss Kiyohara's bravado with derision.

Before much time had passed, the Izu group did break away from Soka Gakkai. Only Mrs. Iida and Mrs. Yamanishi remained faithful, but with Miss Kiyohara's help they soon launched new and successful membership campaigns. Fortunately few incidents of this kind occurred in the provinces, but one even less savory case took place in Tokyo.

In the prewar days, Juro Horibe, then a prosperous lumber dealer in Tokyo, had been a prominent leader of a misguided religious order. After the war, when he was suffering a business recession, he abandoned his old religion and cast about for a new one that showed more signs of being financially advantageous. In 1947, he decided that Soka Gakkai fitted the bill and joined. Horibe was a plump man of jovial appearance, but in fact he was arrogant and vain. During his early years with Soka Gakkai, he treated the leaders of the organization with scorn. As they assisted him and tried to lead him to a more wholesome attitude, however, he seemed to turn over a new leaf. Almost as soon as he became aware of the severe discipline demanded by true Buddhism, his business started to thrive.

Of course Horibe was overjoyed at his return to good fortune, but he was not strong enough to cope with success. Soon he began to despise the many poor people in the organization. This and his conceited belief that he had attained true enlightenment—when he was far from it—irritated Toda to the extent that one day he could no longer hold his temper in check and burst out: "How can I entrust the sacred Gohonzon to a man like you? Return your Gohonzon to the temple at once."

Toda's reproach subdued Horibe for a while. Consumed with ambition to be elected a member of the Soka Gakkai executive staff, he hesitated to show his true nature for fear that it would hamper him in attaining his goal. But his innate arrogance remained with him and ultimately poisoned his faith.

In the fall of 1950, as Toda was being criticized from all quarters, Horibe saw a chance to organize an anti-Toda faction. Since he did not seem to stand a chance of being elected to a leading position in Soka Gakkai, he convinced a number of members to break with the society, establish a new organization, and place him in the top office. Horibe insisted that Soka Gakkai was only one possible lay organization for Nichiren Shoshu and that other similar organizations would be completely valid. But only a few years later, Horibe realized that in revolting against Toda he was revolting against Nichiren Daishonin. Three years after he set up the new lay organization, Horibe's lumber business went bankrupt under most puzzling circumstances.

Toward the end of October, 1950, Toda made a pilgrimage to Taiseki-ji. Arriving in the evening with a group of his disciples, he had dinner and conducted prayer services and discussions. When time came for the late Ushitora Gongyo, Toda went to the Kyakuden with his group. After the service was over, however, he went alone to the Treasure Temple. Wrapped in darkness and surrounded by a grove of shadowy cedars, the Treasure Temple was strangely magnificent in the crisp fall night. Disregarding his weakened physical condition, Toda knelt on the hard, chill stone pavement and began chanting the Daimoku in an even, modulated voice that rang in the night with the strength of steel. Neither the chilly night air nor the numbness in his legs caused by the cold stones on which he knelt affected him. He had come before the abode of the Dai-Gohonzon in a spirit of penitence and confession. He was sweating slightly.

During the five years that had passed since the end of World War II, he had been unable to establish a foundation for the universal propagation of true Buddhism. The structure of Soka Gakkai was still far from stable. Where had he failed? What were the reasons? One by one he sifted through the major events of the postwar period in an attempt to find answers to these tormenting questions.

One of the first important things he had done in 1946 was to institute the lecture course on the Lotus Sutra. This, he felt sure, had been the correct step to take, because during the war many believers in Nichiren Shoshu had allowed their faith to weaken simply because they had insufficient knowledge of the Myoho. Further reflection on his lecture course, however, showed where he had been mistaken.

Tsunesaburo Makiguchi had attempted to explain the meaning of the Buddhism of Nichiren Daishonin by means of the

philosophy of value. Toda, on the other hand, saw that the Daishonin's Buddhism is boundless and cannot be contained within a limited philosophy of any kind. Because he felt this way, he abandoned Makiguchi's philosophy of value and tried to bring his followers to a direct understanding of the teachings of Nichiren Daishonin. But he quickly found that his task was difficult.

At the outset, he had attempted to teach the Lotus Sutra on the basis of the Daishonin's *Ongi Kuden,* but his students found this too difficult. He then tried approaching the sutra from the standpoint of a distinguished commentary called the *Mo-ho-chih-kuan* of T'ien-t'ai. Toda found that this method met with greater success. He therefore elected to follow what seemed the path of least resistance and to use the *Mo-ho-chih-kuan*—which gives greater weight to the T'ien-t'ai interpretation—because he felt that speed was imperative. Now, however, having experienced divine retribution for choosing something other than Nichiren Daishonin's approach to the Lotus Sutra, he saw that he had been wrong. He had been obliged to adhere strictly to the *Ongi Kuden,* but he had not done so.

Even worse, Toda felt that his culpability grew immeasurably in light of the result of his error. Because he had not laid a stronger foundation for universal propagation of true Buddhism, hundreds of thousands of people had been led astray by all kinds of misguided—even dishonest—religious organizations in the past five postwar years. When he realized that he had been responsible for this immense misery, he saw clearly that he deserved death for his remissness.

Moreover, he now understood that the weaknesses and shortcomings of the Soka Gakkai organization itself stemmed to a large extent from his refusal to accept the presidency of the society, in spite of his awareness of his great religious mission. There had, in fact, been no president of Soka Gakkai for over six years; that is, not since the death of Tsunesaburo Makiguchi. Toda had hesitated to fill the position because of the great responsibility it entails. Due to his indolence in this respect, millions of people were suffering misery and misfortune. Failing to perceive the saving light of Nichiren Shoshu, they still labored in the darkness of wrong religion.

Aside from his reluctance to shoulder the responsibility of the presidency, Toda had hesitated to assume the position because, as a businessman, he believed that in a capitalist society monetary success was essential to progress in any field. He had concentrated first on business affairs and had allowed his religious activities to take second place. But it suddenly became apparent to him that he ought to have reversed his precedences: economic success is dependent on the individual's devotion to the achievement of the goal of universal propagation of the true faith.

In spite of the chill night, Toda was burning with fierce new resolution. Still kneeling on the stone pavement in front of the Treasure Temple, he vowed that no matter what hardships he might have to face he would overcome his present crisis. He realized then that he must prove the righteousness of Nichiren Daishonin's teachings. In humility and with renewed devotion, he prayed that the Dai-Gohonzon would forgive him if it considered him qualified for the accomplishment of the great mission that had been laid on his shoulders.

For a while, Toda continued to stare at the door of the temple building as he chanted the Daimoku with his whole body and spirit. Then he heard birds singing. Day was beginning to break over the wooded foothills.

The strain on Toda caused by the collapse of his business enterprises was both mental and financial. Because he insisted on doing everything possible to keep those few employees who stayed with him fed and housed and because he made maximum efforts to pay back whatever he could of the debts incurred by the company, Toda's personal finances began to suffer seriously. He had to economize on everything, including the cigarettes of which he was very fond. Finally, the situation became so grave that his wife, Ikue, had to go to work.

It is true that during his dark hours, many people turned against him. But he had more friends in all walks of life than he had enemies. Aside from the people who had come to know him intimately as a result of religious activities, there were numerous friends who had been captivated by his warmth and charm since his youth. Upon hearing of Toda's business failure, some of these friends were extremely upset. Hoping to help him, they offered a great deal of advice, including the recommendation that he start another business in order to make a living.

After serious reflection, Toda agreed that it would be neces-sary to ensure his family a reliable income. He was still deter-mined to devote his life primarily to religious activities, but he saw that practical needs too must be satisfied. Consequently, he agreed to undertake the establishment of a small finance company of which he would be the adviser. An old friend of his who had experience in business and politics was to be the president. Preparations for founding the company got under way very quickly, though many snares were encountered be-fore it could actually start operating.

Friends and disciples among the membership of Soka Gakkai were of course distressed by Toda's predicament, although he kept matters so quiet that it was not until the middle of fall that the general membership knew just how bad his situation was. For instance, Mrs. Hatsu Chitani, who had played an important part in resolving the quarrel between Soka Gakkai members and a group of unemployed Korean workers a few months earlier, long remained ignorant of Toda's dilemma. She nonetheless noticed that he was looking thinner than usual and that he had almost entirely given up cigarettes.

Becoming alarmed by Toda's appearance, she asked a senior member of the Women's Division what was wrong and learned about the business failure and its disastrous aftermath. Sud-denly Mrs. Chitani was overcome with sympathy and stricken with remorse at not having found out sooner so that she could take steps to help the man to whom she felt deeply indebted. She decided that the least she could do was to give Toda money to buy cigarettes. The next day she went to the bank and with-drew some money, which she gave to the senior Women's Division member with whom she had spoken earlier, asking that it be passed on to Toda. Because she suspected that he would scold her for accepting charity in his name, the woman hesitated. But Mrs. Chitani was so sincere in her concern that it was impossible to refuse her gift.

When he was first approached about the present from Mrs. Chitani, Toda said at once: "I can't take it." But when he learned how concerned and earnest Mrs. Chitani was, he changed his mind: "Well, I can't take it as a gift, but since she wants to help so badly, I will borrow it. Tell her that I am grateful, but tell her to devote herself to her own religious faith and not to worry about me." Toda incorporated the money borrowed from Mrs. Chitani into the funds of the new company he was trying to get started.

Other people too tried to be of assistance. Mr. and Mrs. Katsuzo Oba, owners of a store among the fishmarkets in Tsukiji, Tokyo, had been converted to Nichiren Shoshu quite some time earlier because they hoped to find a way to help their son, who was stricken with infantile paralysis. Their faith was ardent, and Toda offered them personal guidance. But he did more than that—he paid a great deal of attention to the sick child. He bought him picture books and tried to teach him to write. As time passed, the child came to look forward eagerly to Toda's visits, which brought him pleasure and hope. Seeing the improvement he was helping to bring about in their child's condition, Mr. and Mrs. Oba gradually came to regard Toda as the mainstay of their lives. Naturally, when they learned of his unhappy state of affairs, they were determined to do what they could to assist him. Mr. Oba owned a few securities of some value. He sold them at once and gave the money to a Soka Gakkai staff member for Toda.

As had been the case when he learned of Mrs. Chitani's charitable act, Toda at first refused the gift. Later he accepted it—as a loan—because of the generosity and spontaneity of the people making it. This time, too, he put the money into the funds for the new company. He never forgot the goodness of people who had helped him when he was in trouble; and later when he was able to do so, he repaid all these loans with interest.

Toda did not, however, accept all offers of help. He was

especially cautious about taking money from Soka Gakkai members because he could not risk damaging the honor of the organization. He would borrow money when it was spontaneously and warmheartedly offered by individuals, like Mrs. Chitani and the Obas, but he would not accept anything that came from a group. For instance, he turned down financial assistance offered by three of his closest disciples when they banded together to pool parts of their own salaries to guarantee Toda an income.

One day when Toda was resting in bed because of a severe fever, Konishi, Harayama, and Miss Kiyohara called on him to explain their decision to establish a fund for him. Upon hearing the proposal, Toda sat up in bed and shouted angrily: "What do you mean? When did I teach you to do things like this? How dare you treat me this way? I'm surprised to see that you are so foolish. My livelihood is my own business, and I don't need to be looked after by you. I leave everything to the Gohonzon. Don't you understand? Now leave me alone." Kiyohara, Harayama, and Konishi were so dumbfounded by Toda's outburst that they left without another word. As they walked quietly and shyly out the door, Toda turned his back to them. Then, as the three abashed people started down the staircase, they heard his voice calling out, no longer angry: "You look after the other members. Don't worry about me."

It was not lack of appreciation for good will and kindness that prompted Toda to turn down their offer so brusquely. He had his own very good reasons. First, when offers of this kind come from a group instead of from individuals they cannot be completely spontaneous. The opinions of one or more members of the group are bound to influence the others to the extent that they will go along with an undertaking with which they are perhaps not in complete agreement. Toda was resolved to accept kindness only when he was certain that it was inspired by a spontaneous desire to help. Then, too, he was afraid that the attempts of Kiyohara, Harayama, and Konishi might develop into a movement throughout the entire Soka Gakkai. He could not permit this because he could not countenance the use of the organization for anything but purely religious purposes. Never forgetting for a single moment that his faith was the only thing that could enable him to get on his feet again, Toda drew a strict line between business and Soka Gakkai, even at the expense of his personal sentiments. More important to him than his very life was the harmonious functioning of Soka Gakkai and the assurance that its members would continue with their immense task of achieving Kosen-rufu.

Toda's failure in business brought to light the innermost feelings of many Soka Gakkai members and in this way showed who was faithful, who was indifferent, and who was only paying lip service to the ideals of the organization in hope of personal advancement. The nature of a person's faith is mirrored in his reactions to unfortunate people suffering hardships. Some of the believers in Nichiren Shoshu betrayed Toda or estranged themselves from him; these were the ones whose faith was too weak to stand trial. Others were wishywashy in their beliefs and manifested their weakness by either trying to stay neutral on the subject of Toda's troubles or pretending knowledge as they criticized him behind his back. Many believers earnestly prayed for Toda's recovery, but only a small handful dedicated themselves wholeheartedly to helping him through his trials. Shin'ichi Yamamoto was one of the few, for by this time the relationship between him and his teacher and spiritual guide had become closer than ever. As teacher and disciple, the two were inseparable.

On the morning of November 12, before the convening of the fifth general convention of Soka Gakkai in the auditorium of the Kanda Education Center, a memorial service was held to honor the sixth anniversary of the death of Tsunesaburo Makiguchi. Following reading of the sutra and offering of incense, several important people in Nichiren Shoshu and in Soka Gakkai made speeches. Toda was the last to take the platform, and his appearance brought a round of applause, especially from rural delegates who had missed his guidance and leadership at the summer training course at Taiseki-ji that year. He began his speech in a calm, meditative tone: "I met my teacher, Tsunesaburo Makiguchi, thirty years ago. I was twenty at the time, and he was forty-nine. Virtually from the first meeting, we grew very close to each other. As time passed, our relation increased in depth until it would have been hard for an outsider to know that we were teacher and disciple and not father and son. During our years together, my teacher suffered four periods of crisis, and I was at his side each time. The last and most trying period ended in his imprisonment and ultimately in his death."

As Toda reminisced about the trouble experienced by Maki-guchi at various times in his life, especially when he published his four-volume *Value-Creating Education Theory* and later when he was arrested by the police, Toda seemed to have his own current experiences in the back of his mind. When he recalled the final days of Makiguchi's life, there were tears in his eyes. The entire auditorium was perfectly still as he said: "I was completely crushed at the news of his death. I, too, was in prison at the time, and I could do nothing. Bitter anger filled my heart when I learned that there had been only one disciple to carry my teacher's remains to his home. None of the others among his followers would go to help. I don't know whether they were unaware of what had happened or whether they were afraid of the militarist government. But I made up my mind then that someday I would see that proper memorial services for Tsunesaburo Makiguchi were held.

"We are gathered here now to do him honor. And I want each of you to realize that he is here with us. He is immortal. His life is with us, for he has attained enlightenment. And he joins us as we, his disciples, chant the Daimoku under the leadership of the high priest."

After the noon recess, the general convention of Soka Gakkai got under way in a spirit of vitality and fulfillment. Among the items discussed in the opening reports, Toda's resignation as director general and the appointment of Mishima to take his place caused the greatest stir in the audience. Finally, following a number of other talks, Toda rose to address the assembly.

"I have served this organization for twenty-three years as director general, and it gives me immense pleasure to see that now our meetings fill this hall to capacity. I think that I ought to explain to you why I have decided to step down as director general and to ask Mr. Mishima to take my place. During the postwar period, in teaching the Lotus Sutra I have based my explanations on the Lotus as explained by Sakyamuni and have used the T'ien-t'ai *Mo-ho-chih-kuan* when I should have dealt with it exclusively from the standpoint of the writings of Nichiren Daishonin and particularly the *Ongi Kuden*. Since my mistake in selecting a teaching guide is grave, I have asked Mr. Mishima to assume the general directorship. I am certain that under his guidance the organization will continue to make great strides forward.

"At present I am not at liberty to say precisely what my future plans are, but I assure you that I have made a profound resolution in my heart. I am determined to devote my whole life to the universal propagation of the Myoho, to the future of Soka Gakkai, and to the fostering of greater faith in Nichiren Daishonin."

Testimonials and informative talks by leaders of Soka Gakkai, including Director General Mishima and Katsu Kiyohara, who had become a director of the organization, followed Toda's speech. Before the conference drew to a close, Toda was asked to take the platform a third time to make final comments. The theme of this very brief talk was the Buddha's will.

"The universal propagation of true Buddhism is the Buddha's will. In fact, if this were not so, we ordinary men would be unable to bring that propagation about. For each of us, this task is the most important possible mission. I am determined to march toward the universal spreading of our faith no matter what trials and hardships I may encounter along the way. I will strive toward that goal together with you. That is my one wish in this life."

As the autumn weather turned colder, Shin'ichi Yamamoto examined his tattered clothes and worn, thin-soled shoes with chagrin. There was no money to buy anything new. Salaries were in arrears, but he could not allow himself to complain. Now that Toda's new firm, the Daito Shoko Company, was getting started, Yamamoto had more than enough to keep him busy. The liquidation of the defunct credit cooperative was not yet completed; and the first stages of the new firm, located in an old lens factory in Hyakunin-machi, Shinjuku Ward, required intense care. Toda had officially put Yamamoto in charge of the business department—in itself too responsible a task for a young man only twenty-two—but in effect, Yamamoto was in charge of the entire operation.

Still, Yamamoto's faith in the Buddhism of Nichiren Daishonin and the help and guidance Toda gave him sustained him throughout the darkest troubles. Whenever they had a few minutes to spare, they often discussed the future of Soka Gakkai; and at such times Toda shared with Yamamoto a vision that he related to no one else. Though the organization was far from perfect at that time, Toda was convinced that it would grow into a religious lay society of great substance and power. "Buddhism will always emerge victorious," he was in the habit of saying. "Let's fight together, Shin'ichi. Life is eternal; it always manifests itself in some form in this world." He was in essence instilling in Yamamoto the knowledge that, should anything happen to Toda himself, Yamamoto must carry on with the mission.

Toda's faith in the future gave Yamamoto hope. He knew that he no longer cared anything for his poverty, for his lack of clothing, or for the hard work he had to face. With complete confidence he was able to say to himself: "Things may be hard now, but in ten or twenty years just think what Soka Gakkai is going to be! Just think what I may be!" Yamamoto was able to withstand the hardships of his life because of the strength he derived from chanting the Daimoku ten thousand times a day.

Sitting alone one December night in his small, unheated room, Yamamoto thought back on the year 1950. It had been a time of great hardships that only the Myoho could transform into good fortune. Still, he had no regrets. He knew that he had worked as hard as he could. This knowledge and the awareness of a new closeness with Toda gave him a sense of satisfaction. Toda not only had allowed Yamamoto to share his tribulations, but also had confided to him—and only to him—his vision of the future of Soka Gakkai. Yamamoto's one wish was that Toda could extricate himself from his financial troubles and devote himself fully to the march toward universal propagation of the faith. If this would only happen, Yamamoto would do anything to help.

Then Yamamoto thought about what he would do in the year to come. First of all, since he had not been as active as he should have been in the Youth Division, he resolved to spend more time on that phase of Soka Gakkai. Second, he would do more reading and if at all possible would return to his night classes at the school he had attended earlier. Partly because of his ill health and partly because of Toda's request, Yamamoto had not attended night school since autumn. But he remembered his classes and teachers with pleasure, especially Yudo Takada, the professor who had lectured in an original, zealous, and intelligent way on politics and political history. Though Takada was consumptive and frequently absent from class, he was respected and admired by all his students. Since Yamamoto had stopped attending classes there had been no chance to make advances in formal education. This worried him.

For a while, he had entertained the hope that perhaps someday Toda would help him enter a well-known university, but he had given up the idea. Working night and day on two jobs and on Soka Gakkai affairs, Yamamoto had no time for college. But Toda had not forgotten Yamamoto's education. It was only that his young associate had become indispensable to him in the new business, and the opportunity for formal schooling never presented itself. This worried Toda as much as it did Yamamoto.

Then one day Toda volunteered: "I've been thinking about your schooling, Shin'ichi. I've decided to take over your tutoring myself. Leave it all to me." Before long the two had set up a lecture and study schedule. Every Sunday was devoted to Toda's lectures on politics, economics, law, Chinese classics, chemistry, natural sciences, and other subjects. European languages were missing from the curriculum because Toda had little knowledge of them. In other fields, however, he was an excellent tutor, capturing his pupil's attention and inspiring his imagination. Soon, Sundays alone were insufficient, and it became necessary to institute brief study sessions in the mornings before work and sometimes in the afternoons when the day's tasks were over. Toda kept his strict schedule with unvarying regularity, though Yamamoto was sometimes so tired that he overslept in the morning. His eagerness to impart to his young student everything he had learned in fifty years of living suggested that Toda was in a hurry to finish this work because he was afraid that he might die any day. For his part, Yamamoto studied with absorption and attention. The minds of the two men were in perfect harmony in striving for one goal.

Though late 1950 and early 1951 was one of the most trying times in Toda's life, it was the experience of working and studying with Yamamoto that helped him pull through. Certainly, without Toda there would have been no Shin'ichi Yamamoto to take his master's place in later years. On the other hand, without Yamamoto, Toda would have been completely alone in the time of his heaviest spiritual burdens. The trials he was going through were to be the great turning point in his life, comparable to the Tatsunokuchi incident in the life of Nichiren Daishonin, when he was condemned to death by the Kamakura government and miraculously saved. Yamamoto himself was exerting a "billion eons of agonizing efforts in one moment of life," as the Daishonin said in *Ongi Kuden*.

What Toda and Yamamoto were doing at this time influenced more than their private lives. Their suffering and learning became important factors in the achievements and development of Soka Gakkai. They sowed the seeds that were to take root and bear rich fruit. Even at that time, shifts were taking place in the officer ranks of Soka Gakkai. Men of unsound faith gradually left the organization, leaving only those with unwavering conviction of the truth of Nichiren Shoshu. These were the people who would become the Bodhisattvas of the earth of the Latter Day of the Law.

As Toda gradually grew more certain that the time was ripe for him to assume the presidency of Soka Gakkai, he began to visualize clearly the thousand-mile road stretching toward the universal propagation of true Buddhism. Before too much time had passed, Toda did become the second president of Soka Gakkai. Shin'ichi Yamamoto continued to grow in faith. During these trying times, Toda and Yamamoto laid the basis for Soka Gakkai as it was to be in the future. There are two major causes of the startling development and growth in the society during Toda's presidency and following his death. Of course, the greatness of Buddhism and of Nichiren Daishonin is the first cause. The second is the fact that during a period of darkness and trouble two men were able to nurture and care for the sapling that was to grow into the great tree of Soka Gakkai.

GLOSSARY

ARHAT: A saint in Hinayana Buddhism who has learned all things and freed himself of desire and rebirths in this world. Also a Buddhist leader.

BODHISATTVA: A being aspiring to enlightenment or a future Buddha. The Bodhisattva seeks salvation for others and therefore concentrates on altruistic aims.

BODHISATTVA FUKYO: The Bodhisattva Who Does Not Disparage—discussed in the twentieth chapter of the Lotus Sutra—who does not disparage even those people whose slander of the law has earned them damnation in hell. By means of a kind of reverse karma, souls cast into hell for the unforgivable transgression of reviling the law can be born again with the Bodhisattva Fukyo. They will then come to believe in the law and ultimately attain Buddhahood. Fukyo labored to bring to humanity a twenty-four-character version of the content of the Lotus Sutra. In the Mappo era, Nichiren Daishonin exerted similar effort to give to the world the five-character essence of the Lotus Sutra, Nam-myoho-renge-kyo.

CHIH-I (538–97): Also called T'ien-t'ai the Great. A Chinese Buddhist leader and the founder of the T'ien-t'ai sect. He is considered the Buddha of the Zoho, or Middle Day of the Law.

DAI-GOHONZON: The fundamental and supreme object of worship enshrined in the *Sho-Hondo,* Grand Main Temple, of the Nichiren

Shoshu head temple. It was inscribed by Nichiren Daishonin on October 12, 1279, to save all mankind from distress and unhappiness. The Dai-Gohonzon is the embodiment both of the profound theory of the Three Great Secret Laws and of the life of the Daishonin himself.

DAIMOKU: The invocation Nam-myoho-renge-kyo, which Nichiren Shoshu believers chant in their worship of the Gohonzon. By means of this invocation it is possible for a person to draw on the life force inherent in him and thus enjoy life fully.

DENGYO THE GREAT (767–822): The founder of the Tendai sect (Japanese reading of T'ien-t'ai) in Japan. Dengyo the Great completely refuted prevalent misguided Buddhist sects in the presence of Emperor Kammu and achieved wide propagation of faith in the Lotus Sutra in the Middle Day of the Law.

DOMON-ZOJOMAN: *see* The Three Formidable Foes

THE FIVE CARDINAL SINS (Gogyakuzai): In Buddhist teachings the five cardinal sins are: patricide, matricide, killing of Arhats (or other Buddhist believers), hurting the Buddha and causing him to bleed, and disrupting the unity or harmonious organization of believers in true Buddhism. Commission of any one of these is enough to incur damnation.

THE FIVEFOLD COMPARISON (Goju-no-Sotai): Nichiren Daishonin's analysis of religions on the basis of superiority. According to this comparison, Buddhism is superior to religions that are non-Buddhist; Mahayana Buddhism is superior to Hinayana Buddhism; actual Mahayana is superior to provisional Mahayana; Hommon (the true teachings, found in the latter half of the Lotus Sutra) is superior to Shakumon (the expedient teachings, found in the first half of the Lotus Sutra); and the Buddhism of Nichiren Daishonin is superior to that of Sakyamuni.

GOHONZON: The object of worship in Nichiren Shoshu, which is bestowed upon followers, first inscribed by Nichiren Daishonin himself. Since Nichiren Daishonin's death it has been inscribed by successive high priests of Nichiren Shoshu. "Go" is an honorific prefix; "honzon" means object of worship.

GONGYO: The prayer service performed before the Gohonzon every morning and evening. During Gongyo, believers recite the Hoben and Juryo chapters of the Lotus Sutra and chant the Daimoku.

GOSHO: The complete works of Nichiren Daishonin, consisting of religious theses and letters containing guidance to his disciples. Followers of Nichiren Shoshu learn to apply the teachings of the *Gosho* to everyday life in society.

HARITI: A deity invoked for easy childbirth. Originally the mother of a vast number of children to whom she fed the babies of other women, she repented her wickedness after having heard the law from the Buddha and pledged herself to protect the believers of true Buddhism. In Japanese she is known as *Kishimo-jin*.

HIYUHON (Parable): The third chapter of the Lotus Sutra. In it, Sakyamuni explained that every living thing is the entity of the Buddha. He employed the parable of the lotus blossom, which he likened to the law of cause and effect because it contains both the flower (cause) and the seed (effect). This chapter also sets forth the dreadful punishment in store for those people who oppose true Buddhism.

ICHINEN SANZEN: The theory according to which a single momentary existence of life (ichinen) embodies the three thousand (sanzen) worlds of the greater life. T'ien-t'ai Buddhism interprets life as an entity embracing three thousand worlds. This figure is arrived at by recognizing that there are ten states of life—also called worlds—and that each state possesses within itself all ten states, hence yielding one hundred states. Moreover, all life consists of ten factors—form, nature, substance, power, function, cause, relation, effect, result, and consistency. These factors too are called worlds. Thus the one hundred states multiplied by the ten factors results in one thousand worlds. Finally, three sets of circumstances are involved in all life: circumstances related to the physical natures of manifestations of life; circumstances caused by the individual differences among those manifestations; and circumstances caused by the natures of the places in which those manifestations occur. Like the other categories, these sets of circumstances too are called worlds; therefore, the aggregate is three thousand worlds. All three thousand are inherent in a momentary existence of life.

JIPPOKAIJI (Commentary on the Ten States of Life): The work written by Nichiren Daishonin in 1259, at the age of thirty-seven, in which he explains the ranking of religions according to their superiority (*see* The Fivefold Comparison) and, on the basis of the doctrine of the ten states of life, compares the teachings of Sakyamuni prior to the Lotus Sutra, the first part of the Lotus Sutra (Shakumon), the latter part of the Lotus Sutra (Hommon), and the Lotus Sutra of Nichiren Daishonin.

KAIMOKU SHO (On Awakening to True Buddhahood): One of the ten major writings of Nichiren Daishonin. Written in February, 1272, while Nichiren Daishonin was in exile on Sado Island, it was dedicated to Shijo Kingo and other disciples. In it Nichiren Daishonin revealed that he is the True Buddha of the Latter Day of the Law.

KANGYO HACHIMAN SHO (On Admonitions Against Hachiman): The work written by Nichiren Daishonin in 1280, while at Mount Minobu, on the occasion of a fire at the Hachiman Shrine in Kamakura and the imminent threat of invasions by the Mongol hordes. In this work, Nichiren Daishonin berates the Bodhisattva Hachiman on two charges. First, he condemns him for failing the Japanese nation in time of trouble. Second, he blames Hachiman for protecting the Kamakura government even though they persecute Nichiren Daishonin, who is the True Buddha of the Latter Day of the Law. In the second part of the work, Nichiren Daishonin compares the Buddhism of Sakyamuni with the moon, in that it traveled from west to east, and Nichiren Buddhism with the sun, in that it arises in the east and is destined to travel westward through the lands of Asia.

KEJOYUHON (Parable of a Transformed Castle): The seventh chapter of the Lotus Sutra, in which Sakyamuni revealed in a parable how a group of people was enlightened to the meaning of Buddhism upon hearing of the profound relation between teacher and disciple, a relation predestined from a remote time in the infinite past.

KOSEN-RUFU: The attainment of world peace and happiness through the propagation of the spirit and teachings of true Buddhism.

THE LATTER DAY OF THE LAW (Mappo era): The age that began

two millenniums after the death of Sakyamuni and will last for eternity. In this age, mankind can enjoy true peace and happiness through worshiping the Gohonzon and devotion to the propagation of Nichiren Daishonin's philosophy of reverence for life.

LOTUS SUTRA: The next to last sutra expounded by Sakyamuni, it is his highest teaching, though the term also refers to the highest teaching of any Buddha, and its implications may vary with time. For instance, the Lotus Sutra of the Zoho, or Middle Day of the Law, is the Mo-ho-chih-kuan of T'ien-t'ai; and that of the Mappo, or Latter Day of the Law, is Nichiren Daishonin's Nam-myoho-renge-kyo, or the Gohonzon.

MAHASATTVA: A word used to designate Bodhisattvas in connection with their immense courage and earnest desire to perform merciful deeds for all mankind.

MAKIGUCHI, TSUNESABURO (1871–1944): The first president of Soka Kyoiku Gakkai. Accepting Nichiren Shoshu in 1928, he published *Value-Creating Education Theory* in 1929 and established Soka Kyoiku Gakkai in 1930. Because of his antimilitaristic stand, he was arrested and imprisoned in 1943, together with Josei Toda and other leaders of Soka Kyoiku Gakkai. He died in prison in 1944.

MO-HO-CHIH-KUAN (The Book of the Great Enlightenment): This work, called *Maka Shikan* in Japanese, is a compilation of the oral teachings of Chih-i. In it Chih-i sets forth the doctrine that a momentary existence comprises all of the three thousand worlds of life (*see* Ichinen Sanzen). So important was Mo-ho-chih-kuan that it is called the Lotus Sutra of the Middle Day of the Law.

MYOHO: Literally, "the supreme or mystic law," this term is sometimes synonymous with Nam-myoho-renge-kyo.

NAM-MYOHO-RENGE-KYO: Literally, "Devotion to the Wonderful Law Lotus Sutra." Initiated by Nichiren Daishonin, the True Buddha in the Latter Day of the Law, this invocation is the basis of universal life—the most fundamental law of all phenomena in the universe.

NICHIREN DAISHONIN (1222–82): The founder of Nichiren Shoshu, whose teachings are the basis of Soka Gakkai. A fisherman's son, he inherited the doctrine of Sakyamuni and in 1253, at the age of thirty-one, distilled the essence of the Lotus Sutra into Nam-myoho-renge-kyo. In 1279 he declared it to be the supreme guide for people living in the Latter Day of Sakyamuni's law and embodied it in the form of the Dai-Gohonzon, the ultimate object of worship of Nichiren Shoshu. Daishonin is an honorific suffix that is interpreted to mean "the True Buddha in the Latter Day of the Law."

NICHIREN SHOSHU: The Buddhist sect that has faithfully preserved the orthodox lineage of Nichiren Daishonin's Buddhism for the past seven hundred years. Its head temple is Taiseki-ji, located in Fujinomiya, Shizuoka Prefecture, on the southern slope of Mount Fuji. Soka Gakkai is the lay organization of Nichiren Shoshu.

NIRVANA SUTRA: So named because Sakyamuni expounded this his final sutra just before he entered Nirvana.

NYORAI JURYOHON (Fathoming the Buddha's Blessings): The sixteenth and most important chapter of the Lotus Sutra. It teaches the eternity of life.

ONGI KUDEN: The oral teachings of Nichiren Daishonin written down by Nikko Shonin, the second high priest of Nichiren Shoshu. It clarifies Nichiren Daishonin's profound life philosophy by interpreting the important passages of the Lotus Sutra from the viewpoint of true Buddhism.

SANZE SHOBUTSU SOKAMMON SHO (On the Ultimate Enlightenment of the Buddhas of the Three Existences): One of Nichiren Daishonin's important treatises, written at Mount Minobu in 1279, when Nichiren Daishonin was fifty-seven years old. This work explains that the Lotus Sutra itself is supreme in the doctrine of Sakyamuni. It also explains that the life-force philosophy of Nichiren Daishonin, developed on the bases of various Buddhist teachings, is the true Buddhism for the Latter Day of the Law.

THE SECURITY OF LAND THROUGH THE ESTABLISHMENT OF TRUE BUDDHISM (Rissho Ankokuron): The treatise, written by Nichiren Daishonin in 1260, at the age of thirty-eight, that reveals the cause of disaster and unhappiness as being the proliferation of misleading religions and philosophies. This treatise is a remonstrance against the Kamakura shogunate, which then ruled Japan.

SENJI SHO (On the Selection of Time): One of Nichiren Daishonin's ten major works. Written in 1275, it contains Nichiren Daishonin's explanation of the importance of time and his prophecy of the ultimate worldwide propagation of true Buddhism in the Latter Day of the Law.

SENSHO-ZOJOMAN: *see* The Three Formidable Foes

SOKA KYOIKU GAKKAI: Literally, "Value-Creating Education Society." Founded in 1930 by Tsunesaburo Makiguchi, the first president, and Josei Toda. The military government suppressed the society in 1943, because of its antiwar orientation and anti-Shinto policy. Josei Toda, who later became president, reestablished it in 1946 under the name Soka Gakkai (Value-Creating Society).

TAISEKI-JI: The head temple of Nichiren Shoshu, founded at the foot of Mount Fuji in 1290 by Nikko Shonin, the second high priest of the sect.

THE TEN STATES OF LIFE: The states of life that are manifest in both physical and spiritual aspects of all human activities. These ten states are hell, hunger, animality, anger, tranquillity, rapture, learning, absorption, Bodhisattva nature, and Buddha nature.

THE THREE DISASTERS AND SEVEN CALAMITIES (Sansai-Shichinan): Descriptions of these disasters and calamities as explained in various sutras differ somewhat, though in all cases the general meanings are similar. The disasters occur in two categories of magnitude: the minor disasters—war, pestilence, and famine—and major disasters —fire, flood, and storm. According to the sutra known in Japanese as the Ninno-kyo, the seven calamities are: solar or lunar eclipse; abnormal movements of heavenly bodies or the appearance of comets; destruction by conflagration; unseasonable weather, including storms, extended periods of rain, or intense heat or cold; typhoons, gales, or whirlwinds; lack of rain during the rainy season; and the destruction of a nation by internal strife or foreign invasion.

THE THREE EXISTENCES (Sanze): The three existences are the past, the present, and the future, which make up the continuum of individualized and universal life and are governed by the law of karma.

THE THREE FORMIDABLE FOES (Sanrui-no-goteki): The Lotus Sutra says that the worldwide propagation of true Buddhism will be preceded by the appearance of many enemies. The Three Formidable Foes, who will persecute true believers in the Latter Day of the Law, are: laymen who, without recognizing the value of true Buddhism, slander its believers (Zokushu-zojoman); heretical priests who attempt to upset the faith of believers in true Buddhism (Domon-zojoman); and government authorities or other people in high positions who persecute believers in true Buddhism who happen to fall in their sphere of control (Sensho-zojoman).

THREE GREAT SECRET LAWS: Another name for Nichiren Daishonin's Buddhism, which is composed of three vital elements: Hommon-no-Honzon (supreme object of worship as the embodiment of Nam-myoho-renge-kyo), Hommon-no-Daimoku (invocation of Nam-myoho-renge-kyo), and Hommon-no-Kaidan (high sanctuary for the enshrinement of the Dai-Gohonzon).

THE THREE OBSTACLES AND FOUR DEVILS (Sansho Shima): The obstacles and devils that arise to interfere with one's faith in the Gohonzon. The Three Obstacles are mundane desires, opposition to the faith by spouse or children, and persecution by parents or anyone in power or high social position. The Four Devils are sickness; mundane desires; the untimely death of another believer; and persecution by authorities, which devil is also called the Demon King of the Sixth Heaven.

THE THREE TREASURES (Sampo): The Buddha, the Law, and the Priesthood. The Buddha, who possesses the virtues of sovereign, master, and parent, has been enlightened to the true meaning of the universe. The Law is the teachings of the Buddha. The Priesthood is the group of individuals who inherit and transmit the Law. In the Mappo era, the Buddha is Nichiren Daishonin; the Law is the Dai-Gohonzon of Nam-myoho-renge-kyo; and the Priesthood is the clergy of Nichiren Shoshu headed by an unbroken succession of high priests beginning with Nikko Shonin, the immediate successor to Nichiren Daishonin.

THE THREEFOLD SECRET: A teaching, called secret because it has been inherited only by Nichiren Shoshu, that compares actual Mahayana (the Lotus Sutra) with provisional Mahayana (the other sutras), the first half of the Lotus Sutra with the second half of the Lotus Sutra, and the Buddhism of Nichiren Daishonin with that of

Sakyamuni. Nichikan Shonin, the twenty-sixth high priest of Nichiren Shoshu, pointed out that the all-important doctrine of Ichinen Sanzen is to be found only in the second half of the Lotus Sutra and that it is explained in depth only in the Juryohon, the sixteenth chapter of the Lotus Sutra.

Tokugyobon (Virtuous Practice): Part of the sutra of infinite meaning, the introductory section of the Lotus Sutra. In this work, the Bodhisattva Manjusri and others sing the praises of the great virtues of Sakyamuni as a Buddha.

Totaigi Sho (On the Substance of Nam-myoho-renge-kyo): One of the most important of Nichiren Daishonin's writings. In it he identifies believers in true Buddhism with the entity of Nam-myoho-renge-kyo and reveals the inseparability of cause and effect. Although the facts are uncertain, it is said that Nichiren Daishonin wrote this treatise while in exile on Sado Island and sent it to Sairenbo, one of his disciples and a former priest of the Tendai sect.

Ushitora Gongyo: A religious ceremony held each night to pray for world peace and for the earliest possible attainment of world-wide propagation of true Buddhism. Since the time of Nikko Shonin, the founder of Taiseki-ji and the second high priest of Nichiren Shoshu, the Ushitora Gongyo has been conducted every night without a single lapse: at present it is held in the Grand Reception Hall of Taiseki-ji. It now begins at midnight, although its name indicates that it was once held between the hour of the ox (*ushi*) and the hour of the tiger (*tora*); these archaic time designations correspond to two o'clock and four o'clock in the morning.

Vulture Peak: Mount Gṛdhrakūṭa, located near Rajgir, in the North Indian state of Bihar. The sacred mountain where Sakyamuni preached the Lotus Sutra.

Zokushu-zojoman: *see* The Three Formidable Foes

The "weathermark" identifies this book as having been designed and produced at the Tokyo offices of John Weatherhill, Inc. Book design and typography by Meredith Weatherby. Text composed and printed by Kenkyusha Printing Co., Tokyo. Bound at the Makoto Binderies, Tokyo. The text is set in Baskerville 11/13, with Baskerville for display.